Snowbound

Book 2: The Bloodline of Yule Trilogy

Snowbound

Book 2: The Bloodline of Yule Trilogy

Maria Alexander

GHEDE
PRESS

Other books by Maria Alexander

Young Adult Fiction
Snowed, Book 1: The Bloodline of Yule Trilogy

Adult Fiction
Mr. Wicker

Cover art by Daniele Serra.

Published by Ghede Press – Los Angeles, California.

ISBN 13 978-1732454217
ISBN 10 1732454213

In loving memory of my dear friend Len,
who said he was proud of me for doing it on my own.

Prologue

En route to the International Science Base Camp
150 miles NE of Barrow, Alaska

My stomach sinks as the helicopters lift us up above Barrow. I'm not good with heights, like, at all. The only thing that keeps me from hyperventilating is the thought of seeing Aidan again. Chopper blades thunder in the air. Part of me wants to take in the breathtaking scenery below us, but I have to close my eyes to keep from having a panic attack.

It's not just the heights. Last night at our motel in Barrow, I got a surprising email from mom.

Charity,
I don't know what to say. I'm so sorry for pushing you away. I should never have done that. It's been very hard, and I can't cope like I used to. But I'm working on things here living at Grandma Lynn's house, one day at a time.
I want to talk about what happened — with you, your brother Charles, and Aidan. Your dad refuses. And he's right. I need to communicate with you directly. I know you're angry. You don't even have to respond. I know you dropped out of Cornell. Please, baby, tell me what's going on? And what really happened to Aidan? I promise to listen this time.
Love you more than you know,
Mom

I was stunned. And mad as hell. She sends an email out of nowhere after months of nothing? The visual silence of snow stretching towards the horizon reminds me of how it felt when she shut me out. Forever cold.

One day at a time. But maybe she really is getting sober and is ready to face what's happened. I don't even know if AA and that stuff even works, but those few words give me a flicker of hope. Maybe someday, somehow she and Dad can even get back together. But they can't if she doesn't face the truth about what happened on that Christmas.

So, I replied to her email. I think about the words as the helicopter pilot points out the lone polar bear below, hunting for seals on the breaking ice. I'm in total awe. I can only imagine how thrilled Judy and the others are seeing a real live polar bear.

But those words to my mom weigh on me. That email might be the last time I communicate with her...

Mom,

You're right, I'm totally pissed. You bailed on me and then shut me out when I needed you most. I know you love Charles. But please realize that on Christmas Eve, I was the one trying to save your life. ALL of our lives.

Here's the truth for the last time. Take it or leave it.
Remember when I told you how Aidan said his abusive dad was this successful industrialist from "the north" that everyone loves?

The truth is that Aidan's dad is St. Nicholas, aka Santa Claus or just The Klaas. But St. Nicholas is like Dr. Jekyll and Mr. Hyde. His alter ego is Krampus, the monster that punishes bad kids at Christmas, whipping them and throwing them in his sack to take them to Hell. Except there is no hell, just a fortress somewhere in the Arctic. Santa and Krampus are the same person, and he can change at will. But because Aidan's father is evil, he's always Krampus.

Someday, when Aidan's father dies, Aidan will inherit the powers of The Klaas and he'll decide which one he is. You and I both know what that will be.

His siblings, the "elves," aren't exactly the cherry-cheeked elves we see on TV. They're those horrifying, goat-sloth creatures whose corpses filled our living room Christmas morning after the battle. Mom, Aidan fought against his own family to save us. That's how much he loved us.

Speaking of siblings, despite what you might think, everything that happened is Charles' fault. EVERYTHING. If he hadn't sent that letter to "Santa," Aidan's dad would have never known where we were. Leo would have never been killed. You heard the threats yourself when we visited Charles at the detention center — if Aidan had run, we'd all be dead, including you and Dad.

Aidan's dad probably let Charles escape prison on Christmas as a reward for snitching. Charles was terrified of Aidan and wanted to be sure that Aidan was nowhere within reach. Boy, did he succeed! Honestly, you have no idea how incredibly smart Charles is. So stop worrying about him. He'll be fine.

Just know that Aidan surrendered and let his dad take him back home to "the north" in exchange for our lives. He's no doubt being tortured for running away. Maybe worse. It's as true today as when I told Dad over a year ago: I love Aidan. I know you love him, too. And we're going to get him back.

I just hope it isn't too late.

Love,

Charity

Aidan

Chapter 1

December 25
Thirty-six minutes after midnight
On the roof of the Jones house…

"Charity!"

I scream myself hoarse. The only loving home I've ever known has been destroyed. One of my friends is dead. And now I'm being kidnapped by my father to return "home" — the Klaas fortress in the Arctic, where Father will no doubt make me suffer for running away.

To save my sanity, I'm going to write this mental letter to you, Charity, as if you were still with me. As if you weren't lying on the floor of the living room dying yourself from my Father's attack.

My father, Krampus.

He's forced me into an ancient, magical bag that originally belonged to the Norse goddess, Frygg, wife of Odin. The bag binds my powers in its dark interior. I haven't been in this bag since I was a baby, when he kidnapped my mother and I twelve months after he'd impregnated her early one Christmas morning.

My father now jostles the bag violently as he climbs up to the roof of the house where the sleigh awaits. I hear the wind climbers bleating with fear when they see him as they wait with the sleigh. The rest is eerie silence. Sirens wail in the distance. Help is already on the way. It's too late for poor Leo. I pray it's not too late for you…

"You cowardly little bastard," he snaps. The smell of his burning flesh from where you hit him with the mistletoe seeps into the bag. "I would have almost respected you if you had fled and sacrificed your friends for freedom. You would have shown some sense of survival, a true Klaas." He slams the bag into the sleigh. My head rings with agony as it hits the sleigh floor. "Onward, you filthy beasts!" he roars, his lash tearing their hides with a *crack*. The sleigh rises into the air but the trajectory remains low. "One stop, my pets, and then we go home!"

Why would he want to stop? Who else would he want to kill besides us? Maybe Detective Bristow, the officer who investigated Darren's death? Or your father? But your father is in Washington DC, and the sleigh is not headed in that direction — at least, it doesn't seem like it. If I concentrate, I can pick up fleeting details outside of the bag like the temperature. The air quickly grows colder.

We are headed into snow.

Misery and disgust. My father sings the rest of "God Rest Ye Merry Gentlemen," his deep voice booming into the night. He laughs over the line "to save us all from Satan's power," changing it to "Santa's power."

I'm already planning my escape. I vow to you, Charity, that I will not only avenge Leo's death, but I'll return to you as soon as possible.

All isn't lost. At the fortress, there's a very special tome — *The Book of Sigils* — that I used to break the magic seals that held me captive. I'll find the book again and break free once and for all.

That is, if he hasn't already found the book and burned it...

Icy breezes rush over the sleigh until it lands on another surface. Father climbs out. I no longer hear the clamor of his cloven hooves. Instead, I hear the sound of leather soles treading on a thin layer of snow.

He must have transformed into a human.

I hear automatic sliding glass doors open with a hiss and close again.

Snow falls on the sled, flakes dusting the bag. The scent of pines saturates the air. In the distance, a cheap radio plays Christmas tunes. Any moment now all hell will surely break loose. This isn't the first time he's killed someone on this night. I'll never forget the time he returned licking his fingers, his tongue snaking around his hand to

7

savor every last fleck of blood in his fur. That was the Christmas before he killed my mother.

The glass doors slide open again, and two sets of footsteps emerge from the building beneath, one heavy and one hesitant. In the twinkle of an eye, the two sets of feet land on the roof. Someone's teeth chatter between gasps of terror.

"Stop your sniveling," my father says. "You got your Christmas wish. Now, shut up and sit tight."

The bag opens. A blast of shadows as another body plummets into the blackness with me. It closes before I can see who it is. I can't fathom why he'd bring anyone to the fortress. Perhaps instead he'll dangle them from the sleigh hundreds of miles in the air just to hear their terror. I've never seen him do that, but he's that sadistic.

The other person in the bag — man, woman or child — retreats into the abyss. It's as if we don't share the same space at all, but the scent of their fear is stifling. I want to comfort this person, to protect her. Or him. But I don't dare. The scars on my back tingle. He'll soon tear open my flesh again. I have to be stronger than ever.

Despite their treachery, I mourn the deaths of my siblings in the battle. I don't hold it against them. The poor things did what they were told. They had no choice. They're just collateral damage in this family war.

The sleigh soars upward. An intense, misty chill settles on the bag as we break through the cloud layer. I imagine the cold moon above us as we race northward. Home. *You're going home for the holidays.* I saw maps on the computer of my home. The vast stretches of snow layering broken ice stirred by the swirling waters. The ice is receding from global warming. Mankind is slowly killing the Klaas. This is extremely dangerous. More dangerous than anyone knows.

We fly into the eternal sunset of Arctic winter and the freezing air pummels us. The cold worms under my skin, which means it must be very cold indeed. I worry for the other person. If they survive this trip, it's just the beginning of a frightening new life.

As we approach the fortress, the sled's trajectory lowers. On the ice, my siblings howl with glee as they scurry about the perimeter. Some of my remaining siblings might even make it back home now that my father has called off the hunt.

I try not to imagine the punishment in store for me. He might kill me. But why wait to do that?

Arctic breezes buffet the sleigh as it slows to a halt on top of the fortress. The chatter of my siblings swells as they gather around the sled. I gag on the stink of their fur and breath.

"Get back!" he shouts. "Paws off the bag or I'll throw you into the fires!"

A frenzy of fear. There aren't any "fires" per se; they're too simple to realize this is an empty threat. They fall back as he hoists the bag from the sleigh and slings it over his shoulder.

He curses as he limps over the ice, cracking the lash at his adoring children to keep them at bay. The familiar stench of seal meat, rotting plankton and creature piss mixed with the smell of my father's smoldering flesh punches through the bag's magic. I take deep breaths, fighting the urge to vomit.

Their voices echo in the majestic caverns. I recognize how sounds ping ice and stone, especially as we enter the throne room. Sound changes there as if we've slipped underwater, everything loud and muddy. My father's hooves crunch into the ice floor, his breathing labored. His warmth seeps through the sealskin into my body.

The Other person hides. Silent.

"Behold, my wayward son!" Father swings the bag from his back and I spill out of the open top onto the ice. The impact is jarring. Every bone feels like it's about to break. My siblings shriek with joy, peals of cruel laughter needling the air. Their goat-like faces reveal vicious teeth, their bodies something between a sloth and a chimpanzee. The males have twisted horns like Father's. My powers flood back, restoring warmth to my body, and I rise cautiously on my knees. Father laughs, pointing at me.

"Who said you could stand?" With lightning reflexes, he snatches the scourge of chains by his throne and lashes my back. The metallic barbs tear my skin afresh, waves of fiery agony searing my back. I collapse, my chin splitting open on the hard surface. I hold my breath against a wave of nausea.

More laughter floods the room, followed quickly by a ripple of astonishment. I lie there, wondering what's captured the attention of my siblings. Father laughs more heartily than ever.

"Behold, my true son," Father shouts. "He who will now serve and protect me, with the love and respect that I deserve."

A rustle as the Other person climbs out of the bag.

Wobbling with pain, I rise to see the figure crouched by the empty sack, surveying his new home.

I recognize him all too well.

Chapter 2

"Why don't you say hello to your brother, Aidan?" Father asks.

Charles wears orange cotton shirt and trousers with a long-sleeved white shirt underneath and black-and-white sneakers. "Where am I? The North Pole?"

Father's snout twitches and his eyes close. He staggers back, scourge in hand, and drops into the lap of his massive throne. The seat is layered with sealskins. The frame is carved from bowhead whalebone, framed by reindeer antlers. A polar bear skull ends each armrest, jaws open to reveal razor-sharp teeth. A polished mammoth tusk rises from each side of the throne, highlighting my father's own scorched horns. Blood glistens on his scalp. But where you drove the mistletoe powder into his heart, Charity, there's a sunken wound. It looks as though he was stabbed, blood streaking his chest, ribcage and even his abdomen.

He's dying. How long before he succumbs?

When he does, I'll be the Klaas. Free from him, but anchored to this miserable place. I'd hoped to be woven into the fabric of humanity before then. Because, Charity, I wasn't just running from my father. I was running from this entire legacy.

"It's your new home," Father tells Charles. "And I think you're a more worthy son than the one I brought into this world." He sneers at me. "The one who would defy me so he could behave like some poet, sopping up the pathetic sentimentality of humanity. You, Charles — it's as if you were my real son. You have the intelligence and strength I need."

Charles scoffs. "I don't know what this is about, grandpa, but I didn't want to come here to Christmas Land to carry out crazy monster shit. I have plans that don't include you."

"Plans?" Father looks bored. "You mean revenge? You have it. Your sister is dead. Your so-called family who never loved you, truth be told, has been ruined. And the person responsible for the worst of it is right here." He points to me.

He's lying. I know you're not dead, Charity. I detect your presence, however faint, on The List. I just pray the paramedics get there in time.

"You've achieved all your goals, thanks to me," Father continues. "And now you shall reap the rewards."

Charles steps back. "Oh, yeah? How am I supposed to do that? Smear myself with goat shit and build some toys?"

"I will teach you powers you never knew existed. Ancient magic and secrets no other human has ever mastered."

Another lie. Humans can't learn our magic. Or can they?

"Secrets, huh? Go on."

Father raises a clawed finger and Charles rises high up to the glacial dome amongst the stalactites. He screams as he twists to escape the invisible grip.

"Don't you like flying?" Father mocks.

Charles begs to be let down.

"You'll learn to fly on your own. And you'll have the run of the fortress. You can go wherever you want and see whatever appeals to you. As long as you please me, that is." Father leans forward conspiratorially. Charles drops to the ground with a howl, stopping inches from the surface. "Best of all, you can torment Aidan whenever you wish."

Charles drops to the surface and scrambles away from me. "Oh, no. I've seen what that asshole can do. I'm not touching him."

"If he harms you in any way, he will suffer greatly at my own hand. Believe me, he's not strong enough to survive what I have in store." He pauses. "And you can watch."

I wish my father a death worse than Leo's. Eaten alive by polar bears, perhaps. The polar bear can eat Charles, too.

12

Charles walks up to me, staring down with a contemptuous look. He raises his foot, his sole eclipsing his face. I don't flinch. But he changes his mind. Instead of stomping downward, he drives his toe into my stomach. My mind goes white. I open my mouth, but I'm too weak to make any noise.

Charles lets out a whoop of satisfaction. "Well, Santa, that felt great, but this place is still rank as hell. I'm going to turn into Gollum or something living here, it's so dark. So I need to go."

Father indicates one of the fortress openings. "Then you may go," he says.

The entire fortress is surrounded by the Sentinels — that is, the towering monoliths of ice, impenetrable by anything short of magic. So, I'm not sure how he can possibly leave.

Charles doesn't even glance at me before heading toward the exit. The crowds of my siblings part for him. He almost loses his footing several times, the ice ruts tripping him. But as he draws closer to the opening, he shivers violently. He stops several yards from the perimeter of the throne room, cursing and ranting, teeth chattering, doubled over.

"Hey!" he shouts. "You said I could leave! I can't go out there. It's below zero!"

Father laughs. My siblings join in on the humor. Soon, the entire colony is mocking Charles' misery.

"What the hell are you waiting for? Get the sleigh and take me home!"

Father growls.

Charles is flung against up to the domed ceiling, barely missing being skewered on the stalactites. He yelps like a cat.

"Aidan."

I can hardly believe Father just used my name. He says it with such tenderness. Almost with something that resembles love but it's only manipulation. He crouches beside me, his bestial looks softened. His bloodshot eyes glimmer, pale blue like mine.

"Son, I had to teach you a lesson. You don't understand how important it is that you remain here. This is your destiny, not sucking the tit of some girl. You did that enough with your mother."

13

He squeezes his eyes shut, wincing. He must be in extreme pain.

"Hurry up and die, won't you?" I snarl.

His bellow crescendos through the cavern. Deafening. Obliterating. Chaos. My siblings scatter, shards of stalactites breaking loose and falling to the ground. The Mothers in the Taggalaq wail. The entire fortress quakes with his all-consuming rage. My body rises in the air, the scenery blurring. I'm flung against the far wall so hard that everything goes black.

When I wake up, I'm on fire.

Chapter 3

The Taggalaq.

It's an ancient cavern in the sea mountain below the fortress. Unlike the Antarctic, the Arctic has no land, only the frozen ocean waters. However, there are many mountains — it's just that they are underwater rather than above. The fortress sits atop one of those underwater mountains. A labyrinth of tunnels carved by unknown hands burrows down into said mountain. Legends surround exactly where some of the tunnels lead. I'm sure my siblings have explored many of them, if not all. I, however, have only had access to a few.

For the Inuktitut people, *taggalaq* means "darkness." Here, the Taggalaq is where Father keeps the Mothers, trapped in cages for his lurid purposes. Once ancient creatures of the Arctic, they're now imprisoned in the Taggalaq, their voices mournful like whales. Although they're like towering orangutans with mammoth tusks and tentacles, my father ruts with them to produce my siblings. Here, amongst the rotting fish and refuse.

That's where I am, leaning against the filthy cell wall because it's cool like the dirt beneath my feet. Hours of screaming have ground down my voice to a thin rasp. My father has been torturing me by magically setting me on fire. My skin's been repeatedly ravaged by the flames.

I guess he wasn't lying to my siblings. There really are fires.

Another round is about to start. A fire sigil materializes, hanging in the air before me. A sigil is a glowing symbol that hovers at eye level. As this one flares, my skin blisters, my hair smokes. The agony begins afresh. Ears. Thighs. Fingers. Fire climbs from my feet up my legs. Down my arms and over my head.

"NO, NO, NO! Please — stop!" I'm sure he loves hearing me beg. I try not to but I can't help it.

The fire illuminates the horror and sadness of the Taggalaq. One of the Mothers cringes from the light. An infant clings to her, nursing on her bloated, rugged breast.

I try to stay sane by summoning the memory of your unspeakably soft lips and skin, Charity. And the look in your eyes that night when you said, "I love you, too, Aidan the Klaas."

I would do anything to see you again, Charity. If dying would bring me to you, I would do that, too. But I can't die, which means this torture will never end unless my father decides to stop it.

Two blue eyes flash at me from beyond my cell bars. One of my siblings sits by my cell, blinking. She looks away frequently. Shyly. I understand why you were so scared, Charity. They must look so monstrous to you.

"GO...AWAY!" I yell angrily. I squeeze my eyes shut, clinging to the wall, praying to the old gods for relief.

The sigil fades, the fire recedes. I fall to my knees, retching violently as my skin rapidly repairs itself.

My sibling lowers her gaze, as if embarrassed. "You were South. We looked for you."

"I KNOW!" I grab a handful of dirt and throw it at her. She cowers. "You do whatever he tells you, don't you?"

"Young Klaas, have mercy!" She weeps. "There are things we must know about the South." *The South.* Basically anywhere not at the North Pole.

As smoke rises on my skin again, I get an idea. I topple into the dirt, skin aflame as I manage to blurt out: "GET. THE. BOOK."

The Book of Sigils.

She stares at me.

"WILL. ANSWER. IF. YOU. GET. BOOK. LIBRARY."

She scurries off past the veil of smoke as I writhe in agony, choking on the repulsive smell of my own burning skin.

Time passes. I'm not certain how long. The *Book of Sigils* is hidden in the library. Even if she understood what I needed, I don't know if she would ever find it.

Charity, your books have mathematic equations. Mine have magical equations, symbols and words that unlock powers I don't have at my immediate disposal. At least, not at this point. Maybe if I become the Klaas someday I'll have these powers at my fingertips. But for now, I have to use the book. For some reason, I can't memorize these sigils. I wonder what you'd think of me actually having to study.

My memory keeps replaying our kiss behind the gymnasium. The many passionate kisses amongst the trees, the wet blackberry bushes, rain falling gently on our heads. The first time I touched your hand, when I shook it in your living room. I was embarrassed by the things I felt. But not anymore.

My skin heals only to burn again. I can heal like this at the North Pole, but not anywhere else. I don't know how much longer I can take this.

"Young Klaas."

My sister has returned. She slides the book to me through the bars. Astonished, I rifle through the pages. Glamor. Forgetfulness. Deception. Where is Fire?

My fingers smolder and sting. I yank them away from the book.

My sibling reaches through into the cage and clumsily turns the pages for me, one at a time, looking to me for approval. I shake my head. Once, twice, again. The agony builds. Soon, I'll be blind. I yell, "Back!" or "Forward!" for every page turn.

I collapse. Flames creep into my eyes. My thoughts dribble away under maniacal laughter. My babbling echoes through the Taggalaq.

Then, a moment of clarity. Like the minute I gained balance on the bicycle as your father taught me to ride. There. I draw my thoughts together. Father is not trying kill me. He's trying to do something far worse: To drive me mad.

"Fire! Burn! Blister!" I shout, hoping that I'll speak the right magical word from the book. "Wither! Kindle! Sear! Scorch! Conflagrate! Combust!"

My sibling recoils as the book flies open to the page of its own accord. The Sigil of Combustion.

I draw the sigil in reverse in the air before me as I intone the counter hex.

The torment abruptly stops.

"Thank you," I say.

"Young Klaas...now please tell...will we return from the South?"

I shake my head. "Some, perhaps, but not everyone. He should never have sent any of you after me. It's much too dangerous for you guys to be out in the world. But Father didn't care if you got hurt. He just wanted to find me no matter what." Now that I'm no longer distracted by the pain, I realize what a big risk she's taking by talking to me. "I'm so sorry. I should never have run away. It hurt everyone I love. Including you."

The air grows still. My sister cries quietly. "The Cruel One says the humans killed our sister."

"The Cruel One? You mean Charles?"

She nods, her face wrinkled with sadness.

"The humans did kill her. But only because she attacked a young human. They honestly tried not to hurt her at all. Especially Charity Jones. She was very gentle."

My sister rests her head against the bars. "Is it all bad in the South?" she asks, plaintive. "Is there nothing good?"

"I won't lie. There's much bad. The humans believe Father's this jolly gift-giver, which is a tragedy. But there's also good. Earth, trees, plants — nature is wonderful. And rain! Rain's like snow but wetter and it makes the ground smell nice. I know you've not seen these things. It's hard to explain. The best part was that I lived with loving humans who were kind to me beyond measure."

Her expression softens with what looks like hope.

I'm extremely grateful that Father kept her here. She's far smarter than my other siblings. Either she's been pretending to be dumber so as not to draw attention to herself, or Father had a special purpose for her. Either way, my siblings don't normally have this sort of initiative, much less kindness and intelligence. I can think of only one way to repay her.

"Look, you've done me a great kindness at a terrible risk to yourself. I want to give you a name."

She lifts her head and looks astonished. "A name? Like

18

Aaaaidan?" She can't pronounce my name without bleating.

"Better. I think your name should be...Reilly." All my teachers were good people, but my history teacher, Mr. Reilly, was the one who unwittingly gave us our first precious moments alone together, Charity.

"Reilly!" She cavorts about the Taggalaq. I've never seen anyone do that before. "We love that name! Thank you, Young Klaas! Thank you!"

"Shhhhhh! Lower your voice." I crawl toward her. My scalp tingles as it heals. Within moments, a curl droops over one of my eyes. My skin, hair, everything has already recovered. "How did you find it?" I gesture to the book.

Reilly settles by the cell, presses her nose between the bars, and whispers. "The Father found it and hid it after you left. We saw."

"You saw and you remembered."

Reilly nods. "The Father has been trying to teach The Cruel One magic so he may serve."

"To serve how?" I ask.

A series of booms detonate in the tunnels. The Taggalaq shakes ominously.

Chapter 4

Loose dust from the black basalt rock falls on our heads. The Mothers make frightened noises, hiding their babies in the folds of their skin. Even the rat-things flee down holes.

Holding a torch aloft, an imposing figure rides into the cavern on the back of a wind climber. The hooves *clunk-clunk* as the beast draws closer to my cage. I recognize the rider.

Charles.

I quickly hand the book to Reilly, who darts off into a niche tucked behind one of the pens. Is that her secret tunnel into the Taggalaq?

"Jesus, it stinks even more down here!" Charles wipes his watering eyes. The sealskin boots look too big for him, as do his pants, mittens and tunic. The wind climber huffs under his weight, another in tow behind it. Muscular like mules, these goatish creatures pull the sleigh. I don't know where they come from, but they're perfectly suited for our needs. Charles looks me over with that contemptuous smirk. "Shit! I was hoping you'd be dead. Why can't you be dead for once?"

How long have I been down here? A day? A week? A month? My stomach spasms with hunger, nausea forgotten.

"How goes the nicotine withdrawal, Charles?"

"Shut up, asshole. How's it feel to be the real son who can do no right? Pretty shitty, I bet."

"Unlike my father — who's using you, incidentally — your real parents love you," I say. "They always have and always will."

"Yeah, well, they didn't deserve me. They had no idea who I was!"

"Or *what* you were..."

"What's that supposed to mean?"

The ground beneath me tremors. The wind climber bleats nervously. The babies whimper. My father must be raging about the missing book. But why send Charles? Why not come down here himself?

"Come on!" Charles yells, checking the entrance. "We've gotta leave. Your creepy dad wants you."

"I suppose he's threatened to punish you severely if you don't retrieve me in a timely fashion."

"*You'll* suffer. Not me."

The cage bars melt away. Charles' eyes widen. Based on his reaction, I sense it must have been my father who dismissed the prison, not him, although I wouldn't be surprised if my father is trying to teach him such things. The torch illuminates the resentment in Charles' expression.

My hand brushes the wind climber's silky snout in greeting, and I climb onto its back. The treacherous path out of the Taggalaq winds through the sea mountain tunnels. Narrow, slippery, confusing. Coated with a golden bacterial sludge that eats the iron in the mountain's heart. The trailing smoke from the torch chokes me. I don't need this light. The temptation to steal the torch, blow it out and ride off is overwhelming, but I know it will do no good. Not only will it annoy my father, but also the wind climber knows the way back without it.

We ride on until the bluish light breaks across the tunnel opening leading not into the throne room but to the far side of the fortress in a cavern less grand but still stunning. A mosaic of whale teeth embedded in the black basalt wall creates an open eye so detailed and realistic that it looks as if it might blink. The air is thick with the musk of decay. More skins and furs cover a broad bed made of whalebone. Dim healing sigils hang in the air at each corner. They must have been created by my siblings, who have very little magic.

Or maybe Charles, which is bad news. Even a little magic in his hands is a dangerous thing.

Father lies on the bed, beneath the intricate ice carvings in the vaulted ceiling. He coughs violently, flecks of blood staining the matted white chest fur, eyes bloodshot and rheumy. The wound has deepened, leaving an ashen, gurgling cavity. His scalp has turned to gray sludge where the skin has failed to heal. Once imposing, he now lays withered, cheeks hollow, his breath uneven. He doesn't acknowledge me when I slide off the wind climber and approach his bedside.

I've never seen him like this. His frailty scares me because it means my time to ascend is near.

One of my brothers scurries up to me with a platter. A feast of seal meat, fresh water and dried kelp.

"Eat," Father says.

And I do. Ravenously. He doesn't speak until I'm finished.

"That bitch," he says slowly, "made her mark."

It doesn't seem right to goad him now as he's dying. My father. My tormentor. How I'd craved his love. To see Nicholas as the world saw him — a saint. But here he lies dying like a starving polar bear. The mighty Klaas mortally wounded.

"But she miscalculated," he continues, his voice low and gravelly. "I will yet prevail."

"Really?" I ask. "And how will that happen?"

"A cure to this poison lies beyond the Gate of Tatzelwurm. Very dangerous. It's an ash named egg. You must add three drops." His eyes roll up into his head as his body convulses, bluish veins standing out on the backs of his hands.

"Why do I care about this imaginary cure? Or anything about you? You've done nothing but torture me my whole life. Once you're dead, you'll no longer be able to make me suffer."

A low chuckle. "Is that what you think? That your suffering will cease?"

"When I'm the Klaas, your reign of terror will be over!"

He clenches his fist, and my throat tightens. With only a gesture, he draws me close to his face, his breath flush with rot. "I'm not going to die," he says, "because you're going to help me."

"Why should I do that?"

"Because if you refuse to help me, I'll kill you outright. You

22

know I can." At that, he lets go of my throat.

"Then we'll both die," I reply, shocked. "Everyone...will die."

A malicious smile curls on his lips.

I have found astonishingly little about the Klaas as a species in the library. But what I have found in the older manuscripts is clear: the Klaas is tied directly to the life force of Earth. If there is no living Klaas, then the life force will end and the Earth will die. A more recent pamphlet penned by my Grand Klaas — who was considerably happier, as was his father — speculated it's because the Klaas is connected to the poles, and that there'd be an abrupt swap between the North and South poles, which would disrupt the electromagnetic fields on the planet. This would in turn end gravity, and the Earth's atmosphere would be torn away.

But when I was at your house, Charity, I watched a video by a famous scientist named Neil deGrasse Tyson who said that a polar shift would *not* harm the Earth. Does that mean then that the Earth *won't* end with the death of the last Klaas? Or will it merely end some other way? Grand Klaas seemed certain of the latter. I sense he's right.

Father unclenches his hand, his eyes narrowing. "But if you succeed, I will let you go. You can go be with that homicidal little bitch, if you wish."

"Hey!" Charles says. He stands in the entrance, eavesdropping. "You said Charity was dead!"

My father "pinches" the air with his fingers. Charles' hands fly at his lips, trying to pry them open as he moans in protest.

I indicate Charles. "Why don't you send your 'real' son?"

"He is human and weak. I've not been able to teach him the proper spells to make the journey as I'd hoped."

"Which is why you decided to stop torturing me and bring me back."

He nods and parts his fingers.

Charles gasps. "You said I could go with him. To learn stuff."

"You can't be serious! He'd only get in the way," I reply.

"Take him! And I'll know if anything hurts him. If so, the deal will be off, and I'll kill you instantly."

"You're lying. You can't possibly know where I am, much less kill me from afar."

"I don't have to know where you are to end your life." A low growl escapes his throat. "There's so much you don't know."

I wonder if that's true or just a bluff. I certainly believe he'd kill everyone on the planet. His contempt for humanity is that great. I wish I understood why. I suspect something happened after I was born to curdle his disposition, but I was too young to understand.

He's definitely right about one thing. There's so much I don't know. And there's much he doesn't know, either. No Klaas has been beyond the Gate, which means anything could be down there. As I search for this so-called cure, I might actually find something greater: a way back to you, Charity, and a way out of this terrible life for good.

"So, son, shall Charity Jones live?" Father asks, smirking. "Or die?"

His threat isn't idle. You, Judy, Keiko, Michael, Ricardo, your mother and father. Your family. The school. Everyone and everything that lives will be destroyed. Planet Earth shall cease to host life.

And no one will be able to stop it.

But I'm excited. I'm going to find the answers I need to escape this world once and for all, whether or not Father keeps his promise, so that I can be with you.

"Come on, Charles." I rush from the room to prepare for the journey. "We're going to save The Klaas!"

Chapter 5

Deep in the fortress is the Chamber of Niflhel. The chamber is alleged to hold The Gate of Tatzelwurm, a portal in the floor that leads into Tatzelwurm itself. That's where Father says we'll find the antidote to his mistletoe poisoning. Until now, no one has dared disturb the Chamber that I know of. Father's kept the doors magically locked with glyphs – they're like sigils except they don't hang in the air. Glyphs are typically drawn directly onto the surface of something like a door to perform a specific purpose.

But as Charles and I approach, the glyphs fade and the doors open on their own.

I enter, Charles following. The stony walls are unadorned, although someone has carved an opening approximately fourteen feet in diameter in the ceiling to the endless Arctic winter night. Below the opening is a much bigger circle — at least thirty feet in diameter — framed with obsidian stones embedded in the floor surrounding a glassy obsidian surface. Carved into the stones are letters of a language I don't recognize. The letters glimmer as they catch the light from Charles' torch, which he holds in a death grip.

In the Chamber doorway, my siblings murmur and weep, terrified of entering. A hellish blizzard batters the fortress in what must be one of the last big storms before spring arrives. The winds whistle eerily across the opening above us.

Reilly's head pokes above the crowd. "Young Klaas!"

Charles fixates on the stone carvings, his lips moving, brow furrowed. While he's distracted, I turn back to Reilly, who huddles by the door arch.

"Will you not need this?" She offers me the *Book of Sigils*.

"No!" I whisper. "Keep it here. It's too valuable to lose beyond the gate."

"*You* are too valuable to lose," she says. "You'll need it." Her eyes shine with anxiety. I relent and surreptitiously stuff the book in a big pocket inside my sealskin coat. As I return to the gate, Reilly gingerly follows, leaving the rest of her siblings behind at the doorway. "We hear terrible sounds beyond. Do not be swallowed by the darkness," she says.

Charles notices us. "Meh meh meh, don't be swallowed by the dorkness, Aidan," he mimics.

"You must enjoy having your mouth welded shut."

"You wouldn't dare!"

"Don't tempt me!" I stare him down.

He looks away first. "Let's just go, okay?"

While my siblings were packing our food supplies, I spent a precious hour in the library looking for anything that might help guide us in the mountain. I discovered one of my ancestors, an Elder Klaas, left a diary, explaining how "forces" had "bled" the mountain to make way for the underwater mountain range that supports the fortress. But what lies beneath? The Elder Klaas left only riddles and hints.

I step up to the gate and study the strange letters. They're probably magical locks like those glyphs on the chamber door, but much older. I wonder if they're to keep what's beyond from coming up than to keep us from going in. Between micro-evolution and centuries of grotesque Krampus magic, anything could be breeding in this mountain.

I'm more powerful than ever now, Charity, and I'll do whatever I must to fetch this...thing...so that I can be with you. Father called it "an ash named egg." More like "an ash named Ygg." Surely he must realize it's a reference to a poem in the Poetic Edda?

I know an ash
Named Yggdrasill,
A lofty tree,

With white dust strewed
Thence comes the dew
That in dales fell;
It stands evergreen
Over Urd's well.

However, I suspect there is nothing evergreen where we are bound. And if Urd's well or even Yggdrasil ever existed, it's nowhere near here. If not literal, Yggdrasil is at least the symbol of Odin's power over life, both mortal and immortal. The name means "Odin's gallows." It's the only tree that can kill a god.

Nonetheless, Father said I would need a tin for the ash or egg or whatever it is. I found one in the vast piles of gold, artwork, and rarities amassed in his vault. You didn't know that old Saint "Nick" was the biggest kleptomaniac in history? There's a reason he's the patron saint of thieves. He's far more likely to swipe something than leave a present on Christmas night.

I emptied the tin of pearls for this more important item. How odd to think that an old cookie tin is more valuable empty than full of precious stones.

I take a deep breath and step back from the gate, raising an open palm.

"*Machet daz Tatzlewurmstor uf!*"

The Arctic winds blast downward from the opening into the room. The obsidian surface *ripples* like black waters before they melt away, revealing steep stone steps with a crude guardrail that leads downward into what appears to be an enormous, bottomless, circular shaft that bores downward into the mountain. The writing on the stones fades away.

Chaos erupts as my siblings run from the chamber doorway, screeching and howling.

A foul smell wafts up from deep inside. Sulfur. Stone steps with a shaky railing wind downward into a gigantic cavern.

My eyes adjust quickly. But as strong as my sight is, I can only see a few yards inside. A sulfuric scent wafts up into the cavern.

"Do you know what that smell is, Charles?" I ask.

"Your ass?"

"Your death."

A chorus of cries swells from the remaining elves gathered at the chamber doorway as I step through the gateway and onto the stairwell. Backing away from the open gate, Reilly gibbers and howls above them all.

As soon as we have descended below the surface, the glassy black surface reforms above us. The torchlight ignites the textures and colors in the surrounding walls. Mustard, gold, terra cotta, rose, bluish grays and browns infuse the curious stone. The walls are riddled with holes, some large enough for a big dog to crawl through. I peer into one of the holes nervously and see nothing.

The stairs endlessly descend into the mountain. This cavern is so deep, there's no end in sight.

Charles' hand brushes the rocks and his voice echoes. "Is this why you guys are so secretive? Between grandpa's loot vault and this gold mine, this place is worth a million fortunes!"

"Quiet! Whisper if you must but we don't want to attract any more attention than necessary. Anyway, that's iron in the rock, not gold." Something about the rocks bothers me and then I realize what's wrong.

This is igneous rock. We're in a volcano. And the air is warm.

I hasten down the stairs. After a while, with only the sound of our soft shoes brushing the steps, we pass a particularly beautiful patch of golden rock hedged with a sharp, porous black ridge.

"Ow!"

"What now?" I turn to look.

Charles leans over the guardrail, his glove torn open, hand bleeding. "Nothing. I was just touching the wall."

Blood drips from his hand, down into the cavern below. Just as I wonder how hurt Charles has to be to incur my father's wrath, a faint inhuman screech rises from below us.

Scrrrraaaaaay!

My skin crawls at the sound. Even though he's on a higher step, I'm taller. I grab his coat collar and pull his face to mine.

"Don't touch, say or do *anything* unless I tell you," I whisper.

28

"You're going to get us both killed!"

For the first time, he appears scared. He tucks his bleeding hand under his armpit and nods.

Another faint screech. Growing louder.

Louder. Deafening.

Dozens of winged albino creatures shoot from the stone gaps, talons extended. With long necks and viper heads, they have slender, sinuous reptilian bodies that are at least five feet long. Their strange heads resemble a cat more than a lizard. I extend my hand and telekinetically with my will create a buffer between them and us.

The creatures strike repeatedly at the invisible wall of energy I've raised, fangs slashing at Charles, who brandishes the torch. I can hold them off indefinitely but my focus breaks as the cavern trembles, hot air billowing up the volcanic shaft.

I lose my balance. Charles drops the torch as he grabs for the railing. In that split second, the buffer falters and the largest creature dives at Charles, snatching him in its talons.

Without thinking, without any hope, I leap onto the creature's back as it spirals downward.

Down into the endless pit.

Chapter 6

The vicious, venomous swarm envelops us, writhing and snapping at our necks. I push out against them, creating a new buffer. I then slam the beast's body into the wall. Repeatedly. Charles howls with each jolt. His eyes catch mine, wild with terror.

"What are you *doing*?"

"Want. To. Drop. YOU."

"ARE YOU CRAZY?"

The serpent's powerful neck coils, eyes narrowing at me. Its jaws open wide. Fangs lunge at my head. I twist away, barely dodging the attack. I briefly lose my grip. I find footing on his hipbone, pushing myself up.

A landing approaches below. It juts outward from the wall.

I extend my will again. This time, the serpent's neck stiffens, and we hang in the air, surrounded by its kin. A hundred narrowed serpent eyes beam at us with hatred and hunger. I shimmy up the neck to the serpent's head and with my finger I draw a sigil in the air over its skull as I shout the command: "Combust!"

The head smolders, smoke escaping from its eyelids. The skull bursts into flames.

The creatures flee in every direction, darting into the gaps. The headless beast at last drops Charles, wings helplessly beating the air in free fall.

Suspended in the air, I steady myself and then telekinetically grab for Charles. His fall breaks twenty feet below me.

I choke as water vapors engulf us, the hot, moist air forcing us back up the shaft. We've got to get out of here. Clutching Charles by his coat collar, I pull us both to the landing and we run into the open tunnel.

The tunnel floor is rocky. Charles collapses, choking. He's soaked to the bone from the vapors.

"Get up! We've got to keep moving!" I say, moving deeper into the tunnel. It's cooler here, away from the vent. I don't really know anything about volcanoes. Is this one going to erupt? Are the gases a precursor to lava? Or does it only vent hot air? If it's active, it hasn't erupted in a very long time.

A dim light appears in the distance where I suspect the tunnel splits off, but I don't hear anything.

Charles shakes his head. "I can't see anything. I'm going to break my neck!"

"Light," I say, drawing a sigil in the air. An angular "S" formed by two incomplete triangles appears. It swims between us, lighting Charles' pathway.

Charles shivers. "Why can't I do that? What makes you so special?" His lips are already turning blue.

"Shut up," I say, scanning the tunnel, "and hold still." I warm the air around him, stirring it the way Michael's mother did with the hairdryer as she helped us get ready for prom. She teased us for cringing at the goo she wanted to put in our hair. The look on your face when you saw me... My heart sinks at the memory.

Charles dries quickly. "What's wrong?" he asks, suspicion hitching his voice.

"Nothing. Let's go."

The tunnel is barely wide enough for us to walk side-by-side. As I suspected, the tunnel not only splits but forks into three passages. Which to take?

"It's whichever one angles down, dumbass," Charles says.

"It's whichever one isn't full of poison gases, imbecile."

I sniff the air in each passage to check for gases like carbon dioxide. I feel okay, no lightheadedness. Shrieks from the snake swarms rise in the volcano. We've got to choose quickly.

A tiny movement catches my eye in the far right fork. I stare for a moment until the shape solidifies.

"This way!" I motion for Charles to follow toward the shape.

31

"Why?"

"Life."

As we dart into that tunnel, Charles lags, fussing with something in his pocket. What is it? No time to think about it. Must press forward.

"Tell me if you feel lightheaded," I say. "Immediately."

Scrrrraaaaaay! The sounds get louder.

Frogs hop and squirm in the passage. Yellow spotted, blending into the vibrant, igneous rock. I dodge both the ankle-twisting lava stones and innocent frogs. Charles stumbles behind me, cursing.

At least I know he's alive.

We run as the creatures swoop into the tunnel in pursuit, tunnels branching. Charles is falling behind. Again he fumbles with something in his pocket. I just want to leave him to the creatures, but Father will know if he dies. His name will disappear from The List.

The tunnel narrows. Another fork is coming up. Which passage is correct?

A blur of white ahead. Shifting. Solidifying. A figure.

I slow down as Charles catches up. I grab his arm to keep him from passing me.

The white figure seems to be human, head bent, small hands drawn to shoulders. A hood falls over the face.

I've heard of ghosts but I'm not certain I believe in them. You taught me, Charity, to be more skeptical. When the figure looks up at us, the hood drops back.

The face.

It's my mother.

Chapter 7

Aaaaaidaaaan.

My mother's face swims in and out of focus, her long, curly black hair now white and spilling over her shoulders. Eyes no longer bright but dim with despair. Her tall frame floats just above the ground.

"Mum?" My heart breaks. Just seeing her face again – it's overwhelming. What is she doing here?

"What are the hell are you doing?" Charles asks me, clearly unaware of the apparition.

Her expression distraught, she turns from us and starts down the branch to the right, which leads to a steep slope.

SCRRRRAAAAAAY!

I follow her into the passage.

"That passage is too steep!" Charles shouts, scrambling after me.

"You're the one who said we should take the tunnel that goes down."

"But that's suicide! I'm going the other way." He stomps off down the other passage, the light moving with him.

Charity...how did you live with this person? It's like he's compelled to do the opposite of what I say, even if he initially agrees with it.

My mother was the only person I ever loved and trusted besides you, Charity. How can I ignore her? If it *is* her, that is.

I double back and charge after him down the other passage.

"HEY!"

Wrapping him in my invisible grip, I tear him off his feet. He floats like one of those balloons you tied to Keiko's locker for her birthday.

33

"DAMN YOU!" He struggles, but no matter how much he flails, his fists and feet miss me.

SCRRRRAAAAAAY!

The serpents screech as they careen after us, wings brushing the walls as we dive into the other passage.

My mother's ghost has vanished. The walls close in further as the ground slants. Charles drags behind me, howling for me to release him. His protests would be funny if I weren't worried the creatures would eat him alive.

Within moments, the passage squeezes us almost flat, the gritty surface snagging our clothes. The serpents' screeching grows furious as they clog the narrow gap in the shrinking corridor, unable to pursue.

"I told you! This one is wrong!" Charles says. "You're trying to kill me."

"You imbecile!" I yell back. "I just saved you!" But we're trapped. A draft tells me there's more beyond, but behind us, a serpent's cat-like head threads its way into the gap, inches from Charles.

SCRRRRAAAAAAY!

Closing my eyes, I focus on the walls around us. Moss suddenly sprouts on the surface of the igneous rocks. Next, a thin layer of moisture forms on the surfaces.

Stretch. Wiggle. My arm slips against the wall. The wet sealskin slides instead of snags.

"Careful! Go slow," I caution Charles, releasing him from the invisible bond so that he can maneuver independently. He complains under his breath but works his way through the gap, falling on me as he tumbles down the rocky slope. I break his momentum just before his shoulder strikes one of the jagged stone teeth surrounding a tongue of porous black rock and he tumbles into a cavern.

I step cautiously onto the tongue that unfurls into a cavern. Mists obscure the cavern walls, making it impossible to guess how big it truly is.

We're not alone. Hundreds of wraiths bleed from the shadows to crowd around us. Men, women, and children. Faces mournful. Curious.

34

Angry.

Mists have obscured the way we came in. So, I send up a barrier to keep them at bay, but they move through it.

"Do that thing you did with the dragons!" Charles demands. "It's not working!"

A towering woman weaves through the crowd, her head at least three feet above mine, rotting flesh hanging from one side of her face, long white braids swinging below her elbows, gown billowing with ashes, eyes fiery. Albino reptile wings crown her shoulders.

The wraiths part for her.

This can't be real. But it is.

This is the realm of Hel.

Chapter 8

Not to be confused with Hell, the Christian invention of fiery damnation. Centuries before Christianity would organize, another religion was thriving in the wintery northern countries, one that worshipped gods like Odin, Thor, and Frygg while fearing the trickster Loki. Hel was one of Loki's children, or so the story went. She ruled over the realm of the dead, also known as Helheim.

But it seems the dead here in her "hall" are not from the general population. Rather, they are likely the souls of people who have died here in the Arctic. Many are Inuit. Others are explorers from another era. And still more probably prisoners of my father, brought here to serve some purpose and then be killed.

"Aidan, son of Nicholas," Hel says. She towers over us, her albino body draped in flowing coal black robes. Her long, thin serpent's tongue flickers from her wormy mouth, teeth rotted, her very words lingering like the stench of a corpse. "Your father is near death yet it is you who visits me. Did you bring me an offering?" She pink eyes lock onto Charles with undisguised hunger.

Charles ducks behind me.

I remember something from an old book in Father's library. I quote it out loud. "In wrath Odin did seize Loki's daughter and fling her beyond the edge of the Ocean. She fell until she reached the black depths of Nifel-hel. There in the realms of torture became she a queen."

Hel sniggers. "No one has power over me. It seems your father never told you the real story about me, did he? I am your blood, Aidan." She leans over me. A worm drops from her mouth and lands on my cheek. I wipe it away with revulsion. Previously cloaked in her robes, her albino wings open behind her. "I am your many-greats-grandmother. My blood is in you. *I am you.*"

"I believe it, Granny." Charles shoves me. "He tried to kill me and my crew."

"*You're* the ones that tried to kill *me!*" I shout. "And I saved you from yourself!" The pitch of my voice drops. The words pour out like tar. "And for what? I should have let you kill yourself. You're worthless! Pathetic! Evil!" The light of my eyes bathes Charles' shocked face as I turn to him, seething. "Enough talk. Time to die."

My skin stings like a thousand nettles prick the surface. The rage floods my body. Destruction races through every synapse, the violence pounding in my head. Hel is somehow manipulating the part of me that is Krampus, making me lose control of my rage.

By my will, Charles rises above the ground, clutching at his throat, feet kicking. "An-ti-dote," he gasps.

Beyond Charles, in the crowd of wraiths, I see my mother's apparition. Her face is radiant. She mouths three words that ring in my head.

I love you.

"You think I have an antidote to your father's poisoning?" Hel laughs, her body bloating, ivory scales rippling over her skin. The braids meld with her head and neck as her face snakes around me. "Kill this mortal and end this," she urges.

My mother's face shines. That face – I've so desperately missed it – reminds me of my better side. Hers.

The spell breaks. The stinging recedes. I can think again.

End *this*? Not Charles. She means the world. To bring the apocalypse. My ancient kin called it Ragnarok. In the prophecies of Völuspá, a fiery sword rises into the sky and blots out the sun.

Like a volcanic eruption. That would certainly kill us both. Or at least Charles.

Hel transforms into a hideous, bloated monster with pale skin and sickly amber eyes.

I drop Charles and he falls to the ground, crying out as he lands awkwardly. I let the violence rise in my blood, blotting out everything. Everything, that is, except my purpose. I love you,

Charity Jones, and nothing will take you away from me if I can help it.

Hel's wings rise up threateningly, stretching across the cavern, yet she backs away. Her massive jaws open, and heat erupts from her throat. "YOU WANT TO KILL HIM. IN YOUR HEART. YOU CANNOT BETRAY YOUR DESIRES."

"Some desires are stronger than others," I reply calmly.

Hel lunges for Charles, but I throw up an invisible shield. She collides with the barrier. He runs through the wraiths toward the corridor opening on the far side of the volcanic vault.

She then strikes at me, the true source of her frustration. Her powerful wings beat the air, blasting the great cavern, scattering rocks and dust in its wake. The wind stirs, driving Charles toward a cluster of serrated rocks. Wounded, he's easily thrown by the assault.

Summon Yggdrasil!

Urgent and commanding, my mother's voice speaks in my mind.

"How?" I ask out loud.

Summon it!

As Hel lunges at me, I extend my arms toward her and focus on the earth beneath us. Energy swarms over my skin, coppery, blurring, my vision pixelating, temperature rising, light separating.

Expanding...

Chapter 9

Pools of light appear on the volcano floor surrounding Hel. Bursting with green leaves, the massive branches of Yggdrasil erupt from the pools, shooting up to the ceiling. They surround Hel, crushing her in their embrace, and pierce her heavy wings. Blood oozes from the cuts, flowing like lava. She screams with agony.

At my command, one of the branches drives into her neck. Her monstrous wings and body blacken before petrifying into basalt rock. Even her blood hardens in long red streaks from her wounds.

I collapse in shock, shivering violently. I've killed a god! There must surely be a price to pay for that. Did I have a choice? I couldn't let her kill Charles.

The wraiths whisper at my back. My mother approaches me as the others huddle. I fear her reproach. How could I have done such a wretched thing in her presence?

My boy.

Unsteadily, I rise to meet her. "Mum?"

Look at you. So handsome. Like your grandpa.

"Mum, how can this be you?"

I'm so proud of you, Aidan. Hel lied. She isn't your grandmother at all. Your true many-greats-grandmother lies beyond.

Burning tears spill down my face. Overwhelmed with emotion, I reach out to touch her. "I miss you so much."

She places her cool, ghostly palm against my hand. *I miss you, too. But we must go now.*

"But I just found you! Where will you go?"

Her form wavers, as do the crowds beyond. *Now that Hel no*

longer holds us here, I must go where I am no longer anyone's mother.

Grief racks my body. "Please don't go!"

Aidan, don't forget you're the Klaas. The beginning and the end.

And with that, my mother and the other wraiths vanish.

I expect to hear Charles' mocking voice, but there's only silence. He's nowhere to be seen.

"Charles? Where are you?"

After I ensure he isn't huddling behind some outcropping of volcanic rock, I wonder if he re-entered the tunnel without me.

I check The List. He lives. And he means grievous harm. But when does he not? How useful is this "gift" if one is dealing with a perpetually agitated sociopath?

I have to find him before he gets himself — and everyone else — killed.

But first, I slip between the ash trees to petrified Hel. Scattered at the her feet are several blood-red, egg-shaped "stones." They seem to be what dripped from her ash-inflicted wounds. Some of the stones broke apart when they hit the ground, leaving glistening puddles of ruby dust. Despite their egg shape, I don't think these stones are what I want. I'm pretty sure the "egg" is "Ygg" as in Yggdrasil, not Hel's blood. Although, I'm sure Hel's blood has some powerful magical properties.

I remove the tin from my pack and scrape the tree bark into it. The tree heals as I cut. The regenerative power warms my body and my heart. I sense Yggdrasil is a divine being in its own right.

Hel stares down at me with glassy eyes. I shudder.

I slip out from the grove, the tin secured. Listening. Measuring. Without my father's full power, I cannot locate where a person is at all, only that they live. At least Charles is alive. Could he have entered the tunnel from which we entered? Too dangerous, given the threats we left behind. Perhaps he's in that smaller passageway across the cavern, which is little more than a crawlspace. It makes sense he'd go there to hide from the battle.

I crawl inside.

Even with my eyes the darkness is almost impenetrable. My hands and knees scrape the rocks. My ears pick up indecipherable whispers. Deeper within, the crawlspace widens to another cavern. I'm unusually cold and weak. What place is this? I then recall that Charles should still have his light sigil. I see no sign of it. The chasm that lies just beyond the rocky outcropping on which I stand glows softly. I peer over the edge. Breathtaking. Like millions of diamonds embedded in the hollowed earth. It funnels downward to a...burial mound?

Where is Charles? I turn back toward the crawlspace opening. *There* he stands, right behind me —

— and he plunges the knife into my heart.

Chapter 10

The blade drives a burst of lightning into my heart, into my arms, head and legs. I wobble, suspended in time, disbelieving.

Dying.

Charles leaves the knife buried in me, the twisted, ivory narwhal hilt inscribed with a glyph I don't recognize. Using a second, more mundane knife, he snips my pack straps. The pack drops to the ground behind me as I crumple to my knees, shadows swimming in my vision.

"What?" I gasp. "Charles, what are you doing?" Disbelief. Shock.

He snatches up my pack, pats it down, and nods with satisfaction.

Why am I so weak? Why can't I just pull the knife out and heal? My arms hang leaden at my sides.

"Your dad was right about this place. Now we're both rid of you. Have fun dying, asshole!"

Charles kicks me, his toe landing squarely under my chin. Jaw blazing with pain, vision fading, I topple backward over the edge...

...into...

...breathless...

...nothingness.

Constellations pass. Radiant lines crisscross. A million diamonds wink in hushed oblivion. I gently plummet in silence.

At peace.

Perhaps now I'll be with my mother. Somewhere safe. No more heartache or torment. The greatest evil, St. Augustine once said, is physical pain. But I'm free. I feel nothing.

Just bliss.

I, who conquered Hel, am now in Paradise.

I, who conquered Hel, am now in Hell. Because you're not here, Charity Jones. I must return to you. To have you by my side, to entwine your fingers in mine. Your mouth pressed to mine, our two worlds one. Somewhere in the blackberry brambles, nylon book bags soaked in rain puddles at our feet. Everything drenched in love.

But I'm dead.

A heaviness settles over me. Gravity pulling me into the embrace of dirt.

Shadows drift over my eyes, punctuated with soft explosions of light.

A presence approaches as the shadows give way to a heavy fog, stirring and whirling before me. The light intensifies as a formidable man strides toward me. His heavy iron-gray hair and beard drapes over his shoulders and down his chest. A shimmering, silvery robe envelops him, billowing at his feet like a Victorian ball gown as he walks. He holds a fearsome spear in his right hand, a winged helmet crowning his head. Heads cocked sideways as they peer at me, an enormous raven sits on each shoulder.

I rifle through my memory for everything I've read about Odin. Lord of Yule and the Wild Hunt. Poet. The hanged man. Soul-giver.

God of ecstasy.

And fury.

This must be the afterlife. It's the only place where one could meet him.

Greetings, Grandson.

Odin the Mighty. My eyes can barely meet his single azure blue eye. The other eye socket is shriveled and sunken.

The ravens caw loudly at me as they flutter and hop on Odin's shoulders. Their movement seems to disturb the fog, which scatters in their wake.

Fear not, Grandson. These are Huninn and Muninn. They're excited to meet you. They've been away to help a friend, but now they're back with me.

The raven on the left rubs the top of its head against Odin's ear. Odin then smiles at me benevolently as he points to the narwhal knife still protruding from my chest.

A gift from St. Nick, I see.

Indeed, the knife is still sticking out from my chest wound. A rune is crudely engraved on the surface. Yew. Death. A symbol of Hel. It fades. A curse for one use.

"Charming, isn't it?" I say bitterly. "I guess he wins the award for World's Worst Father." It had to be my father who made it because Charles couldn't have fashioned the knife without help.

That fool is almost dead. The mortal boy will die trying to open the gate that leads back into the fortress. There is no hope for humankind.

"They'll die because of me. Because I was stupid. I let my guard down. I'm so sorry, All-Father."

Odin's face softens.

You died trying to save humankind. That is noble and worthy of eternal honor.

"But I'm a god killer!"

He bursts out laughing. The air rumbles, and even the ravens cackle.

So am I, Grandson. So am I.

Odin gestures with his spear and the skies beyond tear open to reveal a hill on which sits an unspeakably beautiful ivory and golden palace that stands tall against a brilliant clear sky. A rainbow stretches from the palace gates down to the ground to admit visitors.

Valhalla.

More ravens circle the skies above, and in the distance, the joyful singing of dead warriors rings out as they feast and fight until Ragnarok, when the All-Father will call on them to join him in the final battle.

But I need to return to life. To you, Charity.

Grandfather Odin detects something is amiss.

Why is it that you hesitate?

"I'm honored that you'd have me join your warriors, but I have to go back, All-Father."

His hand tightens on the spear. He looks beyond displeased.

"I can't let humankind die."

Odin raises an eyebrow.

"It's not just Charity. It's her family, our friends, and their families. Everyone I met. And beyond." I pause and see he's unmoved.

I no longer love humankind. Nor they me. Why should I care what happens to them?

He's right. They only care about Odin except as a character in a film or comic book. He was once one of the greatest deities ruling the planet. And now that other deities and religions have taken place in human hearts, he's no longer bothered.

"I know you no longer care for humans because they no longer believe in you as they once did. But many children believe in me. Even though I have mortal blood, I'm still a god to them. I give them hope and make them happy. Please, All-Father. There must be a way."

He closes his one good eye and seems to meditate as the raven on his right shoulder mutters into his ear. A stillness grips the scene, and I sink into the holy silence. Then, Odin opens his eye and speaks in rhyme. Power ripples from his words like an incantation.

I can return the gift of life
Where you will suffer yet more strife.
But you must give up something dear —
An eye, a hand, perhaps an ear.
Or yet another thing so true,
You'd swear it was a part of you.
A thing that shows your declaration
Is more than just a protestation.

45

He gave an eye to Urd's Well for wisdom. Therefore, I must surrender something for the gift of life. But what? And how could I choose? How will I know it's enough? "All-Father, name whatever you believe is a fair exchange and I will make my decision."

I feel sick with fear that he'll take away your love, Charity. If he does, I'd prefer to go onto Valhalla, but I meant what I said. I feel a deeper obligation, and I'll just have to find a way to carry on without you.

Odin strikes the ground with his spear, causing the rainbow bridge to disintegrate and the skies to turn gunmetal gray. He continues the incantation.

The Charity you cherish so
You'll never know if friend or foe.
You shall no longer know her heart
Whenever you are set apart.

A jolt of surprise. "You mean, you're taking her off The List?" Such a thing had never occurred to me. Or, at least I didn't know if it were possible.

He shakes his head.

You'll surely know if she's alive
And nothing else, although you strive.
Her dearest wishes will be blurred
Unless from her you hear the word.

Amazing! That's easy. I'll always know that Charity loves me. And if she doesn't, she'll tell me. I'm suspicious that the All-Father would ask so little of me. But then, I am his grandson. Maybe he loves me and doesn't want to make me suffer more than I have to.

"So, I'll know she's alive, but I won't know her deepest desires?"

Odin looks to me expectantly.

I know exactly what I'll answer.

46

Chapter 11

Before I can voice my agreement to the deal, I awaken from death to the agony of the knife piercing my heart. I cough violently, blood and other fluids spilling over my chin, into my ears. I grasp the hilt and, with the last shred of strength left in me, I pull.

Slowly, the blade emerges. A blizzard of white pain rises behind my eyes. My screams fly up into the funnel above me, echoing, magnifying. Once free, the knife rests in my hand, coated with my blood. I hold the knife blade close to my eyes, my vision fuzzy.

Blood surges from my wound. My consciousness fades...I fumble with the coat to staunch the flow. I can feel the *Book of Sigils* in the coat pocket. They are useless to me here...must be a way to connect with my power here...before it's too late.

There is...one...way. Charity, you would call it...a conductor? I would...call it...

I drive the blade into the ground. *Connection.* The immense power of this place courses up into the metal, into the hilt, burning my hand, but I hold on, back arching as the power floods my bones to the point of breaking. I drive the fingers of my other hand into the soil to complete the circuit. One word – this time in English – riots in my thoughts.

Heal.

The "diamonds" in the walls turn green and form a network of emeralds. Awash in green light, the entire cavern pulses, the sound expanding by the beat. The energy swims into my wound, pain receding, vision sharpening. The bitterness clears my mouth and I inhale, drawing the strange energy into my lungs, exhaling a peppery mist. With each breath, I hurt less. Strength creeps back into my body. The hope, the terror.

The thirst for revenge...

I live.

The diamonds return to their former dazzle. The cavern is quiet.

I stand up, retrieving the knife embedded in the ground. It sickens me that someone hacked the tusk from a precious narwhal to create the hilt of this knife. And it's not exactly a tusk. It's actually a tooth that protrudes from the narwhal's forehead, twisted like the unicorn. The malice of the act must have given the knife particularly terrible power. As much as I hate touching the knife, I grip the narwhal hilt and wipe the blade on my leggings. I'm going to need all the power I can get to escape this funnel.

Which leaves a bigger question. How did Charles get out of the tunnels? Or did he? There's no telling how much time has passed, but if it's been more than an hour, he has a fantastic lead. Assuming he's overcome the flying creatures and found his way back, he might have already returned and administered the antidote. The List tells me he is still alive. But is he capable of returning to the fortress proper? My father would never have given him this task if it weren't possible to complete.

More importantly...*what is this place?* And how do I escape?

I step closer to examine the diamonds. Nothing is ever as it seems here. The diamond hums as I press it with my finger.

Suddenly, an image expands behind my eyes of a stunning young woman in heavy furs with flowing blonde hair. Focused and dispassionate, she lashes a giant serpent to a cavern ceiling with ropes to a stalactite so that the serpent's mouth hangs over a man bound by intestines to a jagged stalagmite. The man shrieks in agony as the serpent's venom drips onto his face.

It's Loki! The woman must be Skaði, goddess of justice and vengeance. She's the one who was responsible for Loki's punishment, particularly the serpent.

As Loki screams, the scene remains firmly focused on Skaði. She's unmoved by his pain. I'm startled when she turns her gaze directly to me and says, "Remember me, Young Klaas."

I yank my finger away from the diamond. My head clears. Are these bits of divine history kept for prosperity? Like a library? What a weird thing for Hel to have.

I touch another diamond. The hideous image of Hel herself fills my vision. She hisses at me, wings spreading. "You killed me, son of Klaas, and you will pay!"

I pull away, heart pounding. These are dead gods! This is some kind of graveyard. Hence the weakness I felt when I entered, as if my life force were being sucked out of me. But it's not all death here. If I could do it once, maybe I can again...

I look down at my feet. Holding my hands out over the ground, I close my eyes. Praying.

The cavern lights shine icy blue.

Chapter 12

Lightning crackles up the cavern walls among the embedded stones. A gale whips around me. I stand firm, pure violence coiled in my fists, the storm surging inside and out. Caught up in the violent wind, the bone dust swirls like a sand storm, grazing my flesh, burning my eyes. Thunder in my throat.

I back up as the branch erupts from the ground.

Another branch of Yggdrasil, but full with smaller branches lush with foliage.

This time, I grab hold. The ground disappears beneath me as the branch climbs, and I rise from the funnel depths. Within moments, the branch stops and I jump onto the ledge where Charles stabbed me.

Charles. He's still alive.

I thank Yggdrasil and take off for the tunnels.

The tunnels are warmer since the venting. The bright white chalk marks stand out on the dark red surface like graffiti. Bread crumbs leading back. That must have been what he was fumbling with when he lagged behind me.

Brisk steps, shallow breath. Listening. Moving silently.

Several yellow-spotted frogs lie on the ground in a splattered heap. Very strange.

At the landing, the cavern is quiet. I scan the stairway for him. He had a significant lead.

To my surprise, I see him.

Way, way up on the spiral, he closes in on the Gate of Niklaus. The heights are dizzying. Even if he knows the words of power, only a son of Nicholas can open the gate.

I move swiftly up the steps, wishing more than ever that I could fly. Father can. I wonder why the serpents haven't come for him and then realize that he has smeared himself with a yellow substance from head to toe.

The frogs. He must have slaughtered them in the tunnels to put the serpents off his scent. It seems to have worked.

Charles approaches the gate and, clutching my pack in his left hand, he lifts his right, palm upward. *"Machet daz Tatzlewurmstor uf!"*

Wrong phrase. Wrong person.

The onyx of the black gate ripples ominously and showers him with an oily fluid. I "throw" a telekinetic shield over him, but it's too late. He screeches as the fluid burns his exposed skin, even through the sealskins.

Willing myself faster, the cavern spins as I race upward, taking the stairs two, three, four at a time. If only I could fly...

I shout into the cavern: "I've killed your mistress! Serve me!"

A half-second later, a serpent emerges from a hole. A *tatzelwurm*. As it rises alongside me, it lowers its head and extends its neck for me to mount.

I jump onto its back, and it soars to the top of the cavern.

Charles crumples, shuddering and cursing. He tears off his smoldering clothing. But as he throws himself at the brink, feet slipping over the edge, I telekinetically hold him upright.

"You bastard!" His voice is magnified, distorted. *"Let...me...die!"*

My dearest Charity, I confess that I feel a sliver of schadenfreude as he now thrashes and rages.

He drops the pack into the abyss. I "catch" that, too, and levitate it into my hands. The pack's surface is burned but the tin inside is safe. The gate has stopped disgorging acid and lies dormant once again. Nothing can prepare me for the horror of Charles' injuries as we glide to the top of the stairs.

Charles snarls at me, his acid-chewed lips curled. "This is your fault!" he cries. "Your. *Fault!*" Blistering skin melts over one eye, blinking under a hood of puckered flesh. A cauliflower of waxy, oozing cartilage remains where his left ear was. His scalp is scalded;

whatever is left of his hair, charred. Hideous burns splatter his torso, neck, left hand. He shivers. Tears and snot slicken his pitiful face. Forever disfigured.

So far, Father hasn't carried through with his threat. Charles is badly injured yet he hasn't killed me. Perhaps because he knows the cure is at hand, if only we could get through the gate.

The serpent carries me to the stairway and bows its head so I may descend beside Charles. "Thank you," I say, and it flies off. I hastily withdraw the book from my coat.

"You? Had it?" Charles gasps. He lunges for me, but unlike when he had the narwhal knife, I now have my strength back. I "hold" him in place as I search the pages for what he needs. I first try the healing spell but nothing happens. I keep turning pages until I find something that'll work.

"Numb," I intone, drawing the sigil over his head. His breathing calms, his body relaxing. I also warm the air around him so that the cretin doesn't freeze to death. "Well, well. Isn't this what they call instant karma?"

"Shut up!"

I raise my hand to the gate, voice dropping as I unleash the command. "*Machet daz Niklaustor uf!*"

The black stone ripples as it parts for us to emerge in the Chamber of Niflhel.

Reilly and the others surge into the room, crying and shouting. But I know something is deeply amiss before any of them speak. Icicles blister the walls — a sign that his end is near.

"Take care of Charles," I tell my siblings. "Get the trismegistus from the kitchen trove. Melt some ice to make a tea of it and have him drink it."

I run to Father.

The entire fortress is scarred with ice. A hoary frost carpets the throne room. In the bedroom, jagged blades of ice scab over the eye mosaic, turning the basalt wall white. The hoar clumps on the skins and furs covering the bed. The healing sigils that once hung in the air at each corner have disappeared.

The air stinks of death.

Father lies on the bed, his face turned to me, cataract-shrouded eyes barely flickering with recognition as they land on me. Blood and pus matte the white fur of his beard and chest. The wound has deepened, now a gurgling cavity. He lifts a hand to me, tongue bloated as it unfurls from his mouth, unable to speak. The stink of rotten flesh and burned fur is debilitating.

Before I even reach his side, I open the tin and pour the ash shavings into my hand. They shimmer like embers, but they're soothing to the touch. I add three drops of water from the jug by his bed to my palm to make a poultice. His eyes lock onto mine with a look I want to believe is sorrow, even repentance. His breath deepens when I apply the poultice, smearing the shavings into his wounds, but his scalp remains gray, the skin curdled. He struggles to speak but only manages to murmur something unintelligible. The cataracts dissolve, his features relaxing, tongue retracting.

He looks almost human. Cheeks sallow, brows white.

I spread the last of the poultice on his ailing scalp. The medicine radiates like sunset, raising the room temperature. The blades of ice scarring the wall bead up and weep. A good sign.

He grasps my arm, nails cracked, wrinkled lips working to make ghost words.

"I can't hear you," I say. He won't release my arm.

"Your brother..." The words dribble out like pebbles from a child's hand.

"He tried to open the gate on his own and it...*digested* him. But he lives. My siblings are taking care of him. I daresay he's now uglier than you are."

He laughs but it turns into a hideous cough, his tongue unfurling. His hand relaxes its grip on my arm.

I back away from the bed as he closes his eyes. "Keep your end of the bargain. Let me go."

His hand opens.

I feel his will release me.

"Thank you," I say with a mixture of joy and hatred.

Backing out of the room, I can already hear my siblings' frantic activity. Charles has passed out on a hide and they are trying to keep his burned skin from sticking to the fur. As you know, Charity, those sloth-like claws are not equipped for delicacy but rather for climbing ice. I no longer care what happens to Charles. Even if I did, there's nothing I could do. I quickly transfer my leftover rations to a new pack and mount a wind climber.

"Young Klaas!" Reilly calls out, clearly stricken at the sight of me leaving. "We will miss you. We love you. Please remember us."

Her words break my heart. "Reilly, I will never forget you or your kindness. Remember that kindness is the most important thing. Always."

And with that, I goad the wind climber and we gallop out of the fortress. I'm free! A howl of joy crouches in the back of my throat. I don't dare release it yet. In just a few hours I'll be with you, Charity. I can't believe it.

Twilight breaks across the horizon, an umber haze crowning the smoky blue undulations of snow. It must be the twilight of March, the eve of Spring.

But just before the wind climber leaps up to fly over the fortress Sentinels, I hear the most devastating sound in the world. A sound I should not be hearing.

My father's death rattle.

Chapter 13

Torn from the wind climber's back, I fall to the ice. Everything turns muddy in my vision as my body convulses with pain. Black fur flushes the surface of my skin. Arms. Face. Chest. Feet harden into hooves. Mouth widening. Teeth sharpening. Back arching, muscles thickening.

My voice deepens to a bestial growl. My tongue feels as if it's being ripped in two as it elongates, splits, and slithers out of my mouth.

Massive horns tear through the skin of my forehead, blood running into my eyes. Stumbling. Falling. I stagger to my new full height.

And then I go mad.

The List.

Billions of names, locations, ages, desires flood my mind. Before, I had only limited access to The List. I knew names of people before they told me, what they wanted during Yuletide, and whether they'd been bad or good. But now my mind is overwhelmed with the cacophony of humanity – names, locations, connections, diseases, joys, secret passions, hideous crimes, and much more.

"NO. NO. NO. NO. GODS, NO!

"NO. NO. NO. NO. GODS, NOOOOOOO!"

I strike the ice with my fists, splits running under the Sentinels to the open Arctic.

A bestial howl of anguish echoes over the Arctic. I realize that's my voice now. I hate everything I see, feel, think. I hate who I am. And who I could be. I want to die.

I'll never be him. King of Shadows. Father of dark Yuletide. Thief. Murderer. Rapist. But I understand why he hated the world. He could see too much.

My siblings pour out of the fortress. Surrounding me. Lifting, carrying me back into the throne room. The last place I want to be. But I must sit here. I can't get past the Sentinels for another nine months.

As I sit on the throne, sobbing, my human form returns.

That night, my siblings carry Father's body wrapped in sealskin through the Gate of Baldur, down into the tunnel that leads to the crypt. My siblings sing a mournful song in a language I don't know and they might no longer understand themselves. The crypt contains nine tombs. Each tomb contains a long-dead Klaas, his human likeness carved into the mausoleum surface, framed by mammoth tusks. Nothing else denotes who is buried within. Not even the years that they lived. Just the dismal reminder that each and every one bore a mortal face.

Like mine.

I've always hated this anonymous collection of dead Nicholases. I am Aidan MacNichol. My mother gave me a name. I can't imagine surrendering my life for an unmarked grave.

I stop before the tomb that sits empty farthest inside, waiting for my father's corpse. The ninth Klaas. I didn't open it, nor did any of my siblings. This fortress might be frozen yet it's alive with strange, untamable magic. Six elves enter the tomb and place his body in a coffin-shaped receptacle marked with unfamiliar silver glyphs.

The song dies. I enter the tomb and peel away the sealskin to look upon his shockingly human face. I only vaguely recall what he looked like when I was small. When he wasn't violent, when he was far more Saint than Krampus, my mother was quite taken with him. I can see why. Even with the damage to his scalp, his strong jawline and sculpted nose are still striking. And those eyes. They haunted me every time I looked in your bathroom mirror, Charity, because they're mine.

But you wouldn't have known that from your encounter with

him. It's what's happening inside The Klaas that determines whether he looks human or monstrous. You saw him when his heart was ugliest.

I mourn not for his death, but for his life. He was never the father I wanted and desperately needed. And now there's no chance he ever will be. No change of heart. No slow correction over time. He's gone. I thought perhaps I'd been too idealistic, letting the characters in books form my ideas of what a father should be. But then I met your father, Charity, and I realized that I hadn't been idealistic *enough*. Even if flawed, Fathers can be amazing people.

My siblings watch me with shining eyes as I exit the tomb. As if to indicate that the coffin is now forever closed, an ice wall instantly forms over the entrance. Seamless, smooth, impenetrable. Instinctively, I close my eyes, recall my father's human face, and touch the surface.

The ice groans as an invisible force carves Father's features into the wall. I step back to take in the uncanny likeness under the heavy scorch of mourning.

It's done.

When I turn to leave, another tomb has silently appeared beside it. Empty. Waiting.

Mine.

Chapter 14

Brooding over that harbinger of my death, I lag behind my siblings in the procession back to the throne. Reilly stays close by my side.

"Young Klaas," she says, "what will you do until Christmas? We serve you. Do not forget."

The depression lightens a shade. Yes, there's still one night a year that I can escape to be with the one I love.

Christmas.

But it feels centuries away. The only thing that brings me back is the sudden realization that I know where you are, Charity.

Pittsburgh, Pennsylvania. Carnegie Mellon University. That's where you live but you're headed to Washington D.C.

But thanks to the deal I made with Odin, I don't know anything else about you. Are you thinking of me? What are your dearest desires? Your biggest plans?

Like me, are you now changed, too?

It's no matter. I will love you regardless. And I now know precisely what to do.

Meanwhile, I still have my refuge: the fortress library.

Toppled and crushed, the library stacks darkly mirror those at the high school. Even in their best days, they are far less pristine than Mr. Vittorio would ever allow. A long time ago, I'd organized them alphabetically by author and title, separating the maps, journals and nonfiction from the novels.

The bookcases were built by magic but the material comes from marooned ships, abandoned sleds, and other artifacts of humanity I can't identify.

But Father had a tantrum in the library after I escaped. He would never have burned it down, but he certainly damaged it. My siblings bring me food and drink as I spend the next several weeks repairing what was lost, searching for any book I might have overlooked that would help me escape.

I also have to find out why the ash bark and three drops of water didn't work. It seemed to work at first but it ultimately failed. My intuition tells me that an element was missing. But what?

During my hunt for knowledge, I find a copy of *One Hundred Years of Solitude* smashed under a fallen shelf. My heart pounds. This is the book you kept referring to when we were together, the one you were reading in AP English. The book's broken spine shifts in my hands, the ripped pages filthy, but I consume every word right then and there the moment I pick it up. I need to know the images that touched your imagination. So this is where the butterflies came from! They flutter in my mind's eye as scorpions fill the tub. The secret trysts of Mauricio and Meme sweeten my memories of our romantic hours as we trespassed on your neighbor's property.

I wish more than ever I could talk to you about the book. I crave your intellectual companionship as much as, if not more than, anything else.

When I'm not reading or researching, I spend hours of meditation every day learning to focus so that The List doesn't drive me mad. Your name is a beacon that helps me cull, separate and suppress the names I don't need from those I do. I learn to find Michael, Ricardo and Judy, and then deftly let them go. Your parents, too. They are no longer together. The strain of Charles' imprisonment had been terrible, but the aftermath of Father's destruction, my kidnapping, and Leo's death was too much.

I hope you'll forgive me, but in some ways my mind is warping with this access to The List. While I can't measure you, I measure your friends constantly.

Obsessively.

So closely, I can almost hear your heartbeat behind theirs. Your name crowds out the billions. I sent you dreams once without trying. Maybe I can again.

Summer passes.

The sun rises and sets until it stops setting altogether. The fortress is filled with joy. The elves play and sing boisterously day and night whenever they're not hunting, gathering lichen to feed the wind climbers, or clearing away refuse. I can't help smiling when I hear them. They sing Christmas carols, of course, as well as the ancient songs.

I don't watch them eat. It's really unpleasant.

The elves also bring me some of the letters that accumulate in the Chamber of Ivory. A great many of them entertain and delight me as children put pencil to paper to express their Christmas wishes, which I already know. Many letters offer lists of toys and other diversions, but others ask for a parent to stop drinking, to find a real home instead of living in a vehicle, or for a relative to stop abusing them. These break my heart. How could my father have been so cold to these requests?

And then it happens. Reilly brings me a letter from you in May.

Dear Santa,
I've been a very good girl this year. I want two gifts for Christmas more than anything.
    1. Aidan.
    2. Your head.
See you soon.
Sincerely,
Charity Jones

"YYEEEEEEESSSSSSSSSSSSSS!!!!" I dance around the library, punching the air and crowing with happiness. My voice reverberates through the entire fortress, probably across the Arctic Ocean, too. I hug Reilly – something I've never done before. She looks relieved when I let go.

"Charity Jones wants me, Reilly. Gods, I can't wait to see her! She'll be so happy to know that Father is gone."

Elsewhere in the fortress, the elves burst into a new song.

Infinitely more hideous than Caliban and as treacherous as Iago, Charles plagues the fortress. He vacates his bowels and bladder wherever he wishes, sometimes right in his food. He does it to anger me. He wants me to put him out of his misery. Suicide by cop, as you Americans say. Or, in this case, suicide by Krampus. But I won't. I can't bring myself to do it.

He spends most days sitting in the fortress entrance, huddled in sealskin, staring at the Sentinels with his one good eye. He hasn't spoken much since Father's death except that he does seem kinder to the elves — probably because their healing arts and my magic are what keep him comfortable. I can't seem to heal the damage Charles incurred beyond the gate, and I don't know why.

Nonetheless, two elves guard the library at all times to keep him away from the more magical books. They tell me that he mostly reads stories of the old gods and the occasional map. It seems harmless as long as he doesn't harm those books.

I also let him ride the wind climbers as long as he's gentle with them. He explores and spends time in the air above the fortress. The wind climbers are forbidden to take him beyond the Sentinels.

Meanwhile, I'm heartbroken that I can't free The Mothers in the Taggalaq. Having been imprisoned when they were young and therefore much smaller, they are now far too big to fit in the tunnels. I do dissolve the bars and visit them every day, trying to learn their language. So far, no luck.

When T.S. Eliot said that April is the cruelest month, he clearly never lived in the Arctic. On Hallow's Eve, I'm daydreaming in the library, wondering what books you're reading and who you're meeting. *See you soon.* You think my father is coming, no doubt. I wish I could put your mind at ease.

Thoughts of surprising you on Christmas entertain me when a book hits the floor. And then another.

Charles.

His expression disdainful, he yanks books from the shelves and drops them. I will them up and back into their original places. He reaches for another book but I hold up my hand. His fingers hit an invisible barrier.

I already know what he wants for Christmas.

"Take me back to prison." His is voice hoarse. Tears pour down his cheeks. "You don't need me. Your old man is dead. I'm just an eyesore."

Never taking my eyes off the books before me, I reply. "You think I'm going to drop you back in a juvenile detention center after what you did? You committed murder at the fortress. And since the only law here is mine, *this* is your life sentence. That is, until I tire of you and feed you to the polar bears. Lord knows they need a good meal."

A leather-bound pamphlet made of parchment is wedged between two fatter tomes. It's at least five hundred years old, I'd say. I push apart the two bigger books and slide the pamphlet from the shelf. As Charles broods for a moment, I examine the pamphlet's pages. Woodcuts. No words. Depictions of images from the Edda.

And then I see something. It's one of the drawings of Yggdrasil with the worlds of Asgard, Midgard and the rest at different levels. Beneath the tree and Niflheim, the tree's roots weep three white drops.

Why didn't the drops of water work in the poultice for Father's wound? Perhaps it's not water...

Charles continues his tearful pitch. "It would make my mom happy. Do you really want to hurt my mom any more than you've hurt her already?"

"Did you know that your mother and father had to pay for your incarceration?" I reply, heated. "No. I'm sure you didn't. And you didn't care. I'm freeing them financially by keeping you here. *That* is love. If you ever cared about how they felt, you would have treated them with more respect."

"You don't get it!" he cries. The burns on his face make his pathos hideous to behold. "You grew up like this. Isolated. It's like being in never ending solitary confinement. This isn't normal. It isn't human." He leans back against the books, staring up at the ceiling. "Please give me a chance to make things right in my world. With my parents. I was on medication that was helping me cope until you arrived. But I couldn't cope with you. You were too perfect. You were everything I couldn't be. My broke-ass self couldn't compete, and I saw my parents rewarding you for being everything I couldn't be. And your dad? He accepted me as I was. He appreciated and rewarded me for who I was. I didn't have to get straight A's, conform to someone else's idea of perfection, or anything. Do you understand?"

Emotional pain radiates from his entire body. I've never seen so much as a tear from him until now. Is this manipulation? It feels real. "Why are you telling me this now instead of months ago?"

"Because I was too angry to talk. Frankly, I'm surprised you're even listening to me. I didn't think you'd hear me out."

I wonder if I should let him go back to the detention center. Maybe keeping him here would interfere with the human world. Then again, letting him go could also bring people here. That is, if they believed him. But what would he tell them? Would he tell them the truth? Or make up something damning about me?

"Charles, I can't take you back. I can't leave until Christmas. If I could leave, why would I be here?"

"I figured there was some holiday rule."

"Well, it's more than that. I physically can't leave now that I'm the Klaas. And even if I could, how do I know you wouldn't betray the fortress?"

"I promise I'll keep my mouth shut!"

"Look, I believe you about my father. If I'd been more like you, he'd have treated me better." Charles looks directly at me now, listening. "But this is the first time I've had any indication that you aren't a complete psychopath. I can't trust you until I know you're trustworthy."

"And you think my sister is trustworthy."

"Your sister proved she was so from the beginning."

"You only knew her seven weeks!" His laughter sounds more like boards breaking. "Try fifteen *years*. I watched her stupid life every single day. I know her better than anyone, and it was no secret she crushed on every smart guy in school. If you hadn't come along, she'd still be drooling after that faggot, Michael. She's forgotten you, man. Face it." He moves closer to me. "You're history, Santa."

I spend the next two months making him wish he'd never said that.

Chapter 15

It's Christmas Eve. Midnight is almost upon us.

Charity, I shouldn't have let your brother's voice into my head. It's done a lot of damage to my peace of mind. It's more important than ever that I see you this Christmas. My desire to be with you is overpowering.

Bound to the wall by a glyph, Charles whimpers in one of the corridors. His muscles have atrophied over the last two months. We feed him *muktuk*, frozen whale skin and blubber that's rich in vitamins humans need like Vitamin C. He despises it but he's not entirely refusing to eat.

"Taaaaake meeeee hoooome!" he cries, followed by curses. "You hate my mom! And my dad! YOU'RE A MONSTER!"

His ugly words in the library two months ago still sting. Reilly is in charge of him. She'll make sure he's taken care of while I'm gone.

The elves retrieve the sleigh so that I can awaken it for the journey. Made from rosy Finnish pines and consecrated with potent spells, the magnificent, 20-foot-long, two-seated sleigh glides out of its secret port on the Russian side of the fortress. Scarred mammoth tusks are mounted to the front and back. Ancient runes grace the sled's front lip, black as pitch yet calligraphic like medieval manuscript. They're words from that lost language. I've seen such markings in some of the library's books, but I can't begin to translate them.

The sight should be exciting but it fills me with dread. The wind climbers seem at ease, though, chasing each other and playing in the ice flurries, rising higher in the air with each leap. In the dead of winter, the fortress is steeped in night save the spectacular wraiths of eerie green light dancing on the horizon. Do you see why I'm dismayed with humanity's fantasies of this place? Bathed in this grisly light, I feel far more like Frankenstein's monster preparing to flee the pitchforks and torches than jolly Saint Nick hopping in his sleigh to sprinkle presents beneath tinseled trees.

As I watched Father do many times, I slowly circle the sled, striking the surface with the lash, intoning words that have meaning for no one save the dead men in that permafrost crypt, and maybe a few gods. With each hit, the runes smolder and spark to life.

The wood grain crackles, and then the vessel hums with a bass trill so deep the vibrations creep under my skin. Bones buzzing. Teeth chattering.

Electricity races down the massive steel runners yet the ice beneath does not melt. The wind buffets the scene, obliterating the horizon with snow. A weird chorus of spectral voices rises around us.

Older than the eye of Odin, this terrible craft has brought naught but nightmares for decades. I'll try to change that starting tonight — that is, if I can get the damned thing off the ground.

As you say, Charity: No pressure.

"Wind climbers! Let's go!"

The animals line up so that the elves can harness them to the sleigh with the reins placed near the fortress wall. Undaunted by the hellish winds, the elves lift the reins together with military precision and coordination to harness each climber. For the first time, I wonder how old my siblings really are. Maybe this is a special ritual for them. I've never seen them work with this kind of deftness.

Anxious and beyond excited, I climb inside. The wide front seat cradles me with black velvet cushions. I sit down uneasily, reins in one hand, the lash raised in my right. With a flick of my wrist, the lash unfurls over the wind climber heads. A crack explodes in the air.

Nothing.

"Come on!"

The wind climbers bleat helplessly.

I look to the elves. I thought they'd clamor to come with me, but instead they clot together, shuddering and whimpering.

"What's wrong?" I ask. "Somebody tell me, please? I quite literally don't have all night."

One of my siblings reluctantly breaks away from the pack, eyes tearing. The rest gibber as he lopes toward me, extending to me the handle of the magical narwhal knife. He then tilts his head to one side and exposes his neck to me.

"What's this for?" I ask with growing annoyance.

"Each new Klaas must baptize the sled in blood," he says. "We want you to see Charity Jones. So, we offer ourselves to you."

Revulsion washes up into my mouth. I can't hurt him, Charity. But I want to see you so badly that my heart is torn in two. What am I going to do?

The elf remains in position, knife handle extended.

They *expect* this? They must have watched my father slaughter one of them when he became The Klaas, or at least heard about it.

The blade catches snowflakes. Its narwhal handle reminds me of not just my own death, but that of the innocent whale. Blood and tooth magic.

Do I love you, Charity, more than my own conscience? Could I do something unspeakable just so we can be together for a few hours? Would I still be the person you loved if I did?

No. I wouldn't. I want to drag my father's carcass out of that crypt and rip it to pieces. He was a bully and murderer from the beginning. And now this. Not that it was his fault. This ritual's existed for some time, it seems.

But I bet he was a coward. What if he killed one of the elves because he was too craven to cut himself? That would explain a lot. It's not like the Klaas can die here at the fortress — well, except apparently in the graveyard of the gods, where Charles stabbed me. Which begs the question: how much blood does the sleigh need? A whole elf? Or will some of my blood do?

I guess it's time to find out.

With the blade tip, I rip open my left coat sleeve. Bluish veins stand out on my wrist, which I hold out over the sleigh lip. Don't think. Just...

Slash.

The elves shriek with surprise.

White light explodes behind my eyes. The blood sprays the wood, which drinks it up greedily. I slump over the sleigh front, blinded, legs weak, thunder in my ears, arm throbbing.

After several moments, my vision returns, grainy at first, building as the sleigh stirs. The runes blaze so brightly they project over the wind climber's heads like a signal.

And with that, the front wind climbers rise up into the air. One, two, three, four, five, six, seven, eight. The sleigh lurches upward. I fall back into the seat, scrambling for the reins. The storm drowns out my thoughts, voice. The reins cut into my unhurt hand, I grip them so hard. My wrist is already healing, but a thick scar remains.

The fortress disappears below as we spiral into the sky. The elves cheer and wave. Are we flying?

OH, GODS. WE'RE REALLY FLYING.

Someone must surely hear my hoots of elation. The poor wind climbers probably think I've gone mad. I rock the sleigh until it spins upside down. The wind climbers bleat joyfully and corkscrew in the sky. I can't even fall out! More shouts of glee. The flaps of my coat open, the air blasting my bare torso. The tie has been ripped from my hair, the long curls loose in the wind, whipping into my face. And I don't care. I stand in the stirrups and raise a fist, triumphant.

I'm free! Of the fortress walls. Of everything!

We circle the perimeter of the fortress grounds until I realize that, of course, I have to tell the wind climbers where to go.

Before I see you Charity, there is someone else I must visit first so that I can properly prepare to see you.

Michael Evan Allured.

Chapter 16

An explosion of stardust.

Nothingness.

A rush of wind.

Soaring ecstasy.

Scent is the first sensation to return as we materialize over our target location.

Sea brine. Car exhaust. The intoxicating aroma of spicy grilled meat, rum, and cigars. The stink of marijuana.

And then sound.

Jangle and jive. *Merry Christmas, Baby.* The gritty voice of a popular singer on an iPod player drifts up from an open window somewhere. Car tires peel out. Police sirens swell and fade. Swell. And fade.

Miami, Florida.

A metropolis materializes, skyscrapers lit green and red creeping out into the ocean. It's unbelievably warm. You might find this temperature perfect for wintertime, Charity. I find it abhorrent.

Then again, I'm a bit prejudiced.

The city percolates with celebrations on rooftops, in apartments, on affluent terraces soaked with spilled champagne, cocaine, and red glitter.

But Michael is not in any of these. The tiny house where he and Ricardo are spending Christmas squats behind a two-story suburban home on the worn edges of the city. A light flickers in the living room where people are drinking and talking, cigarette smoke drifting into the dingy backyard through the window screens. A delicious, aromatic smell of roasted meats, beans, and rice lingers in the air from the kitchen. The children dream in their sleeping bags and spare beds, restless with Christmas wishes that tug at my heart.

No one sees or hears the sleigh land on the tiny house roof because the Klaas can conceal his presence in the sleigh. The wind climbers paw and sniff at the shingles, nuzzle one another, crane their necks to get a glimpse of the ocean. Even I can't resist taking a moment to watch the waves. I then climb out of the craft and survey the yard: rusty car parts, a broken washing machine, bicycles, balls. A hoop nailed to a pole. Bald patches in the crabgrass. Low voices in the house trickle out. The white paint chipped with age.

Then, the light in the larger house switches off. People say goodnight. The kitchen light turns on briefly but soon everyone is settling in for the night.

The neighborhood is quiet, the air tinged with the smell of seawater. Insects sing under the distant roar of waves and car engines.

My feet hit the grass beside the tiny house. Michael and his boyfriend Ricardo are inside. I can hear the soft clicking of Michael's keyboard accompanied by Ricardo's oiled cloth gliding over rifle steel.

Bars on the windows.

A telecom is mounted to the right of the door. Mounted above is a black surveillance camera. Multiple red lasers stream across the opening at ankle, hip, and neck height. The lasers extend into the yard and beyond. Heavy artillery is hidden in the bushes to either side, as well as in the eaves. And in the piles of junk. Even on the rooftop of the bigger house. Each weapon shoots poisonous European mistletoe. Concentrated. I can smell it from here.

They're armed this way because they're expecting my father to come finish what he started last Christmas. It's just a matter now of convincing them I am who I say I am.

Reaching between the lasers, I knock on the front door.

Sudden movements within. Ricardo swears in Spanish. He

pumps the rifle. Michael's voice crackles from the telecom.

"Look, *Kramps*. You're not fooling us. If you take one step toward the other house, you're gingerbread toast. Got it?"

"Michael! It's me, Aidan! I know you can't trust what you see. But, please, test me. Ask me anything. I don't have time to explain, but you have nothing to fear and I desperately need your help."

Silence. They're probably exchanging texts.

"Oh, yeah? Then how did Aidan escape Santa Land?" he asks. "And why didn't he come sooner?"

If I tell him the truth – *I'm now the Sinterklaas* – he might assume I've changed for the worse. I have to make them believe I'm the same Aidan. "I stole the sleigh. It won't work any other time of year, and I couldn't escape otherwise."

Dead silence.

"Before I see Charity," I continue, "I need to clean up because I smell like elf dung and my hair is probably frightful. Look — turning invisible will only solve one of those problems. So, please, you guys, I know you can help. You've got a shower, don't you? And a toothbrush?"

"He does look amazingly hot," Ricardo says in the background.

"Penis doesn't get a vote, honey," Michael says. He then addresses the telecom. "Okay, if you're really Aidan, and it would be beyond awesome if you are, what was the name of the band I made you listen to that you hated?"

"Someone named The Beeper."

Silence. And then raucous laughter.

"Or was it Beiber? God, I hated him. I also detested that man singing 'trolololo' or whatever. What a torment! I've still not forgiven you for that...earworm...by the way. I might've brought you a lump of coal."

"One more question," he asks. "Where'd my mom get the top hat?"

"I don't believe it was ever your mother's. Your father loaned it to me," I reply. "He wore it on his wedding day. We talked in the living room one afternoon about what it means to love someone so much you would turn inside out to be with them. I then described the suit I wished to wear to make the night perfect. How inspired I was by illustrations in books. I didn't tell him where I'd seen those books, of course. He asked me to follow him to the garage, where he then took the top hat out of storage and said I could wear it to the Winter Dance."

The scene replays in my mind, Dr. Allured's kind face smiling at me. His soft, low voice. The way he patted my back, telling me I was a "good kid." Like your father, Charity, he was loving, kind, and smart. I wish I'd known him better.

And then I suddenly realize Michael's father is no longer on The List. The feelings of loss well up. Strange that I'd shed tears for someone else's father and not my own.

"He passed, didn't he? I'm so sorry, Michael. He was a good man."

The lasers disappear. Deadbolts unlatch. And the door opens.

Chapter 17

"Holy jingle bells, Batman! We thought we'd never see you again!"

Michael pulls me into a bear hug. His DEFCON T-shirt is rumpled but clean. He's lost some weight. In a white undershirt, Ricardo has not changed except his hair is now cut very short. They both wear baggy shorts, feet bare.

"Whew!" Ricardo waves at his nose, laughing. "You using seal piss for aftershave? Not that you've been shaving."

I'm dizzy with joy. The little house overflows with electronics. Surveillance screens. A master control system. Weapons of every kind. Machinery unrecognizable yet formidable. The musk of male sweat punches the air, offset by microwave cooking smells from the kitchenette. More of the same kitchen smells from the bigger house plus macaroni and cheese, pizza, soda, and cereal. Boxes and dirty dishes are stacked, crammed, stuffed on every counter.

"I'm so sorry for your loss. How's your mother holding up?"

"Not great. She's coming in tomorrow, although I can't see her until the twenty-sixth. You know. In case your dad makes an appearance." He has dark circles under his eyes. "She didn't want to be alone in the house for Christmas."

"Well, don't worry. He can't come without the sleigh." I want to allay their fears and unite them with their families, but I can't just yet. Once I'm with Charity and see how she reacts to my transformation, I can let them know. She's really the only one who can reassure them.

Michael perks up as he assesses my sealskin coat and pants. "Where'd you get this stuff? Eskimo Target?" He shakes his head, looking disgusted. "Don't worry, pal. We'll fix you up. But you can't hold out on us. We're dying to know how you got past your dad!"

Michael ushers me into a tiny bathroom with only a shower and toilet. He gives me a towel, toothbrush, comb and electric razor. "We might need to cut the hair," he says. "The whole Arctic Fabio thing looks good on you, bro, but it's maybe a little too Tarzan."

I nod.

"While you shower, we'll let Charity know you're coming," Ricardo says.

"NO!" I clamp my hand on his arm.

Ricardo's eyes widen. "We've got to tell her. She's going to be armed to the teeth. Even if you somehow get in, you'll be dead before you get anywhere near her."

"You have no idea what's happened to her since you last saw her," Michael says, his voice lower. "It's like her genius went into hyperdrive. She's making stuff that would give Tony Stark self-esteem issues. I only know because she's got me on the hook for some of the software."

"And the tank is crazy secure," Ricardo says.

"The tank?" I ask.

"The think tank where she works. Volertech. It's a place where mega-Mensa types make things for the government. Except in this case, the think tank is also an engineering lab wired with loads of high-tech security. Shit so sophisticated even we've barely heard of it. That said," Ricardo continues, looking to Michael, "I'm not sure we can even get through. Cell service's been sketchy over there. Did your last text go through?"

Michael shakes his head. "She has to surrender her cell phone while she's in the tank. I sent her an encrypted email."

"And you haven't heard anything back?"

"No. Nothing. She's probably on the scope. It's some kind of internal surveillance drone she made for them."

I close my eyes for a moment. "What's Judy doing?" I ask. "She's not here, is she?" I catch myself from saying exactly where she is. Old Aidan wouldn't have known that.

Michael and Ricardo both shake their heads. I can't get over how grown up they look, even though Michael's still just seventeen. Ricardo might be nineteen now.

"Dude," Michael says, "she refused to tell us. I don't know about her sometimes. One minute she's hella brave. And then the next moment she seems suicidal."

Another story I want to hear — Judy's life post-Krampus and how she has or hasn't coped with the loss of Leo — but there's no time. This is much harder than I thought it would be.

"Anyway," he continues, "why can't we just send her a message saying, 'Yo, Stark! Someone's coming to visit who isn't Krampus'? She's got to know, or she'll never lower her shields."

I start shaking. Flustered, I shut the bathroom door.

The truth is that I'm scared blind to see you, Charity. What if you no longer love me?

You're history, Santa.

Charles has gotten into my head in the worst way. All these months, I've thought of little else than seeing you, Charity. But now I'm terrified that he was right.

I can ask the guys what they know after I clean up. Maybe that will give me some confidence.

I've forgotten how heavenly the sensation is of hot water running over my skin. It's not enough to calm my nerves for more than a few moments. I ruminate about my fear and everyone else's. I could at least end theirs. I could tell them what happened, but I would risk everything. It's not just that I think they're not ready. I'm not sure that *I'm* ready for them to know.

I comb out the tangles, heat myself to dry, and emerge in the towel. Michael's planted on the sagging brown couch with a laptop. Ricardo sips an energy drink as he sits crisscross on the rug, reading a *Soldier of Fortune* magazine. They both stand to see me off.

Michael hands me a bag. Inside is a pair of cargo pants and a T-shirt. "You'll have to free ball it, but I think you'll be fine." He admires my torso. "Damn, you're ripped! What've you been doing? Benching polar bears?"

Ricardo slaps me on the back. "Nice work, you. Must be that Atkins sushi diet you eat up there." Suspicion dims his eyes. Michael may be brilliant, but Ricardo is the warrior. I worry that he can sense I've changed. Ricardo then puts his arm around Michael lovingly. "So, how did you know where to find us? I thought only Daddy could do that."

I blurt out another half-truth. "The sleigh knows." It's true, the sleigh knows how to get where I want to go, but I tell it where.

"The *sleigh*?"

"He mentioned that outside," Michael adds. Ricardo nods. "We gotta see this!"

"It's a marvel. You'll love it," I reply, relieved to have dodged that question. I close the bathroom door once more to dress, but I keep my boots. When finished, I enter the little living room. "Thanks, you guys. This means everything to me."

"No problem, man," Michael replies.

I crinkle the bag in hand. "I can't thank you enough."

"Dude, it's nothing." Michael smiles, standing. "Won't you at least let us tell Charity you're coming?"

"I didn't just come here to clean up. I need to ask you both something. Am I being foolish?"

Michael frowns. "What do you mean?"

"Do I still...*mean* anything to her?"

The two burst into weeping hysterics. Ricardo gently pats my cheek a couple of times. I think he wants to slap me, actually. "You are so cute."

Michael wipes his eyes with the palms of his hands. "You tell *us*. What does she want for Christmas?"

I say nothing.

They look at one another, questioning.

"What's wrong? You getting a bad vibe or something?" Michael asks.

I shake my head. "On the contrary..." I hesitate, wondering how to tell them. "My father" — another half-truth because it *was* the All-Father — "shut off my ability to measure her. I didn't even know he could do that. I haven't totally lost the ability. For example, I know you want to see your mother," I say to Michael. I turn to Ricardo. "And you want good news from your sister's upcoming doctor visit.

But I can't begin to tell you what's in Charity's heart." I want to tell them about the letter, but that was seven months ago and we're wasting time as it is. "I didn't think it would be that big of a loss, but it's a nightmare! How do you humans live like this? Now I know why men write all of those miserable, insecure love songs."

Michael says after a moment, "That's rough, man. Well, to be honest? We haven't talked with her since, when hon'? Early October?"

Ricardo shrugs. "It's been awhile. We texted recently about tonight. I don't think anyone thought you'd break out."

"Something's going on, though," Michael says. "She wants us all to get together in person after the New Year to talk because she's been hella tight-lipped about everything, especially online. I do know she's obsessed with more than her work gig. The stuff I've been doing with her is totally extra-curricular. I'm just worried she's gonna *have* to drop out of school because of Volertech — who, by the by, is a contractor for the State Department. And they don't care if she graduates as long as she can design crazy machines for them."

"Screw that school," Ricardo says to Michael. "I told you. They're just taking her money and using her to get alumni contributions. She's already got a career. Like you! Why do you care if she graduates?"

An old argument, apparently. Michael waves him off, gaze fixed on me. "So, you're afraid of rejection? That's it? Not to downplay your feelings, bro, because rejection is pretty much the worst, but it's kind of normal. Then again, I guess you're kind of the opposite of normal, aren't you?"

"I understand this is a big favor, but please promise me that you won't tell her you saw me tonight until I let you know how it went?"

"You don't want her to know you got cold feet?" Ricardo frowns. "Dude, I can't seriously believe you'd do that. Besides — can't you just hang out with us for a few days? You've escaped! You don't have to go back, do you?"

"I don't know." I start to sweat, even in my palms, my heart pounding. I *do* have to go back. I've heard the consequences for not returning are grave. Anyway, this fear of finding out Charity doesn't love me is madness, but I can't control it. And the longer I'm here, the more questions they ask. "It'll probably be okay, but please. Promise me."

The two exchange reluctant, annoyed looks. "Okay! I promise," they each say. I feel something pass between us. I can't put my finger on it, but I worry that I've done something I shouldn't have by making them swear an oath to me.

"Just keep us updated before the end of the day, man." Michael gives me a soft punch to the bicep. "I'm sure everything'll be fine. And I'll call my mom. Thanks for helping us be together on Christmas."

We exchange hugs and goodbyes. They follow me outside and watch me toss the bag up before leaping onto the roof. I then snap my fingers dramatically and make the craft visible to them.

Ricardo's face beams with awe. "Hooo-leeee shiiii—"

Michael yells over him. "SIIIIICK! IT'S THE SATAN SLEIGH!"

Doing my best Kris Kringle imitation, I wink at them and crack the lash. The wind climbers rise into the starry Miami night before disappearing into stardust.

Chapter 18

Arlington, West Virginia.

The sleigh lands on an office building rooftop in an industrial complex. The rows of tilted solar panels that surround us, as well as the hive of air-conditioning condensers hugging the southeast corner, are all coated with a thick layer of snow. A pile of snow sits in the gaping mouth of a massive black satellite dish tilted skyward in front of us.

Compared to Miami, this city sleeps like a babe in the nursery. It's well after midnight, the black sky raining shiny droplets that bead on the wind climbers' hides. A handful of people guard warehouses and other buildings nearby.

This is it. Am I going to test my luck and see if you still love me? Or should I flee?

A security camera mounted on the rooftop is pointed directly at us. Others are positioned around the perimeter, aimed outward at the surrounding parking lot and grounds. But the one fixed on the sleigh is paired with another perched on the opposite wall facing a maintenance door I suspect leads to a stairwell. A keypad and sensor are mounted on the wall to the right of the door handle.

Light streams under the door just before it swings open and a man emerges, shouts, points a rifle.

"HANDS IN THE AIR! YOU ARE TRESSPASSING ON PRIVATE PROPERTY!"

I slowly raise my hands, although I'm fairly certain they can't see us. If I don't want someone to see the sleigh, they don't. At least, that's what I've been told. Although someone could walk between them if they wished, the solar panels are a barrier to one of them straying directly into us.

Wearing bulky jackets, four security personnel with large semi-automatic rifles cautiously circle the sleigh. They look around but not at us. Plastic curlicues of transparent communication headsets wrap behind their ears. I don't sense any mistletoe in those bullets, but the memory of wounded Noah falling, abdomen bloodied, flashes in my mind's eye.

They lower their weapons.

"Did another goddamn bird set off that sensor? I see nothing. Do you?" asks one of the women. Her name is Diana.

"Negative," a man responds, stepping between the solar panels. His name is Bill. A wind climber sniffs him. He's oblivious to the animal. Thankfully he steps away.

The other two groan with annoyance at the mistake.

I relax. Still, it troubles me that their technology was sensitive enough to detect the incoming sleigh. There must be motion detectors in addition to security cameras.

Obedient and trusting, the wind climbers keep position, the personnel creeping around just a few feet away. I worry what would happen if a wind climber were injured. Would we be able to make it back? What would happen if I couldn't get back in time?

I don't want to find out.

Images of people — family, close friends, coworkers — flicker around the security personnel like the ghosts in Hel's cavern. The List identifies everyone. I know their names, locations and, of course, Christmas wishes. Most of the personnel just wish they were home instead of working, and their families want the same.

Not everyone has a Christmas wish per se, as not everyone celebrates Yule. But I can sense that person's deepest desires. On Christmas, the impressions are strongest.

One of the security personnel wants an excuse to kill someone. Not just at Christmas. Always.

It's the tall blond male named Josiah.

"Let's get out of here," the other woman says. Tina. Then, to her earpiece, "The roof is clear. Please file motion detector malfunction with facilities."

Holstering their guns and chatting about how they wish they could break out the whisky, the personnel exit the rooftop and file through the open door. The last one through is Josiah. He glances back twice before reaching for the door.

Split-second decision: Do I leap out of the sleigh to grab the door before it closes? This might be my only chance to slip inside an open door. But I can't risk being seen. And if it doesn't lock immediately, there might be yet another alarm.

Do I even want to do this?

A wind rises, gusting over us. The door closes, deadbolts sliding into place.

You are inside, somewhere beyond that door. The terror gives way to overpowering desire. How could I be so stupid? I need to see you more than anything. I can't run now, not with you so close. No matter what the outcome.

I was so overwhelmed with fear that I didn't ask any questions about this place before I left. Michael and Ricardo tried to warn me. And why I did land on the rooftop? I guess old habits die hard, even if they're not yours.

The building has three other entrances: the front lobby, the loading dock, and the back entrance. There's also a door into an underground bunker at a sister building nearby, but there'd be too much distance to cover to get back here. Too many chances for something to go wrong as I try to find my way out of the bunker. The back entrance and loading dock are locked down from the inside. But one entrance is surprisingly accessible: the lobby.

A man guards that entrance. He is lonely and bored. I know exactly what he wants for Christmas. And she's not his wife.

Chapter 19

Benjamin Cain sits inside the lobby at the reception desk, reading a newspaper. When he isn't on duty here at Volertech, he sometimes works at Ronald Reagan Washington National Airport, wheeling disabled passengers for Delta Airlines. A tall and wiry man with a gold-capped molar and wide smile, he has three grown children who in turn have given him six grandchildren. Almost all have descended upon his and his wife's home in the suburbs of Arlington County for the holidays.

He doesn't seem to mind the quiet. That said, I'm about to turn his night upside-down. You see, I've transformed into someone Cain fantasizes about constantly in order to get past his guard and into the building.

Her name is Genny. She's his wife's youngest sister. Married. Involved in many illegal business activities. Her Christmas wish is to travel next year to exotic places. Tonight she's home, but I've taken on her likeness: high heels, tight red dress, hoop earrings and long nails. And her bulky purse. It's like carrying a dead baby seal under my arm.

I hate deceiving people like this. I hated it whenever my father would change form. When he took on the likeness of your father, Charity, it enraged me. I've heard that the previous Sinterklaas used the power so that children wouldn't catch Santa putting gifts under the tree — they'd instead see the image of their mother or father.

This is encounter won't be nearly so innocent, which is why I feel a bit less badly about the deception. Unfortunately, I'm completely inexperienced in shifty encounters, unless you count what I've read in Dashiell Hammett stories. I sense that approach might be amusing but dated and conspicuous.

At any rate, I've parked the sleigh in a safer place: the empty next-door parking lot where there are no guards.

Benjamin is absorbed in a magazine as I approach the glass doors and tap on the surface. An RFID reader is mounted on a short pylon beside the right door for after-hours access. His head jerks up, startled, eyes wild, only to widen when he sees Genny. He mouths her name.

I wave back, smiling.

He slides out from behind the reception desk and, unhooking the gleaming cluster of keys from his belt, he scurries through the metal detector to the door.

"What are you doing here, missy?" he asks, cracking open the door.

I shrug as I modulate my voice. "I...was thinking of...you." I try to smile.

"Me?"

"Yeah. You sound surprised."

"Oh, I ain't too surprised." A touch of bravado in his voice.

"Good. Because I thought I'd drop by and...party."

"But baby it's...it's work. And almost one in the morning!" He stammers with surprise, but he's clearly pleased. His eyes trail up and down my body. "What's Dan doing?"

"Sleeping?" I reply. This is harder than I thought it would be. "He had a lot to drink."

Benjamin simply stares, mouth open.

"Can I come in? It's kind of cold out here."

"Uh...yeah! But hang on." He goes back inside, fiddles with something at his desk, and then returns. "Just for a few. I'm not supposed to be lettin' anyone in who's not authorized. You know. High security and all."

I nod. He holds open the door and I enter, relieved to be inside but confounded that this man would jeopardize his job for this woman. His obsession with her is worse than I thought.

After locking the door, he leads me through the metal detector into the spacious reception area. Black marble covers the floors. A large fish tank is embedded in the wall, teeming with delicate, colorful creatures. Security cameras watch everything in the lobby, which is secured from the rest of the facility. I wonder how long they keep the video. Twenty-four hours? A week? Indefinitely?

Benjamin strokes the thin strands of hair stretched over his scalp as he evaluates the situation. He then motions for me to follow him across the lobby to a small, dark office. Perspiration soaks his armpits and neck.

No way. I can't get trapped in a room. "Baby, I need to...powder my nose," I say. *Keep focused. This is for Charity.*

"Uh...sure. It's over there." He points down the hallway to an alcove, above which is posted a sign with male and female icons. As I turn away, he grabs my arm and pulls me close. "You did bring some *stuff,* didn't you?"

Stunned, I stare at him, and then I understand. Drugs. She's his dealer. Yes, he's obsessed with her. He wants to sleep with her. But she supplies something other than sex.

"Don't worry. You just get comfortable there."

I head toward the restrooms. He watches me walk down the hallway and doesn't go into the office until I enter.

Or, at least I pretend to. Ducking into the alcove, I open the door and let it shut. I then wait, listening. He's moving furniture around, tidying up. I silently slip out of the alcove, take on the semblance of the female security guard who cursed — Diana — and head back toward the elevators, passing the office where Benjamin busies himself straightening papers and cleaning off a couple of chairs. I hear him stop what he's doing, checking to see who walked by.

I give him a curt nod before I step into the open elevator.

Inside is Josiah.

Chapter 20

Josiah assays me with his piercing bluish-grey eyes. Evil oozes from his pores. "I thought you were patrolling the labs. Didn't I just leave you there?"

"I was. I mean, I am," I reply. "I'm on my way back right now."

"This is going up." He holds his hand in the doorway and looks at me expectantly. The doors remain open. This is just the mezzanine. There are three floors above us and two below.

"Correct," I say and step out. "Have a good evening."

He presses his thumb somewhere to the right of the doors and they slide closed.

I call another elevator as Benjamin frantically searches the lobby. He sweats heavily as he sits at the desk. I notice a surveillance screen sitting below the counter, switching between cameras. A computer screen is running software that monitors alarms. Motion detectors must have alerted security about the sleigh.

Benjamin avoids my gaze.

"Problem?" I ask, trying to sound official.

He shakes his head. "No, *ma'am*. Not a creature was stirring. Not even a mouse." The gold tooth gleams as he tries to appear cheerful. His eyes belie his dread that I've touched on his secret.

"Good." The open elevator provides the perfect escape. This is the first time I've ever been inside an elevator. Its steel walls are polished to a high sheen. It reminds me of Father's icy mausoleum. I quickly decipher the control panel and press the button for the lowest floor. When the door closes, I assume the identity of Josiah now that I know the woman is patrolling below.

Focus. Where are you, Charity?

The labs. Of course! But you're not alone. Others are with you. Young. Late teens. College interns. One from California. Others from international destinations. Almost everyone is awake.

Especially you, Charity. You're expecting a visit from Krampus.

I have no plan to draw her out. I just hope a strategy will avail itself when I locate her, as it did with Michael and Ricardo.

The words "Touch ID" light up in red on the elevator button panel above a slick black plastic square. Fingerprints. My index finger tentatively touches the black square.

Nothing happens.

I can fool people. It's much harder to fool machines. But I have an idea.

I switch back to Diana's form and open the elevator. "Benjamin. Something's wrong with the elevator. Can you help?"

"Yes, ma'am!" He races to the elevator. I explain that it's not working. He presses his thumb against the pad, and green lights appear beneath the floor numbers. "There you go! Not sure what's wrong. Must've been a glitch."

I dismiss him with thanks. He looks genuinely relieved as the doors close between us.

The elevator drops to the lowest level. Doors open to a pristine white corridor. I stroll purposefully down the left wing past one locked door after another with plate-sized round windows. At first I breeze past these rooms but eventually I can't ignore the contents.

Robotic exoskeletons. One metallic suit is suspended in the air above a circular platform. Wearable military weaponry. Rifles, lasers, protective helmets and body gear. Soldiers of the future. Bloodless death machines. Each lab room is more terrifying than the last.

And then I find myself standing before two tall sliding glass doors, peering into an enormous underground bunker.

Drones and missiles.

Missiles as big as a car and as compact as a baseball. Some of the drones are hard to distinguish from the missiles because both are aerodynamically designed for long-range flight. Yet many are unmistakable weapons of mass destruction.

A snowy white drone with an elliptical body the size of a football glides soundlessly through the bunker, scanning the various projects with its camera. Its inky Cyclopean eye is set on a vertically mounted track so that it can change position on the drone. The eye closes in on the glass doors, hovering before me.

Watching me.

Charity Jones. You're guiding it. You can see me.

Mesmerized, drowning in emotion, I raise my hand to touch the glass where the drone hovers. Remembering that day you introduced me to your "friends" Mr. Spotty, Ms. Yoyodyne, and Les Femmes Nikitas. Quaint yet brilliant automatons. And now these machines of war...

I imagine your eyes peering into mine.

I wish more than anything I could drop this façade and show you it's really me, Aidan, but you wouldn't believe it. You're expecting my father, who once before masqueraded as someone you love. All that matters is that you're on the other side of the lens. I'm dying at the thought of it.

I need to move up one level. But the real Diana must also be on that level, and she's heavily armed.

This level has no stairwell — at least, not in this part of the floor. I would much prefer stairs to the steel coffin. Backtracking to said steel coffins, I decide to keep this form in case I run into another guard like Josiah. Inside, "Touch ID" lights up.

This is bad.

Since I don't actually have a communication headset, I can't call anyone for assistance. I could press the "Call in Emergency" button, but I don't want to draw any more attention to myself than I already have. I could wait. Another guard might call the elevator. That would mean standing here for at least another hour, possibly two or more, until the guards change shifts in each building segment. (And that assumes they actually do change.) Meanwhile, time slips away and the sleigh sits in a parking lot. It's not safe. The entire situation makes me nervous.

After several nerve-wracking moments, I remember something you once said, Charity, when we were preparing for battle in your living room. Something about how my father and I could manipulate gravity and "other natural forces."

Other natural forces...like electricity, maybe?

My palm covers the black square. I close my eyes and will the electricity to run through the circuits that enable the elevator to move up one floor. Gently. Carefully. *Don't short out the console.*

The elevator rises. One floor.

And then the doors slide open.

Chapter 21

The aromas of Chinese food and beer hops hang in the air. Young male voices alternately laugh and murmur in the distance to my left.

I move away from the voices, listening for Diana, hoping to find you somewhere away from them all.

You are here. So close.

Like the floor below, this one stretches far beyond the ground floor boundaries. It's a labyrinth of hallways with rooms, a bunk that doubles as an office for an engineer. Cots, bookcases, a small restroom with sink, worktables piled high with tools and works in progress, whiteboards and computers occupy each room, doors labeled with the engineer's first initial and last name.

The rooms cluster around sitting areas with gaming consoles, refrigerators, giant white screens, and fishbowls overflowing with candy, pretzels and energy bars. Bathrooms. Showers. A modest gym. The fully equipped kitchen offers industrial coffee makers and soda dispensers, as well as packaged snacks and fresh fruit piled in wire baskets.

I continue to wander the halls. With every step, every moment I spend this close to you, my desire for you amplifies. The mental effort it takes to hold this illusion become more burdensome. My mind keeps drifting to memories of how your skin felt against mine. Your lips. And the sound of your laughter.

If I were on The List and shielding myself against my father, where would I be? I would barricade myself behind one of these closed doors in an office with a bathroom for twenty-four hours. It would not even be my office. I would choose one that didn't have my name to confuse the enemy, even if only briefly. Inside, I would — as Ricardo mentioned — be well armed. If your genius has blossomed as Michael says, you have no doubt developed far more sophisticated weapons to deploy European mistletoe.

Although, the deadly blow to my father came not from a machine but from your hand.

You would be with others of your kind. Not to endanger them but to assure yourself that normalcy will return. To guard your sanity. A reminder of life to fend off the fear of death.

Circling back toward the voices, which lie to the western end of the floor, I stay to the south, closer to the elevators. A green "Exit" sign hangs over a door at the end. A stairwell up.

"Hey, hey, Di-AA-*naaaa*!" one of the interns sings out. His name is Kamal. The other interns laugh.

I duck into one of the offices and crouch behind the door.

"Very funny. Did you just discover Michael Jackson?" The real Diana replies. Apparently she's patrolling their area.

"For your information, we listen to American pop music in Pakistan," Kamal replies. "Including Madonna, Taylor Swift, and Avril Lavigne."

"Those are probably the only women you knew there," Diana replies.

"Burrrrrn," another intern says. Eugene. Like you, Charity, he's from California. San Mateo. He snaps off the top to another beer bottle. "Hey, *mucho gracias* again for the Christmas present, by the way," he says.

"No problem," she replies. "Anything to keep you eggheads happy and out of trouble. I have enough to worry about."

"Might not be enough to keep *me* out of trouble," another intern inserts. Sergei. He has a heavy Ukrainian accent.

"And you're in heaps of it. Your prototype sucks," Eugene needles.

Sergei responds. Boasting. "You wish. My friend, you're just jealous of my prototype and my lady."

"Your *lady*, huh?" I can practically hear Diana roll her eyes.

"What are you talking about?" Kamal asks.

"My lady, Charity, and I. We're in love."

"What?" Kamal says. More of a statement. "You and the Ice Queen? No way."

"She may be obsessed with snow, but she is not cold. She simply prefers her men to be impervious to the winter climates."

"For fuck's sake, Sergei. How old are you?" Diana asks.

"Nineteen. But we are born men in the Ukraine, not boys."

"And how old is Charity?"

A pause.

"Seventeen. Maybe," Eugene says. "Total jailbait."

"Not necessarily," Diana says. "Age of consent is fifteen in this state if you're both underage, but it's illegal to have sex with a minor over fifteen. Maybe only a misdemeanor, but you could get in trouble, even deported. Not to mention, it's against company policy."

"Besides, she can *totally hear you lying about her*," Eugene says, raising his voice. "Hey, Charity! Shut this clown down, will you?"

"Is she denying what I am saying? No."

"How can she? She's asleep," Kamal says. "She went to bed before midnight."

You are not asleep.

I measure Sergei. He's lying about the sex, but he honestly believes you love and desire him because one terrible truth swims up from the his emotions:

You kissed him earlier tonight.

"She sleeps like the dead," Sergei says, "because I wore her out earlier."

Snickering and banter.

"I don't want to hear this." Diana starts walking away.

"When? While we were picking up dinner?" Kamal says. "Ah, so *that's* why you two didn't want to come with us."

"Don't jeopardize your future here, Sergei," Diana continues. She heads back toward the other end of the floor. "You'll never have another chance like this again."

"Wow. You and Charity, huh?" Eugene says. "You're definitely the man, Sergei. I'll back off in my pursuit of the Amazing Miss

Jones and wish you two lovebirds a Merry Christmas!"

The young men wish each other Merry Christmas, clink bottles.

Merry Christmas.

Chapter 22

This heartbreak is far worse than when Charles plunged that narwhal knife into my chest. In fact, I wish I'd never pulled it out. I thought being taken from you was unbearable, but this eclipses every wound I've suffered so far. The loss of my mother, torture in the Taggalaq, dying in Nifel-Hel...nothing was as painful as this is.

I should have tried to measure the people you were with before I came here. It didn't even occur to me to do that. Or was I just afraid?

I'm *so* stupid.

I want to die.

My face is hot and wet. Waves of darkness crash against me.

Charles may have intended merely to hurt me but he was right. You have moved on here in this place with so many young geniuses. How could I have expected you to do otherwise? But...what we shared was so powerful. A part of me disbelieves you could have moved on so quickly. But did you have a choice? When would you ever see me again? Of course you assumed my father was still alive, coming back on Christmas to finish what he started. I have brought you nothing but misery.

I still love you, Charity Jones. Thoughts of you kept me sane through the worst. This is destroying me.

My skin ripples with dark fur. No! I can't lose my form now. I try to go invisible, but that doesn't work, either. I'm too upset.

Diana's footsteps stop. She speaks into her headset.

"In the elevator?" A pause. "Are we having electrical problems? Or...?" Another pause.

Two questionable events in an hour. And if they check the elevator camera, they will see either me or Diana doing strange things to the console.

I crack open the door and peer out. Far down the hallway is the EXIT sign. The elevator is much closer, but so is Diana.

The thought of doing anything except curling up in a ball of agony feels impossible, but I have to get out. Now.

I step out of the room. Silently, I make my way to the elevator, watching for Diana. No one notices me step into the elevator lobby but I do hesitate to get a glimpse of Sergei. Dark hair. Fair skin with a shadow of stubble. Regal nose. Haughty brown eyes I want to gouge. Jealousy blinds me to everything except him. Arrogant bastard. My fists clench, nails cutting into my palm. The urge to lash out and rip his head off swells inside me.

I turn back to the elevators, but I'm startled to find Diana standing behind me, not ten feet away. Eyes wide. One hand touching the headset. The other reaching for her gun.

I've forgotten to change form. I still look like her.

The elevator is no longer an option. I run for the EXIT sign as she reports the intrusion.

"Stop! Or I'll shoot!"

I raise a shield at my back as the bullet bursts from the gun. Deafening. It deflects, embedding in a wall. She shoots again.

The interns run for their rooms, cursing, shouting, bottles crashing to the floor. Doors slam.

A figure emerges from the door under the EXIT sign.

Josiah. Gun aimed at my head. It doesn't matter that it's "Diana." He shoots.

I dive into a maze of bunks and living spaces. The bullet flies past my shoulder. My ears ring. A strange chemical smell obliterates the smell of Chinese food.

"Stop shooting, dammit! You're going to kill the real me!"

"How do I know it's you?" Josiah shouts to Diana.

"What?"

"HOW DO I KNOW WHICH ONE IS YOU?"

"We keep talking," she says. She's out of sight, somewhere

northeast of my location. "I don't know what kind of bullshit this is, but stay in my ear."

No windows on this floor. One more level up.

Diana and Josiah continue to prowl, she at the north and he the south. I weave in and out of the offices, assuming the form of the other male security guard, Bill. I try to cut across toward the EXIT.

Josiah turns the corner and spots me. "Get the hell back upstairs!" he growls, lowering the gun. "Cover the lobby as instructed!"

I hold up my hands, nodding, and run to the EXIT door.

"Who is it?" Diana asks.

"Just Bill," Josiah says.

"NO, IT'S NOT. I'M TALKING TO HIM DOWNSTAIRS," she shouts.

More shots. Deflected bullets shatter framed artwork, game console screens. One grazes Josiah's head.

"Sonuvabitch!" Josiah reflexively covers his bloody ear.

I close in on the EXIT door. Just within reach. Diana runs up behind Josiah, pulls him back. Mutters into her headset.

Bill kicks open the door, gun drawn. I'm caught between the three. No more hiding.

With a gesture, I tear Bill's gun out of his hand. It flies to the left, hits the wall. I then hurl him back through the EXIT door. He slams against the far wall in the stairwell, slumps to the floor unconscious.

Diana shouts into her radio, "Cut off the exits!"

Once through the door, I pull it shut and wrench the steel handle to render it useless.

More armed security guards crowd the lobby and pour into the stairwell. I race up the stairs, police sirens wailing in the distance. The goons stop, guns drawn.

"Hands in the air! You're under arrest!"

I refuse to hurt anyone else. Instead of a shield, I throw up a thick barrier of moisture. Bullets pepper the barrier. But instead of deflecting and ricocheting in the stairwell, the rounds swim into the heavy air and then drop. The guards hesitate before charging after me, confused, the discharged rounds falling with a splash. The steps are now wet, slippery, and covered in bullets and spent shells.

Second floor. Third. Electronic locks *click* as I pass the stairwell doorways. Locked. By me.

Coming up on the rooftop. Helicopters swarm the building, one directly above. Blades grind the air. No exit that way.

There is only one way out now.

When I reach the fourth floor, I rip the door from the frame and race down the hallway. Into the open floor of office desks. A helicopter swoops past. Thunderous. I run straight at the wall of windows —

— arms crossed over my face —

— and I smash through.

Chapter 23

Summoning.

Falling.

Landing.

The sleigh catches me mid-fall. I land hard on the front seat, wincing from the glass cuts. Raindrops and blood soak my clothes and hair. Police lights flash in the parking lot below, red and blue reflected in the scattered glass shards. The surrounding trees bend in the wind. Officers pour into the building while others remain outside, watching and searching. They can't see us because the sleigh has been cloaked the whole time. Police pour into the building, some stand below staring at the gaping hole in the bank of windows, puzzled. The wind climbers pull away from the chaos, far away from the two helicopters with searchlights plowing over the scene.

"Thank you, my friends. Circle here a bit."

My hands curl around the reins, arms covered in painful cuts. My whole body feels traumatized from the jump. The sleigh drinks up the carnage, stains vanishing as soon as the droplets bead on the cushions.

Here, in the isolation of the sleigh, my soul, my life shatters. Every dream and hope I cherished, that kept me alive and sane, is gone.

Never mind that I exposed myself to humans. My true form is

probably recorded on multiple security servers. I don't care. They don't know who I am. They will never piece together the truth without Charity. Even she might not realize what has happened. Like what happened with Charles and his friends, they might not tell her – or anyone – what they really saw.

Tears burn my eyes. It feels like someone has thrust a torch into my gut. I've never felt anything so excruciating in my life. I suppose this is the heartbreak that poets write about, but on an order of magnitude greater than I would have ever guessed.

Should I return to Michael and Ricardo? They might console me, but seeing them would just remind me of her, making it hurt even more.

I don't deserve this after everything I've suffered. Love true to the very end: that's what I'd hoped for. That's what kept me going. And what do I get? The best thing that has ever happened to me has turned to ash.

The sleigh crosses the Potomac River. I crack the lash and the wind climbers circle the dome of the White House before flying toward the Washington Monument. The capitol of the greatest nation in the world seethes with tremendous power. Charity has tapped into this grim grid that reminds me of the constellations within the graveyard of the gods. The power here is dark. Will she one day be my enemy?

Now what? I don't want to return to the Arctic. I have this one blessed day to be free. I once read a marvelous story by a man named Ray Bradbury called "All Summer in a Day." What if you lived on a planet where the sun came out only once every one hundred years? In my life, I have freedom one day a year. It would be cruel to lock *myself* in a closet during that time.

Even if the sun is eclipsed.

Darkness. Rage. The perverse need to strike out and somehow "get even" with Charity is overwhelming. It's hard to admit how angry I am at her. How can I avenge my feelings — or at least make myself feel better — without destroying everything in my reach?

The sleigh leaves the Capitol Mall and, turning south, follows the mighty Potomac River, widening as it approaches Quantico. I know where to go. And whom to see.

A year ago, nothing would have hurt Charity more.

Chapter 24

The night air sweetened by rain and pine releases a deluge of memories and feelings. Oak County sleeps as it did that night one year ago, with perhaps a few more security systems installed by those who dimly recall a disaster that befell a family with a troubled son and a brilliant daughter who captured the monster that menaced their community. But from the sleigh that sweeps over the wooded hills, it seems peace on earth and goodwill towards men prevails.

Neither of the Joneses lives here any longer. They have parted ways — Mr. Jones having moved to an apartment near his work while Mrs. Jones lives with family in Texas. Almost everyone else remains, especially Charity's classmates who are set to graduate this coming June. So few of them even came close to her genius, except Michael and Judy. No one had any hope of escaping school before the designated date.

Especially not Beth Addison.

How she annoyed me at school. I ignored her but of course I *noticed* her. Long strawberry blonde hair that brushed her hips, leafy green eyes, and lips the color of peonies. I discovered peonies quite by accident as I was searching online for pictures of roses to send Charity. Roses seemed so pedestrian that I thought surely my true love must like something more interesting. It turns out Charity was not imaginative that way.

Beth eventually became quite forward in her flirtations despite purportedly mourning her murdered boyfriend, Darren. Had I not been completely taken with Charity, I would have been just as fascinated with Beth as every other boy in the school. Charity never knew about the minor skirmishes I had with football players. Darren's so-called friends went into a frenzy for her as soon as he was out of the way, but it seemed Beth had eyes for only one person.

Me.

I won't lie. Her attention could be intoxicating. My ego enjoyed it but she really was no one compared to Charity. Her lack of subtlety and wit at times was embarrassing.

Now things are different. Is it really revenge if Charity will never know? Either way, I need to staunch this wound with an ego boost. Fortunately for me, her family is asleep. She, on the other hand, is awake.

The sleigh lands on the roof of her house, a sprawling three-story mansion that includes a three-car garage, a pool graced by a waterfall, a fire pit, and well-manicured grounds surrounded by towering fir trees. And no fewer than three glorious chimneys.

Not that I will need them.

The roof lends me plenty of handholds for an easy descent, but I choose to leap down onto the soft grass. My wounds have healed, leaving my clothes and hair stained with blood. Stripping off my sealskin boots, I climb the steps up to the top of the waterfall. Past the deck with its rattan furniture, the cozy living room is dimly lit by a row of recessed lights over the rosy marble fireplace adorned with Christmas stockings, the windows smothered with flowing golden drapes. Beth sits on the couch, transfixed by her cell phone, wearing a thick, red velvet robe and slippers.

I dive into the surprisingly cool crystalline waters. A few moments of swimming do the trick. One cannot do much for the bloodstained clothes but it helps.

The water feels extraordinary, although not nearly as invigorating as the Arctic Ocean. I climb out and sit on the pool's edge, feet dangling. Beth stares at me, slack-jawed, through the sliding glass door. My body reacts strongly to seeing the exposed skin of her legs and cleavage. With Olympic effort, I calm myself.

Aidan? I see her lips move.

I run my hand through my hair — which must be a mess if

Michael called me Tarzan — and approach the glass.

Her eyes drink me in. Shock. Fear. Delight.

The thin, wet cotton clothes cling to my body. Soaked to the bone in the cold winter wind. I smile and pretend to shiver.

The glass door slides open.

"Aidan MacNichol, what the hell are you doing in my pool?" She manages to look both appalled and amused. "Have you been working out? You're seriously shredded. Where did you go, anyway?"

I shake my head. "Good evening, Beth. It's quite cold. May I come in?"

She steps out of the way, lets me inside, and shuts the door. I stand dripping on a straw doormat lying on the terracotta tile. "Don't move. You'll get water everywhere." She retrieves a bath towel and robe for me. "I must be crazy letting you in like this." Her eyes widen again as I strip off my shirt, and she bites her lower lip.

Slipping my fingers around the waist button on my trousers, I raise an eyebrow.

"Sorry," she says, turning around. Her head jerks when my pants hit the floor but she doesn't look until I have on the robe. "You're insane. You know that?"

"For what, pray tell? Swimming in your heated pool at night? Is that not considered a pleasant pastime?"

I stroll into the living room, my feet sinking into the plush carpet. Framed photos of her handsome if exceedingly homogenous family members adorn the walls. A Christmas tree with gilded ornaments and blinking lights glitters in the far corner of the room. A painting of Jesus on the Mount hangs to the left of the tree. A "God Bless Our Home" sign is mounted over the front doorway. On the coffee table in front of the couch where Beth was sitting lays a thick, leather-bound Bible.

A memory tears me away. The Christmas tree in the Jones house that I decorated using their science fiction ornaments. Mrs. Jones' ill reaction to the holiday transformation of her home. The tree falling in the battle...

"You're insane for trespassing. My father could have woken up and shot you."

He won't wake up. No one will while I'm here. For I'm now the Klaas. And I won't forget who I am.

Chapter 25

"Perhaps," I say. "But was it insane to visit you? Am I not welcome?"

"No. I mean, yes. Of course you're welcome. I just thought you left town. They said your dad took you away last Christmas. Nobody thought you'd come back."

"I didn't think I would return, either. But here I am." I step closer to her. My skin is heating up, my skull feeling tight, vision narrowing. The robe cinches her waist, emphasizing her hips and breasts. I feel my breath drawing up, hitching.

"So...have you heard from Charity? She left school, you know." Beth looks down at her feet. "They say she graduated early but she dropped out, didn't she?" Without waiting for confirmation, she rattles on. "Doesn't she work for the government or something on the east coast? She doesn't want anything to do with this place. I get it. She never fit in, anyway."

Charity's name slices into my heart. I falter, gutted. "I know."

"All her friends left," Beth continues. "It's like a different school without those guys." She pauses. "I mean, *you* guys."

Even though I'm withering at her last comment, I step closer. She frowns, narrowing her eyes. "What happened to you? You look different. You sound the same, but..."

"But I'm back now. Today was my first chance to escape...family obligations. So, I chose to come here."

"But why? Aren't you with...someone?"

I hold out my hand. "Not any more."

The words sever my soul from my heart. The part of me that

loves Charity is shut away. It bloodies its fists as it bangs at its prison door. But here I won't find rejection.

Beth's warm hand grasps mine. Holding her gaze, I bring her hand to my lips. Gently. She gasps, her eyes breaking from mine, attention wandering upstairs.

"Don't worry. They can't hear us," I assure her.

"How do you know?" She squints, suspicious. "Did you murder them or something? My mom's a light sleeper."

"They won't awaken because they have sugar plums dancing in their heads." I wonder if this is how my father appeared to my mother. Did he seduce her, ever the gentleman devil?

"Sugar plums, huh?" The gold flecks in her green eyes flicker in the tree lights. Floral scents release in her hair as my fingers rake into silky strands. Her skin smells fresh, as well. No makeup on her lashes or cheeks. She draws closer. "Your hair is a hot mess," she says, pleased, playing with the strands. "Smells like chlorine."

I hear her but the words no longer have meaning.

"Is this a Christmas booty call?" She laughs.

"It's whatever you want it to be." My breath slows. I turn over her hand and kiss her wrist, moving closer to her, my other hand dropping to her waist. She does not move for a moment, transfixed by my eyes. And then, she closes her own, her lips parting.

I kiss her.

A jolt as the chemicals surge through my body, an unholy confluence of lust and sadness. I feel black bristles pricking through the skin of my back. I fight the transformation and will them to retreat under my skin. My heart thunders, arousal building.

She pulls away abruptly. Confused, I say nothing, but her intent is soon clear. She takes my hand and draws me upstairs – not to the elegant wooden staircase by the front door, but back toward the sliding glass door where a white metal staircase spirals upward. We swiftly ascend to the third-story loft with a window overlooking the pool. I silence my steps but my feet tickle. Black bristles are sprouting from the tops almost as fast as I force them back. Gods, I've got to hold myself together. I can't turn into Krampus now!

We crest the top floor and enter a lounge with more plush

carpeting, an entertainment center, bar and a bed neatly covered in a thick brown comforter tucked back into an alcove. The dim downstairs light casts shadows in the room.

Beth throws back the comforter and turns to me, tugging the sash of my robe. It falls open, exposing my body. I feel both vulnerable and invincible at once.

My temples ache. My forehead throbs, but it doesn't diminish my excitement. She drops her robe on the floor, her thin daffodil nightgown revealing every nuance of flesh. She murmurs assurances that everything is "okay" because of "the pill" she's taking that her parents don't know about. Meanwhile the bittersweet, haunting moments I shared with Charity twist and condense into a singular hunger burning me up from the inside out. I can think of nothing but her, feeling the love we shared every moment of every day we spent with one another. I'm not with Beth. I'm with Charity despite wanting to erase her from memory.

Beth and I tumble onto the soft bed, and then the sensations blur in the heat. The ache of embarrassment mingles with the unbearable pain of Charity's rejection as Beth guides my inexperienced hands. She gives more assurances. Everything feels *so good*, she says. Again and again.

So good, and so terrible at once.

And all at once, to my absolute horror, I transform.

My temples explode with pain, and any pleasure dissipates in the light flooding the bed from my eyes. My teeth thicken, sharpen. Lengthen. Monstrous horns erupt from my skull. Rip through my skin. Blood drips warm from my forehead onto the pillow and her hair. Perhaps she mistakes it for my sweat. Eyes closed, she's oblivious until I gasp with shock at my transformation. I can't tear away from her fast enough.

And then Beth starts screaming. I'm already fleeing, horns and fangs retracting.

"I'm so sorry, Beth," I blurt, savaged by guilt. Over and over. I shouldn't have even been here. "I'm so sorry. Please forgive me."

Hooves melt to feet. I jump to bypass the spiral metal staircase, dropping straight down to the first floor. I want to comfort her, to assure her that it's still me, that I never wished her any harm, but I can't without upsetting her more because I haven't regained myself. I don't know how long it will take, either. The lush black fur covers my arms, spreading up my neck and over my cheeks. My fingernails are thick, sharp claws.

It must have happened because of my arousal. I'm even angrier at my father — if that's even possible — for not telling me about these things.

I snatch the damp clothes from the floor and run outside, collecting my sealskin boots from poolside before climbing to the roof. I hear Beth sobbing uncontrollably, traumatized, repeating my name.

Shaking, I climb into the sleigh. I have still only partially recovered my human form. Blistering tears of regret and heartbreak soak my cheeks as I crack the lash overhead.

"Home," I whisper to the wind climbers, yearning for the momentary oblivion of stardust.

Chapter 26

The sleigh arrives to the cheers of my siblings. I never thought the sight of the fortress would be so welcome. Isolated from humanity, this refuge is perfect for the Keeper of Sin. I can't hurt anyone here. I can bring trouble to my siblings, but they aren't human and loyal to a fault.

No doubt my disposition reminds my siblings of my father's moods after each Christmas night. How foul he was when he would return. They scatter as I leap out of the sleigh and throw the lash into the snow. No one asks any questions. Even Reilly avoids my gaze and proceeds to care for the wind climbers. The others gather in jabbering clumps. While they're not very intelligent, even they must know something is terribly amiss.

I wish I were made of ice. It would make my duty so much easier. It really makes no difference whether I am Krampus or St. Nicholas — the world goes on as it does the other three hundred and sixty-four nights of the year. The sins of humanity multiply while I hide in the murk of Arctic midnight. I only contribute to their misery by interfering in their lives. I may be happy for an hour, but at what cost? It's as if I can still hear Beth screaming. I'm both relieved and completely wrecked at the thought that no one will believe her. If she doesn't find a way to cope, she could easily end up hospitalized.

And it's my fault.

Inside the fortress, the ice cracks under my heavy footsteps as I make my way across the throne room.

Charles' laughter echoes from the hallway. "Welcome home, Santa! What, not feeling so jolly?"

I try to ignore him but his words are burrowing under my skin.

"I take it Cherry wasn't so excited to see you? Well now you know how it feels to be rejected by the Jones family. Welcome to my hell, motherfucker!"

I hesitate in the throne room, wondering if I should kill him. But I don't want to give him even a moment of satisfaction. Not even a hint that he might be right. Because if I do, he wins. That murderer doesn't deserve to win anything.

However, if I don't get rid of him, he will torment me. Any reminder of Charity must be eliminated. Of course, I don't have to kill him myself. I could ask Reilly to do it...

No. I'm not my father, despite what just happened.

Then again, there's more than one way to get rid of him.

I throw silence at Charles. My siblings can still hear him, but I can't. This way I can save my sanity without taking his life.

Despondent, I wander the hallways of the fortress. Anguish. Guilt. Everything I have done has gone wrong. The icy walls throw back my reflection. More ghost than god. Neither Krampus nor Kris Kringle. Just a stupid boy with nothing left to live for.

I stop before the doorway of the room where my father died. I could stay here, under the soft skins. I've never wished that I could sleep, but now I wish it so desperately. I recall how blissful my mother looked when she slept. Her dreams carried her away from this living nightmare, far from my father's abuses. I had the library at least.

I crawl into the skins of the bed and wrap myself in them. I have no wish to heal. I just want oblivion and soothing seal pelts.

Many hours later, Reilly stands in the doorway. My other siblings gather behind her, their fearful whispers rustling in the hallway beyond.

"We are sorry to disturb you," she says gently. "May we bring you some food? Or water? Perhaps a book!" She waits for an answer but I give her none. "Is there anything we can do, Young Klaas?"

"Don't call me that!" I cry. "My name is Aidan. I want nothing more to do with this curse."

"As you wish, *Aaaaidan*," she says and leaves.

Long after they leave, I wonder if I am wrong to push away this part of my life. I should embrace it, or at least take the form I am meant to have to match this mood.

Let the beast out.

And so I transform fully into the terrible creature I so despise. At least my appearance is not a lie. No one will love this form. I can't break anyone's heart. And they can't break mine.

But it's not enough. The List still scrolls through my mind, tormenting me with certain names. Michael Allured. Ricardo Zepeda. Judy LaHart. Mr. and Mrs. Jones. Mr. Reilly.

Can I just remove them from The List? It's never been done before, as far as I know. But there's much I don't know.

Focusing my intent, I delete them all from The List. They live — and they may live well, for all I know — but I will not be aware of them nor will I be able to measure them. Ignorance is bliss, they say. If I can't sleep, at least I have ignorance.

And finally I delete Charity. I will love her as long as I live. But being able to measure her when she no longer loves me is a greater torment than the fires.

Goodbye, Charity.

Charity

Chapter 27

April 15
Approximately 1.5 years after Aidan's kidnapping

International Science Base Camp
150 miles NE of Barrow, Alaska

I stand before a massive fortress of ice floating on the horizon, blue shadows carved into the towering slabs crowded together to form the surrounding wall. The freezing wind punishes my body with crippling blows. Smokey goggles cover my eyes, ice crusting my eyelashes. Despite the extraordinary layers of clothing, my bones burn with cold. I shout into the wind until I'm hoarse.

Enraged. Dying with desire. I'm shouting in a language I don't understand.

Dream words.

The ice beneath me rumbles. One of the towering slabs shatters and crumbles, chunks of blue ice spilling before me. I stagger backwards.

A figure emerges from the new breach in the fortress wall. Tall. Dark. Long curly hair...

I awaken with a start and kick off the blankets after a night of tossing and turning on my hard bunk. Grey twilight from the bleak Arctic icescape seeps around the edges of the heavy blackout curtains on the base camp window. It's 5:23 a.m. The sun rises in half an hour. When it does, it'll be up for almost eighteen hours.

Outside, a helicopter approaches the base camp. The rumbling would have woken me up if the dream hadn't.

The dream. I haven't had variations of this one since Aidan first told me about the fortress. The ice slabs are new. If they're real, we need more equipment if we're going to get through that. Hopefully we'll find him inside the fortress.

And then kill his father, Krampus.

We chose this date to start out for the fortress because the weather is warmest yet still cold enough for the ice to support snowmobiles towing sledges with the precious cargo for our mission. This morning, if the weather is clear, we board a plane that will fly us with our snowmobiles and sledges to our destination coordinates, twenty miles from the fortress.

Aidan. My butterflies and scorpions. At times I miss you so much, I think I'm going to dissolve on the spot. I have not for one moment stopped loving you, craving your touch, thinking about those milky blue eyes. I miss the way you laugh, the dorky yet ingenious things you say, dark curly hair spilling over your forehead. I wonder if you think I've been naughty or nice given everything I've done to get here. How I used that guy Sergei I work with at Volertech to make contacts. I let him kiss me on Christmas Even — but only a kiss. I told him I needed to stay pure for my wedding day. He bought it. The poor jerk brags that I'm his "woman," telling everyone that I'll soon return to Volertech and be his "bride."

Whatever. Loser.

"Guys!"

Ricardo blinks awake as I shake his strong shoulder. He rubs his upper left arm as he sits up. Michael grumbles in his bunk, asking what time it is.

"It's almost time to get up," I say. "But I have to tell you something. We might need more equipment." I tell them about the dream, specifically the ice slabs.

Judy rolls over in her bunk and stares at me, eyes bleary. I can't get used to seeing her without her piercings. "So, it's not enough that it's in the Arctic. It has to be surrounded by crazy ice slabs?"

Michael throws a look at Judy that makes her glare at him. He and Ricardo both have grown beards. I can't get used to that, either. Not only does it make them both look a lot older, they'll need the facial hair in the cold. "Snow be crazy," he says and kisses Ricardo. "Morning, hon."

"Morning!" Ricardo swiftly dresses. "Those 'slabs' are probably pressure ridges causing the snow to pile up. It *can* get pretty high. If it's making formations like that, we've got axes to hack out a path."

Judy sighs, shaking her head. "Maybe there aren't any slabs. Maybe it's just a symbolic warning that there'll be obstacles. I think Aidan sends symbols, not literal images."

"Like the rose petals cupped in his hands in that first dream I had?"

"Yeah. Which you first thought was blood, remember?"

She has a point. Even though I'm a skeptic, I'm not immune to my emotions affecting how I interpret what I see.

We do the most delicate packing last: four, first-generation Kel-Tech Sub2000s. They're freaking cool, collapsible semi-automatic weapons that are clearly not for killing polar bears. If the Canadian government knew we had them, they'd certainly take a dim view of us bringing such a thing to a peaceful scientific expedition.

But they're not our biggest problem. I brought Ghost, my Volertech prototype, the most sophisticated and effective Arctic drone ever developed because of its anti-icing technology and advanced GPS capabilities. I named her Ghost because she's an echo of her original back at Volertech. I made this one from the spares. To some, it might look like a toy. The trained eye, however, will see it for what it is: voice-activated, twenty-first century spy tech that will change warfare against Russia forever. It's enough to get us in massive trouble with both Volertech and the State Department, not to mention the rest of the U.S. government.

I know it was a ridiculous risk, Aidan, but you're worth it. And everything will be fine. Ghost is, as Michael says, *sick AF*. They'll never know we had her, especially since her original is safe at Volertech.

So, we have to stay under the radar, although it's proven

increasingly difficult as the longer we've been stuck here, the more questions we're getting from everyone here. They're an interdisciplinary team of Canadians, Russians, French, and Chinese scientists working together on climate change. We've lied and said we're graduate students from Carnegie Mellon studying Arctic ice melt with Dr. Arnold Haggerty. He's our "cover adult" pretending to be a climate scientist who brought us here for his Arctic study team. But there's no real team or study. And that's not his real name. He's an actor who wanted a free trip. The helicopter took him away this morning before we woke up.

We worried that someone would check his credentials, but no one cared as long as we paid. Now that we're here, though, we've got to get onto the ice before anyone figures out anything. Bad weather has delayed us a couple of days, but we have the go-ahead this morning to get on the plane.

I keep lookout on the surveillance micro-cam secretly mounted in the hallway outside our bunk as we finish packing. The cam feeds to my phone.

We did a week of cold training in Switzerland, followed by a course in polar survival taught by this retired Swiss soldier who really liked yelling. I'm sure Michael and Judy will forgive me as soon as we hit the ice. Ricardo said the training was non-negotiable, that we'd die without it, and I know he's right. He found the people through his Krav Maga sensei and had already started his survival certification when we three arrived. Our course included snowmobile training, but Judy kicked our butts and really showed us how to ride. I still don't have my driver's license but I can take jumps on a Ski-Doo in three-foot drifts.

Today the blue skies soar above us. But as I've peered out the window the last few days at the Arctic winds kicking up snow on the endless ice, I've wondered if we've learned enough. I've watched the snow flurries rise and scatter in blinding clouds, like ravenous ghosts tearing across the horizon. The worst snowstorm in Pittsburgh was nothing compared to what we've seen since we arrived at the base camp. Somewhere out there is Aidan's dad — the monster that killed my friend, kidnapped the person I love, and sent his own children to

115

their deaths, all while terrorizing humanity with impunity once a year.

Krampus. He knows our deepest desires include wanting to blow off his head. So, he's expecting us.

We're sending the drone to the coordinates that Aidan has been projecting into my dreams. The "Magical" North Pole is just north of the Healy Seamount, over six hundred miles away from the geographical North Pole. For months, the GPS coordinates have haunted my dreams, no doubt some kind of SOS from Aidan.

While I'm thrilled that everything's come together in such an amazing way, deep down I'm worried sick about how this expedition was funded. The bulk of the expenses were the equipment, weapons, and plane charter. I'm pretty sure the plane charter alone could feed a third-world country for a week.

Michael's parents supplied some of the funds, but I suspect most of the funding came from work Michael did for a mysterious client on the Dark Web, which makes me heartsick. Rumor has it there's even a new Silk Road. But, seriously, what's worse? Krampus or drug money? Unlike the War on Drugs, the War on Christmas is at least winnable.

I wonder how Ricardo got his share of the funds, but he's not talking, either. He's the one who paid for not just the survival training and shooting lessons, but the weapons, the snowmobile rentals, the gear, the sledges, and even the special ammo. I thought his family was struggling. When pressed, he says he's got "connections" and "called in favors" but nothing more. I feel like an idiot for even questioning him. I should be grateful for the help — and I am — but I've got to worry, if not for myself then for Ricardo.

Judy's folks released her trust fund. She won't tell me how she convinced them to do that. She's loaded but she reminds me that she can only use so much at a time, and she can't take money out of the actual portfolio investments until she's twenty-five. She paid for her own travel and supplies. And her gun. Interesting fact: did you know there's no minimum age for possession of firearms in either California or Alaska? Neither did I. Of course, the gun needs to be obtained legally. I'm pretty sure Judy's wasn't.

Ricardo leaves to use the restroom and then forage for another axe. He returns with one, looking grim.

"I think there's a problem. The pilots were having a big argument. It might have been about the helicopter that took away Jules." That's the actor's real name. "Kept hearing the word *elly-cop-tear.*"

"French guys always sound angry," I said.

"Nooooo, this was *way* angrier than the usual. I thought they were going to rip out each other's throats. I just wish I spoke French."

"*Je parle français!*" Judy reminds him.

"I was just going to say, maybe you should scope it out, Judy," Ricardo says. "Whatever it is, it's not good."

"CJ," Michael stands close to me. He wears everything but the thick parka and the gloves. "No matter how we pack it," he whispers, "it's too heavy. And I don't know what to let go."

The weight of our sledges is critical. We can't exceed 100 kilograms. Every tiny bit counts. We weighed the tech carefully before we shipped it. We smuggled the parts for the guns and other tech in sports gear, and it came in under fifty pounds — or so we thought. When we first arrived, our French scientist contact brought the potent brew of *viscum album* for the bullets that he'd created to my specification. The four of us created the rifle ammo from that in our bunkroom. (It was surreal, like an episode of *24* set in the Arctic.) But that shouldn't have affected the weight that much. Michael and I then assembled the smuggled parts to the KEDs (Krampus Electron Disruptors) as Judy and Ricardo double-checked our packed supplies. No chance we'll be able to put together anything in the cold wearing woolen gloves under a set of waterproof mitts.

"Take fewer weapons," I say. "Dump the bigger rifles. It's not like we're going to see any polar bears."

Ricardo throws me a warning look. "Aidan will survive friendly fire if it's just a bullet. Not V.A."

"We need to lose the guns. I don't want to end up in death water," Judy says. "Again."

She's referring to the survival training where we had to jump into a water hole carved from an icy lake and to learn how to climb back out. We didn't all jump in, just Judy, being the smallest of us. They taught us how to strip her down and warm her so that she'd survive. The problem is, a person might survive falling into winter water just outside the Arctic Circle. But where we're going, it could kill you if you and your team don't do everything just right.

"Besides, I've still got my prezzie from Uncle Anyu for those little creeps." She pats the holster under her arm that holds the handgun she picked up in Barrow from an Inuit arms dealer (Uncle Anyu) who propositioned her sixty-three times. *I like blue hair*, he said with his unusual accent.

Judy's gun makes me nervous. I still shiver at the memory of finding the stolen gun under Charles' bed and shooting "my dad" — or rather Krampus, who had taken the form of my dad as he tried to bring down our guard before he attacked us.

"Well, Judes, hopefully you won't need that." Michael pushes aside the bag of standard rifles and ammo boxes.

She glares at him again and says nothing. I sense that look is about more than the gun. She hasn't spoken to him since last night. They went to the mess together for a snack and stayed gone a while. When they came back, Judy was acting strange but she wouldn't say why. I want to ask what's going on, but I don't. There's simply too much to think about that's more important than a spat.

Ricardo picks up one of the rifles and leans it against the wall. "We have to take at least one rifle. I mean, you're right, CJ. We don't need tons of ammo, but we do need protection. You never know what's out there. We don't even know what's in that fortress exactly. There might be more than elves."

"Fine," I say. "One rifle. Minimal ammo." Just as Ricardo unties the rifle bag, two men appear on the micro-cam. My blood chills. "No way."

A banging on the door.

"Who the hell can that be?" Michael says under his breath. He opens the door and my jaw drops.

Sergei.

Chapter 28

"Surprise!" Sergei grins like he's won the lottery. He wears a bright yellow and blue knitted cap that flattens his enormous ears, and a red parka with a massive fur-lined hood. Behind him stands a brawny guy with small blue eyes, blond beard splintered with gray bristles. Something about him smells official. Actually, Sergei just smells, period.

"What are you doing here?" Panic shoots through me.

"*Moya milachka*, I could not bear the thought of you going into the most dangerous wilderness known to man without an expert guide."

"Who the hell are you?" Michael asks.

"Charity has not told you?" Sergei looks at me expectantly like I'm going to introduce him, but I'm too angry to speak. "I am Sergei Petroff, an intern with Charity at Volertech." He clears his throat. "And...her boyfriend."

"What?!?" Judy laughs. "Oh, my god, he's serious!" Everyone except Sergei and his pal cracks up.

Sergei's face wrinkles with confusion. "And...this...is Vasily Ivanov." He indicates the man standing behind him. "We will be joining you on your expedition. The pilots have given the go-ahead for our flight."

"Oh, HELL no." Ricardo pushes forward. "Charity is leading this expedition. And you need to leave."

Sergei looks Ricardo over like a zoo specimen. "You have no choice, my friend, whoever you are."

Ricardo looks like he's going to rip this guy's head off but he keeps quiet and looks to me for backup.

"I'm the lead," I say, shaking with rage. "And this is a private expedition."

"We're here to protect the prototype. We wouldn't want it to fall in the wrong hands."

I freeze when I hear this bombshell. How he figured out I had a copy of the prototype, I don't know. All I know is that he's blackmailing me — not for money, apparently. Maybe just to spend time with me? Or to get something else?

This is very bad.

"Like hell they did," Judy says before I can speak. "You're only here because you have the hots for Charity. You don't care if you ruin her trip."

"We'll not interfere. Just observe." Sergei's smugness is nauseating.

Anger and indignation are mushrooming inside me. "I don't know what you're talking about. You have no business being here," I say, shaking.

Vasily yanks Judy' bag from the floor. He frowns at her.

"Hey! Put that down! NOW!" Judy shouts.

"Is not just sleeping bag. Is too heavy."

Vasily has a gloomy, *basso profundo* Russian accent. He sounds like he needs to listen to about ten years of Tony Robbins seminars.

"Drop it!" I order.

Judy pulls it away from him. He lets her take it. The others look ashen.

"You need to leave *right now*," I say.

Vasily seethes. Sergei, though, plays it cool, approaching me directly. "My beautiful Charity — "

"Don't give me that crap!" I back away. "You're threatening me! Get out of here!"

"Either you let Mister Ivanov and I join you, or we call Volertech and the State Department. Your choice."

"So *he's* with the State Department?" I indicate Vasily. "Let me see your credentials."

As Vasily scowls, Sergei moves closer to me, face softening, lower lip quivering. "Besides, *moya golubushka*, don't you miss me?"

Oh. My. God. I'm seriously going to throw up. I took advantage of this Neanderthal's attraction to me, but I cannot hate him more than I hate him now.

"Look, Moscow," Michael fumes. "Do you seriously think we're going to let you babysit us? You need to get the hell out of here before things get ugly."

Ricardo edges toward the rifle propped against the locker. Vasily rests his hand on the gun holster bulging out from under his parka.

Heavy footsteps in the hallway interrupt us. A grizzled face appears in the doorway as Viktor Chernikov sticks his head in the room. A former Russian military commander, he runs the Arctic research base camp. He's totally hands off on the science team activities, just overseeing the day-to-day operations. So, it must be bad if he's here. He looks annoyed. "What's the problem?"

Clearly startled, Sergei responds rapidly in Russian, which of course we don't understand.

"English, people!" I glare at Sergei.

Viktor, who's been a gruff grandfather to us since we arrived, looks apologetic. "I'm sorry, Charity, but they have clearance to be here."

"But they *don't* have clearance to join my expedition!"

Viktor doesn't look worried. "Dr. Haggerty should be able to settle matters."

"Who's Dr. Haggerty?" Sergei asks.

Oh, crap.

"He's the scientist running the experiments we're helping with," I explain. "But he's going to meet us on the ice. One of our machines isn't properly calibrated. So he's taking care of it in Barrow so we can get going rather than delay the expedition any further." Where did I learn to lie like this? I'm sure Aidan knows. I hope he can tell the difference between hurtful and harmless lies.

"Ah, so you are *not* leading the expedition, rather it's Dr. Haggerty," Sergei says, looking hopeful. "He might not mind some extra help."

"JUST GET OUT!" I'm losing my temper. "Help us, Viktor!"

Viktor's response sickens me with disappointment. "You need to resolve this peacefully or I'll be forced to have the Mounties escort you all back to Barrow. Now," he addresses the group, "your plane is ready. Good luck."

The Royal Canadian Mounted Police are no joke. They're the last people we want involved.

I didn't come this far to let this dangerous, lovesick jerk in his goofy wool cap keep me from Aidan. "Fine. You want to follow us? Knock yourself out. You better hustle. We're gone in thirty minutes. And we're not sharing any supplies."

After Sergei and Vasily leave, we try to come up with a plan. Fortunately, no one lynches me for agreeing to the new company.

"Can't we ditch those a-holes?" Judy asks.

"Not until first camp. Middle of the night," I say.

Ricardo groans. He's the navigator, going ahead of everyone to look for thin ice and plot pathways around ridges if possible. "Traveling when we're exhausted is really dangerous."

"So are they," Michael adds. "We don't know who that Vasily guy is. Or his real intentions. Or even Sergei's. I mean, does that guy seriously think he's your boyfriend?"

"I had to lead him on a little to get the Russian contacts. But I would never in a million years have told him about Ghost. I didn't even tell you guys. I don't know how he figured it out. I don't even know how he got the resources to get here. He must have convinced someone I was doing something wrong and needed a tagalong. I don't know who that guy is, but he's probably not from Volertech. This isn't how they do things. They're super direct and corporate about everything."

Michael falls face first on his bed with a whimper.

A continuous white blur of snow and ice stretches for hundreds of miles below us. I try to steady my breathing because I think I'm totally having a panic attack in this small plane. But then the spectacular Arctic icescape takes my breath away with its striking palette of grays, pinks, blues, and whites ignited by sprays of golden sunlight. Judy drinks up the colors, taking photos and chattering nonstop about how the snow and ice create an incredible canvas for the light. Her folks gave her some highly sophisticated camera equipment for the trip, thinking that she wasn't going any further north than 60 degrees.

She also says the pilots were arguing because of the hazards Sergei's plans created for them. A second plane has to follow ours, as there isn't enough room for two more people with snowmobiles and packed sledges. The pilots don't want to weaken the ice with a second landing, and with whatever B.S. leverage Sergei has, he's demanding that he land close behind us. I'm hoping they're far enough behind that we can lose them.

Michael fights airsickness, head between knees, while Ricardo peers out the frosty window, idly rubbing his upper arm, silently scanning the horizon. He's probably calculating, scheming, trying to figure out how to ditch the jerks.

I'm trying *not* to think too hard about the fortress until we see it.

My stomach flops up into my throat as the plane descends, but the landing is surprisingly gentle. Still, Michael's face is pale and sweating. Ricardo helps him breathe. Judy packs away her camera. Already, the cold steals through the metal doors of the plane like wraiths with razor fingers.

"*Il fait frois, non?*" Our French pilot, Henri, laughs with his co-pilot, Olivier, who says more I don't understand.

Judy wrinkles her nose. "*Tu fermes ta gueule, connard!*"

The pilots look surprised, and then they laugh hard. "*Une vrais française, alors!*" Henri says.

"*C'est ça,*" Olivier replies with a wink.

When I nudge her to translate, she just shakes her head.

The digital thermometer on the pilot's dash says it's -30°C on the ground. Could be worse. I read about how the British polar explorer Ann Daniels and her all-female team suffered record-breaking lows of -46°C when they tried to go to the North Pole on foot. One of the three expedition members had to drop out because her toes were chewed off by frostbite. Another lost use of her hands and needed help going to the bathroom.

It's one thing to read about that stuff and quite another now that I can feel death pinching my cheeks gleefully, like Aunt Bellina when she's had a couple glasses of wine.

I wonder if I'll ever see Aunt Bellina again. Or Mom and Dad, for that matter.

This could be the end of the line.

Chapter 29

The two pilots tumble out of the cockpit and open the plane doors. The icy air clobbers me. When I inhale, the cold singes my insides. I wear four layers of clothing, a helmet, a balaclava (aka face mask), smoked goggles, a pair of woolen gloves under a set of waterproof mitts, and a double layer of socks in my waterproof boots. Yet it's barely enough to keep the cold from eating me alive.

Even worse, every scar on my body from where Krampus dug his claws into me during the battle feels like someone is plunging a chilled knife into it. Those wounds never healed quite right.

Everyone is stunned as we look around. We're here. In the Arctic. We're surrounded by three hundred and sixty degrees of What The Hell Am I Doing Here? I'm freaking out big time yet it also feels weirdly natural. If someone had told me two years ago that I, a California girl, would be standing on the Arctic Ocean, I would have locked myself in a closet forever. But then I would have missed seeing the sunlight spilling liquid gold on the powder blue ice. It reminds me of pictures I've seen of the moonscape except it's ivory, and instead of craters, the surface is packed with snow.

Crack! Crack!

Gunfire?

"What the hell?" Michael says, startled.

"Eez zee ice," Olivier says. "Eet eez a leeving theeng! Eet moves. Eet talks."

The ice *is* alive. And it's really loud. A series of booms echo across the ice, followed by a groaning, grinding sound. Like someone is opening and shutting the oldest, rustiest doors in the world.

"Crazy," I say. "Someone totally needs to sample that." Judy and Michael nod in agreement.

Ricardo does jumping jacks. "Come on! Get your circulation up!"

We do as he says. As best we can, anyway, layered up in so much wool clothing. (Cotton equals death, or so said our Swiss cold survivor instructor. If it gets soaked with sweat, it freezes.) I wince with the movements as the skin of my sensitive scars pulls. But if I don't move, I'll get frostbite, and then it'll truly be game over.

Henri and Olivier unlock and open the cargo doors, lowering the ramp. We all help unload the snowmobiles and sledges as the second plane arrives, landing a couple hundred feet away. To each snowmobile we hitch a sledge packed with supplies, ensuring the contents of each sledge are secure. Judy's sledge has the tent, which is critical to our survival. We've spread out the other supplies — food, water (one day's worth), cookers, basic mechanic's tools, first aid kit, gas and engine oil — between the sledges in case we lose one. And we're all wearing bottles of petroleum fuel under our coats so that they don't freeze. We have to cover twenty miles one-way. Anything can happen. And will.

My dirty, scraped-up Ski-Doo is yellow. Michael's driving an orange Polaris and Ricardo a red Viper. We hopefully won't lose each other by sight unless there's a whiteout.

Judy approaches me before she climbs onto her black Viper. A strong machine, not fast or fun, but it'll pull her sledge. "I could push creepy intern dude into an ice crack," she offers. "Just sayin'."

I laugh. "You have both sets of GPS coordinates, right?"

"Of course! Relax," she says and hugs me tight. Then, in my ear: "You're going to see Aidan soon. It's going to be epic."

For the first time in a long time, I burst into tears. We hug for what feels like an eternity. "I miss him so much," I whisper back. Remarkably, my tears don't freeze. At least, not right away. We break when we hear the buzz of Sergei and his buddy approaching on their snowmobiles. "Are you and Michael in a fight?" I ask. "You don't look like you're getting along."

She makes for her Viper. "It's better to talk about it in a tent with hot tea," she says as she climbs aboard. "Right now, we need to think about surviving and ditching you-know-who."

That answer worries me. We need team spirit and high morale to survive the cold — both of which are already compromised by the jerk-holes pulling up to us.

I feel that familiar ache as I double-check the GPS coordinates for our reconnaissance camp to find Aidan. It won't be as the crow flies because there'll be pressure ridges and open water to navigate around, but at least we know exactly where we're going: first the reconnaissance site (which no one was supposed to know about) and then the fortress. I tug the balaclava up to make sure it covers my nose, adjust my goggles, and switch on the ignition.

Everyone is seated, snowmobiles rumbling, except Sergei, who stomps through the snow to me. "Where are we going? You give us GPS coordinates for destination!"

I give him my middle finger.

We launch in "flock" formation. Ricardo is out ahead, scouting. We watch for hand signals, following closely in his path. Fist up means he sees thinning ice or open water, so we need to stop.

The Ski-Doo balks, the sledge tugging the hitch until the snow loosens the friction. I wince. That alone is going to suck up gas.

Sergei and Vasily lag far behind, scrambling to catch up.

The wind rises, stirs, and then blasts our crafts with snow. How I used to wish that I could get away from Oak County and the BFJs. Now the wind throws me around rather than bullies. I long for the days of stealing kisses with Aidan in the old kitchen.

Blistering winds from the east howl, pummeling us like a boxer's speed bag. Everything blurs. My body seizes up with the sudden drop in temperature. The sledge fishtails behind Judy, threatening to jackknife. The wind tries to throw the Ski-Doo off course.

Blizzard.

Judy moves her snowmobile away from mine, giving everyone berth. Ricardo pulls forward. Sergei and Vasily are not even in formation. They lag behind Michael's tail like scavengers. I try to hold the Ski-Doo on course, but I can't see the GPS without holding it close to my goggles. Winds like this demolish campsites in seconds.

Ricardo's fist goes up. He motions to form a protective line with the snowmobiles. We do. We then stumble toward one another, leaden feet sinking in the snowy depths. Throwing our arms around one another for shelter.

Barely visible in the storm, Sergei and Vasily skid to a stop somewhere nearby, battered by flurries. The snowmobiles tilt, wrenching at the hitch.

Snow chokes my goggles. Wondering if we should get the tent material and zip up in it, I press my head to Judy's as the guys hold us. Every muscle tenses as we fight to stay upright. I try to jog in place to keep my body temperature up. Everyone starts moving, creating a weird bubble of hopping and stomping people. My body soon tires, legs heavy, each breath dragging more needles into my lungs.

An image of Aidan flickers in my mind of that night at the dance, lifting his palms to the sky...

Snow.

I would pray except I don't believe in God. Still, there is someone who can help. If only he could hear us.

Aidan, make it stop. Please.

Can't see more than three feet away. The two closest snowmobiles tumble over, the hitches threatening to break.

Whiteout. We can see nothing beyond a few feet. The barbed-wire winds tear into my layers of clothing.

We'll all die if this keeps up.

Ricardo drops down and starts digging with just his gloved hands, throwing and packing snow up and around us. I get it! He's building a wall of snow as a shield. We join in. Within a few minutes the snow is waist height. If we squat down, the ivory walls block the winds. My body warms a few degrees although I still shiver deeply. Painfully. We continue to move our arms, do squats, anything to keep moving. When that fails, we cling to each other, rubbing limbs.

Hrrrreeeeeeeeeeaw!

A weird, high-pitched cry cuts above the rough winds, more mammal than bird.

"What the hell is that?" I shout, hoping it's just yet another sound of the Arctic ice.

Crack! Crack!

Or is it gunfire?

Michael motions for us all to squat and huddle.

Two mysterious "flares" hover above us in the howling whiteness. But if they're actual flares, they didn't launch properly. After a moment, the twin lights disappear.

Hrrrreeeeeeeeeeaw!

And then someone wails like they're being eaten alive, driving *t*error into my heart.

Several minutes later, just as I wonder if this is the end for us, the winds fade. Sunlight breaks sickly yellow over the solid white, the horizon appearing, clouds parting.

The ache of hope, exhausted by cold and fear.

Michael whoops. "We live! Woooohooooooo!"

"That was *way* too short for a blizzard," Judy says warily. "And I don't think Vasily and Sergei were making those noises because they found a bouncy house."

"How long are blizzards supposed to last?" I rise to my full height, legs and butt aching. The snowmobiles tilt in the drift, the sledges in disarray, tarps loosened. Mini-shipwrecks. We examine our crafts, but nothing seems lost.

"Hours, maybe? Not minutes," Ricardo says.

Judy nods. "Exactly. This is super weird."

As we push off excess snow and set our snowmobiles upright, my "Spidey" senses tingle.

"The jerks," Ricardo says. "Where'd they go?"

"Who cares?" I push my sledge upright and secure the cover. "They must have taken off."

Except their snowmobiles and sledges are still here...

"NO!" Michael yells. "No no no no!"

A hand reaches up from under the snow. It's not moving.

We run to the site and burrow into the drift until we uncover the body.

It's Vasily. His wide eyes stare up at the sky, his mouth wrenched into a scowl. One hand clutches his chest. The other reaches out to us. His cheeks are flushed red, nose tinged blue. Michael places his cheek to the man's mouth, probably checking for breath. Nothing. He removes the dead man's glove on the outstretched hand to reveal red fingers.

"Wow! He looks sunburned!" Judy says, shivering. I put my arms around her and we hug away some cold.

"He didn't die from the blizzard," Michael says, examining the man's wrist. "He went into cardiac arrest."

"How can you tell?" I ask. "Hand clutching his chest?"

"Yeah. That and his skin's flushed." He unzips the dead man's parka, digs into the pockets until he finds a dark blue booklet, which he opens. A whistle as he brandishes it. "His real name is Dmitry Stepankov. He's Russian Interpol, kids."

An international police officer. My brain silently explodes. "That's not State Department. What is he doing here?"

"It's not like we're breaking any Russian laws," Judy says. "Even if we want to kill a polar bear, that's not against the law in Russia. Besides, he couldn't have known that we want to kill something other than a polar bear."

"Maybe he did somehow," Michael says. "Sergei knew about Ghost."

I scan the horizon as they talk. Where's Sergei?

And then I see the grisly trail. I let go of Judy and trudge through the drift about thirty feet, following the gory flecks until I find Sergei's blood-soaked blue and yellow cap.

Judy gasps behind me before I even announce what I see. "Oh, God!" she cries.

The chunky streaks of Sergei's torn body stain the freshly fallen powder. His head lies beyond, his spine raggedly protruding from his neck. A rifle lies nearby, the heated barrel melted into the snow.

I fight the pressure rising in my throat. The surrealism of the gruesome scene is numbing. Maybe it's easier for me than everyone else because of what I went through with Darren. The others vomit onto the snow, cursing, gagging, crying. All I can do is close my eyes and hug myself. *Here we go again.*

"What the hell could even do this?" Michael yells hoarsely,

spitting into the snow.

"It's not the elves, is it?" Judy asks. "Could they have done this?"

Michael is losing it. "And why didn't it get us? We were RIGHT. FREAKING. THERE!"

He's right. It doesn't add up. Something passed through here and tore Sergei to bits, scaring Vasily — or Dmitry — to death. Yet it ignored us. Why? Is it a warning? Why not just finish us all off?

Ricardo says nothing, jaw set, eyes behind his goggles strafing the ice and horizon for clues. He idly rubs his upper arm again. I wonder if he's hurt.

"We need to call the base," Michael says, making for the snowmobiles. "I'll get the satellite phone."

"NO!" Ricardo grabs Michael, holds him back from the snowmobile. "Think for a second."

"He's right," I add. My legs are rubbery. This is the second person I've ever hated that I've found dead. And it's as horrible as the first time, with even greater consequences. "If they send someone out here, they'll accuse us of murder."

"But we couldn't have possibly done this!" Judy says.

"Who packed several axes?" Ricardo points to himself. "And if anyone heard us arguing with those two — Viktor knew we weren't happy — we'll be in prison forever."

Michael starts hyperventilating, clenching and unclenching his hands.

"I don't know," I reply. "Technically, we're in international waters. There are no laws here."

Michael calms. "Wait. No laws and...no crimes?"

"That's not true," Judy says. "Russia could convict us of the crime because the jerks were Russian nationals."

"Ukrainian. Well, Sergei is. Or was," I add.

"How do you know so much about this?" Michael asks Judy.

She directs her answer to me, not Michael. "Remember the French mistletoe my dad smuggled in? Well, guess what? That's not all he smuggles. And nobody here needs to know more than that."

I stare at her. This explains a lot. The abandonment for "holidays abroad." Her isolation. How could she get close to anyone with this

131

family secret?

"They don't think I know what they're doing or how they make so much money," she continues. "But I do know. And I sometimes worry they won't come home from one of those trips, that they'll wind up in some foreign prison. That's how I know international law — worrying about my parents."

Michael's so freaked out by this revelation that the whites of his eyes appear behind his goggles. "Okay, then," he says. "Judy McSmuggler says we're going to hang in the gulag for killing an Interpol cop."

"Well, at least I'm telling the truth!" Judy yells.

"Stop it, you guys, okay?" I say, annoyed. "Michael, do you really think a coroner would convict us of killing Sergei? That doesn't look like an axe attack."

Michael sighs. "You have a point. So, we're going to call?"

"No. And here's why. We don't really know why Sergei was following us. He might not even be who he says he is. Maybe he's not Ukrainian. Maybe he's Kiev. Maybe he was forced to do what he did. Or maybe he was going to kill us for the drone. Point is, if they killed us, they could've gotten away with it because we're in the middle of nowhere. They could've broken a hole in the ice and literally stuffed us down the memory hole. No one would have ever found us." I slow my breathing, deep breaths, calming myself, thinking. "But we're obviously not going *that* far. We're just going to leave them here and not tell anyone so that we can buy enough time to get to the fortress."

"CJ, you're not seriously thinking we should abandon this site," Michael says. "Two people have died. One has been brutally murdered!"

"That is exactly what we should do," I shoot back, resisting both the guilt and nausea. "But not before we take their gas and food."

Chapter 30

We're fugitives for something we didn't do. Was Sergei Russian, not Ukrainian? I read online there's a big difference between the cultures, that Ukrainians are more open-minded and that Russians tend to be xenophobes. Volertech wouldn't have hired him if he was Russian or the citizen of any other enemy nation. Which makes me wonder what exactly did they want with us? Why didn't they just arrest us at the base? They must have wanted to know where we were going really badly. One thing I never, ever did was transmit those coordinates electronically. Despite the encryption I was using, it's remotely possible that they hacked my phone or other equipment to get certain information about our cargo, but not that.

Did Volertech send them? Or someone else? Whoever they were, they didn't plan very well. They should have planted someone in our group, gotten our trust, and betrayed us. Maybe they realized that we were too tight knit for that.

One thing I do know is that someone infiltrated Volertech on Christmas. The official memo from the CEO said that there had been a breach of security protocol, and that a couple of security personnel had been injured pursuing the intruder. However, no suspects had been taken into custody because the intruder had purportedly jumped to his death. I don't remember hearing anything about the identity of the body. But then, they wouldn't have told us anything, anyway. They would have done exactly what they did do: double down on security and forbid us from talking about it.

When the actual infiltration went down on Christmas, I was wearing headphones, listening to my jams as I patrolled with the drone down in the hangar. Only one goon with a gun had been assigned to the alternate entrance in the sister building, whereas four patrolled *our* building, in addition to the security guard at the front entrance, who's since been let go. If Krampus were coming to kill me, he would logically take the entrance with fewer people. Less resistance.

When I heard the gunshots, I immediately thought Krampus was in the building. I had been stupid enough to post that "letter" to him on my reconnaissance trip on the icebreaker. But it couldn't have been Krampus because it sounded like whoever had broken in was pursued on foot by security. Krampus would never run. He can deflect bullets and annihilate everything in his path. So whoever it was must have infiltrated the building thinking no one was there. That still makes no sense when anyone on 4Chan could probably get more information using a laptop while sitting in a café in Hong Kong rather than risking a full-body break in. Unless, of course, the thief wanted to steal some tech. Still, that's incredibly risky. Or stupid.

Whatever they were after, maybe Volertech now thinks I had something to do with that. Again, though, why not just arrest us? Why have an Interpol agent bully us into leading him to our site? They can't possibly know about Aidan. And even if they did, so what? Aidan was kidnapped as far as everyone is concerned. In fact, why not enlist our help? We'd all be on the same side.

After we claim the gas cans from the dead men's sledges, as well as the petroleum bottles that they'd been wearing. Ricardo ensures we each have a loaded rifle ready to use before we continue on the mission. No telling what killed Sergei and scared Vasily to death. And even if we don't veer near polar bear territory, it's good to be ready. Anywhere there's open water, there might be polar bears. But that's not what killed Sergei.

Michael states his official objection to the course of action but surrenders to the group vote. Judy is glaring at him again. I don't ask because I just want to get going.

Although no one has recovered from the sight of Sergei's body, we force ourselves to take water and food breaks. It's a tad warmer now at -27°C. The human body needs around five thousand calories a day to survive these extremely cold temperatures. I've packed plenty of peanut M&Ms in my meal packets, not just because they're high in protein, fat and calories, but in honor of Leo.

Man, I miss him.

The bone-aching cold is unreal. Between that, the drudgery of hauling our sledges over rough ridges when they get stuck, and the constant fear of thin ice, I've never felt so perpetually close to death. But as I think of Aidan, the breathtaking beauty of the Arctic comes to life. The sunlight etches periwinkle blue and gray swirls into the undulating icescape. I feel at ease. Even happy. But then I realize that in fifty years this extraordinary wilderness will be gone thanks to climate change, and my spirits crash.

What then will happen to the Klaas?

Three hours later, with still another five miles to go before we can stop for the night, we halt at a long break in the ice — this must be what polar explorers call a "lead." Black seawater foams and flows in the three-foot-wide crack. Soon a gray film of ice will cover it, but it'll be a while before it's safe to cross. Judy volunteers to explore the lead for a crossing point. We unhitch her sledge and she soars off like a hawk, following the break until she's out of sight.

Ricardo broods, his back to Michael.

"What now?" Michael asks. "Dude, talk to me."

Ricardo shakes his head, rubbing his upper arm. He looks like he's about to have a breakdown. Then again, we probably all look that way because of the cold. "I'm just thinking."

"About what? You've been totally acting strange this whole trip. What's going on with you?"

"Enough!" Ricardo explodes, his voice echoing across the ice.

"Fine," Michael says, sounding wounded. He doesn't look fine.

I go pee behind my snowmobile, my butt and other parts seared by the frost until I can clumsily pull up my layers of pants. It's ridiculously hard doing anything in these gloves. And everyone always has to pee. The cold makes your body wants to get rid of the toxins ASAP.

As I stand, I hear it.

Hrrrreeeeeeeeeeaw!

A mist rises on the horizon. And an ominous rumbling.

"It's coming!" I shout, jumping on my snowmobile. "IT'S COMING!"

Michael gasps.

Ricardo shoves him toward his snowmobile. "*Go go go!*"

"What about Judy's gear?" Michael asks, mounting.

Hrrrreeeeeeeeeaw!

"Forget it!" My heart crashes against my rib cage, adrenaline burning up my body as the wind rises around us. "We'll come back for it!"

That might be a lie.

We race along the crack's edge, the bizarre blizzard at our backs, lashing us with scorching cold winds. I push the snowmobile to fifty miles per hour, struggling to keep it on course, hoping we don't hit an ice pan or worse. The craft skids and careens as it hits ice. I can't breathe. I slow down, terrified I'll lose control but more terrified that the creature will get me. Ricardo pulls ahead.

Where's Judy? How far did she travel? It's like she just disappeared and fell through thin ice.

I glance back at the storm and wish that I hadn't. Two eyes burn like hellish fires in a snow flurry. My thoughts blur in the rush of hysteria as I try to make sense of what I'm seeing.

A towering figure emerges from the flurry, lurching toward us. Enormous reindeer antlers crown its skull, its body emaciated, limbs long and clawed. Michael and Ricardo scream, *go go go*, snowmobiles speeding forward, swerving in the freezing gales and snowy tendrils. The flurry overtaking us...

Hrrrreeeeeeeeeaw!

HRRRREEEEEEEEEAAAAAW!

Chapter 31

Then, something even more bizarre happens. The blizzard creature turns south. Shrieks fading. Winds dying.

And it's gone.

I yell to the guys, but they can't hear me over the snowmobile engines. No one dares slow down. We have to find Judy ASAP.

Eventually Judy and her snowmobile appear. The craft sits near the spot where the crack narrows to a passable point.

"The *hell* was *that*?" Michael is out of breath, as if he'd run the entire way. He doubles over on his Ski-Doo.

"It's probably what killed Sergei," I reply. "I saw those fiery orbs during the blizzard, but I didn't know what they were."

"Whatever it was, I don't think it even saw us," Ricardo says.

"Maybe it found something better to kill," Michael replies. "Again."

Judy seems oblivious that we just avoided death as she fixates on whatever is flying high above the Arctic. I slide off the snowmobile seat, boots crunching in the snow. "Jay! We almost died!"

"Shhhhh!" she flaps a gloved hand at us, holding her binoculars in the other. "Look!" She points up to the sky.

A flock of brown birds flies overhead in a jagged line.

I frown, annoyed. "What the hell? Bird watching?" Although, I'm not sure birds come this far north.

Judy shoves her binoculars at me. The look on her face tells me I'm being an ass. I take them and focus on the migrants.

They aren't birds. They're large goat-like creatures, swishing their legs like they're running on the wind.

And they have babies. Adorable, flying "kids" cavort after the elder goat-things, doing back flips and "running" circles around the adults' legs. The babies open their mouths like they're bleating. An adult periodically attacks the face and ears of a little one with his or her tongue for an impromptu bath. Midair.

I'm so stunned, Michael has to gently pry the binoculars from my hands. Then, even he appears traumatized when he passes them to Ricardo. That's when I remember that Michael and Ricardo caught a glimpse of these creatures before the battle at my house, when Krampus' sleigh was on my rooftop. I've never seen them until now. Popular legend is that reindeer pull Santa's sleigh, but it's not reindeer. It's these goat-like creatures. They'd almost be cute if they didn't work for Krampus, too.

"That can't be real," I say, shaking my head.

"Right?!?" Judy replies. "The evil flying goats have had evil flying *baby* goats. I think they're returning to the fortress."

I want to start sobbing as I hand the binoculars back to Judy. A crack of doubt wider than the one in the ice opens in my mind about this mission. "Guys, there is no way I'm hurting those animals, even if they're evil."

Ricardo places his hand on my shoulder and looks me in the eye. Sometimes I think he understands me better than Michael and Judy ever will, and it's not just because he's been "othered" in society like I have. "CJ, you know as well as anyone that war means casualties. To accomplish your mission, you might have to hurt things besides Krampus. A lot of things. You know this. You've done this." He looks like he wants to say more but he just pats me on the shoulder.

"Okay, we'll try not to kill flying goat babies, but we're still takin' down Krampus," Michael says. "Besides, we haven't even seen inside the belly of the beast. There might be bigger fisher." He waves us to the snowmobiles. "Onward ho, Eldorado!"

I climb onto my machine. The engine beneath me sputters to life. "Really? *Heart of Darkness* references?" In Joseph Conrad's book, the Eldorado Exploring Expedition disappeared without a trace. "Dude! Not helping!"

Chapter 32

We retrieve Judy's sledge. As we then eat our twenty-five hundred-calorie lunch of energy bars and peanut M&Ms, we discuss the blizzard creature. Nobody has any ideas. The Arctic is deadly enough without this thing.

And progress is, well, glacial. Between the frequent bathroom breaks (because the cold makes your body vacate waste faster), the constant need for food and water, refueling, and fumbling around in our mittens, it feels like we're hardly moving. Even my brain is frozen, thoughts crawling around in my skulls until they trickle out of my mouths.

We repeatedly encounter places where the pressure ridges smash up against one another, creating walls of snow rubble. Sometimes we go around, like when we hit the open water, but then we come to a pressure ridge that seems to go miles in each direction. Determined to move forward, Ricardo and Michael take turns with the machete chopping out blocks of ice to make a passage for our crafts. We help each other push our sledges over the ridges. It's grueling work, worsened by paranoia. I check the GPS periodically to make sure we are, in fact, moving in the right direction. At least twice we have to adjust course because the ice we're on is moving southeast of our target at almost as fast a clip as we're riding.

We'd been warned Arctic ice is like that. Constantly moving, usually in the direction you don't want to go.

The ice creaks, bangs, and moans ominously as we're forced to stop on an ice pan — that is, an expanse of blackish-white ice — to refuel. I hastily pour gasoline into my snowmobile as the ice breaks away behind us. If anyone had been behind me, they would be afloat and we'd have had to wait for the ice to settle.

After seven exhausting hours of travel, we cover just over ten miles. We're still just under ten miles away, with less than four hours of sunlight left, and we're super tired. So, we set up camp.

My legs, butt, back, shoulders, hands, and neck are incredibly sore from getting our crafts across the ice and from then sitting for hours in the snowmobile. My lips are already chapped. My head hurts, but mostly from worrying the entire time that the slightest wind might be a prelude to the blizzard creature. At times, the wide-open expanses alternately take my breath away and play havoc with my apparently latent agoraphobia. Although, maybe it's not that I'm afraid of open spaces as much as I'm realizing we're hundreds of miles away from any kind of help.

We're insane. I know because I've read everything I can get my hands on about Arctic explorers. At the moment, thinking about each person helps me focus my racing thoughts about how crazy this all is. We're not the first. Others have tried and made it.

Like Ralph Plaisted. Way back in 1968, after failing the year before, he was not only the first person to ride a snowmobile to the geographical North Pole, but his was the first undisputed surface conquest of the North Pole. Robert Peary, Frederick Cook...they both claimed to have made it to the Pole but they had no proof. Ralph did. And because he encountered all the crazy problems that we did today and more, he failed the first time in 1967. But dude learned a lot from his failures. The following year, it took him only forty-three days to go over four hundred miles, leaving from Ward Hunt Island. (Hundreds of miles from here, but still.) And then there was Wild Bill Cooper, who traveled something like five *thousand* miles by snowmobile, from Minnesota to Greenland (thanks to the surrounding ice sheet).

Those guys must have all had iron butts. I can barely move, and I'm a champion sitter-downer. I'm sure the freezing cold is making everything worse.

Snow stings our faces while we ride. The bottles of petroleum get heavier by the minute lashed against our bodies under our coats. Every word we say is punctuated by puffs of white air escaping our mouths. It's a good thing I put on ten pounds eating those snacks at Volertech. Poor Judy looks as miserable and exhausted as I feel, but she doesn't complain. If anything, her eyes look hard and focused.

After almost snapping one of the tent poles in half as we wrestle with them in the blistering winds, we four manage to put up our yellow and red pyramid tent. We opted for one big one so we can sleep next to one another. Michael triumphantly points out the ventilation tunnels that let us cook inside without getting carbon monoxide poisoning. Judy and Ricardo together find snow to melt for drinking water, soup, and cooking water for the freeze-dried meals. Both highly experienced campers, they work like pros with the cookers, eventually conjuring an appetizing aroma of potatoes and beef. The cookers also warm the tent. Michael cracks open the sleeping bags, cringing.

"Ah, crap! They're frozen!"

He and I remove the guns, ammo, and KEDs from the sleeping bags, and then spend at least twenty minutes beating the frost out of the bags. My spirits sink at the thought of trying to slide into a frozen bag tonight. Not that any of us were going to sleep much anyway, but we need rest to make good decisions. Once the bags are a little less crunchy, Michael lays them out, putting Judy and I in the middle of our Arctic cuddle puddle.

Even in the murky tent, the gadgets gleam. Deadly and beautiful. A thrill works up inside of me because we *made* these things. Us! The VA mix is meant to be potent at -30°C, but the problem is that ammunition tends to lose power and accuracy when it's that cold. I've added metal shavings to the mix for the VA powder. It should help.

The KEDs are my special weapon against Krampus' ability to manipulate electrons, in particular to shield himself from attacks. The KED fits on the wrist and works a lot like a Taser, shooting out what I call a "squid" that erupts into a spray of electrically charged tentacles.

The charge disrupts the holding pattern of the electrons to allow gunfire through. If a team member is in his invisible grip, another member simply has to shoot a squid into the space between Krampus and the captive. Or just shoot Krampus while he's distracted. That works, too.

Meanwhile, I set up the computer and unpack the drone. Even if she isn't as high-powered, she's still going to tell me what I need to know:

How to save Aidan.

Chapter 33

Michael fusses over Ghost as I lift her from the packing material.

She's a white disk about ten inches across with four rotors, weighing a tad more than a TV remote. The earlier prototype was shaped like a football with a sliding elliptical camera. I discarded that design because I wanted Ghost to be able to fly through tight spaces like the Millennium Falcon. She's also solar powered, with specially designed panels covering the top of her disk. She has a shocking amount of juice, enough for a 24-hour surveillance run — both in air and on ground — before she has to sunbathe again. Best of all, she's really quiet.

The project I signed on to develop for Volertech was a drone that could withstand extreme cold, with a range of one hundred miles from the control station. I've been designing one on my own since I was in the hospital. She doesn't look like much. But believe me: no one has been able to develop an Arctic drone anywhere near as sophisticated this. Most Arctic drones look like Mr. Spotty. The U.S. government wants to buy Ghost's sister – ostensibly to survey our interests on the extended continental shelf in the Arctic. But what they really want is an army of small drones to spy on Russia.

Everyone watches as I check each part to make sure nothing broke in transit. My thumbs up gesture triggers a collective sigh of relief. She's utterly perfect. Can't wait for her to light up the fortress.

That is, if we can find it.

Our dinner of beef stew and cocoa with cinnamon — thanks to Ricardo — is hushed by exhaustion, hunger, and anxiety. Every squeak, moan, or "gunshot" sound startles us because it could signal that the ice around us is breaking away. On top of that, we listen for the screech of the blizzard creature approaching in the distance.

The survivalist instructor warned us that, since the ice totally changes topography overnight due to the ocean currents beneath us, we have to find a solid place to camp. Being instructed is one thing. Doing it is another.

Judy checks the satellite phone. "It's working," she announces. "No one's called."

"That's because they haven't found the bodies," Michael says morosely.

"Stop it!" I say.

"Stop what?"

"Stop trying to guilt us for leaving them." My spoon drops into my plastic bowl. I already feel guilty. No need for reminders.

"I'm not!" He rubs his stubbly cheeks with his gloved hand.

Ricardo gathers empty dishes, carefully staying out of this. Smart guy.

"Good. Because we have enough to worry about," Judy says as she doles out extra chocolate.

"But they're going to call," Michael says. "What do we tell them about the Russian guys?"

"That we lost them in a storm," I reply. "It's true and simple."

Michael rubs circulation into his arms and hands, shaking his head.

The laptop boots with a comforting hum. I munch on peanut M&Ms as Michael's tracking software starts. No hitches. The screen opens with Ghost's view. I have two controllers: one that straps to my wrist and the other is a modified tablet. Both are available and ready.

I switch on Ghost and pretend to stroke her back as she purrs.

"Awwww! Ghost makes me miss Miru," Judy says with a head tilt. Adorable Miru, her fat marmalade cat that ignored us while I had my emotional breakdown over Aidan on Judy's couch. I wonder when Judy was last home?

The camera comes to life. My tired, cranky, frozen face lights up the computer screen. Heartbeat spikes, legs weakening. I look to Michael. He crouches behind me.

144

"Ready?" I announce. He nods.

We don our balaclavas, parkas, mittens, and fur hoods before we unravel the complicated tent exit, carrying Ghost. The wrist controller clings to my arm over my coat sleeve, programmed, ready to receive commands. I gave it voice controls because I knew it would be too cold to use bare fingers. Our boots crunch into the snow, winds conjuring wraiths from the ground as they lift the powder. The freezing wilderness stretches out of sight under a canopy of brilliant blue sky.

It. Is. *Freaking!* Cold.

I nod to Michael and toss Ghost up at the sky.

Ghost spins in place above us, capturing the complex set of satellite signals that calibrate her location. The wrist controller reads our GPS coordinates. And then Aidan's...

"Go," I say to the controller. And Ghost flies away.

Chapter 34

Everyone crowds around the computer screen, blowing on steaming cups of cocoa as the Arctic icescape sweeps beneath Ghost. Her camera lens captures the endless drifts and graceful, wind-carved waves of snow. Sun sprays pure light over the sparkling bluish ice.

The microphone isn't working. At times we hear the rush of wind. Other times nothing. Frustrating. It's close to sunset by the time Ghost reaches the foreboding circular wall of ice slabs.

"Wow!" Ricardo announces, excited. "Those sure aren't pressure ridges. They're definitely not remotely normal." As everyone else cringes with despair, he adds, "We'll find a way inside. You'll see."

But there's nothing within the circular wall, which is as big as Cornell's sports stadium. Just more drifts divided by a widening crack of open water littered with jagged pieces of floating ice.

"This can't be true," I say, growing more anxious by the second. Ghost circles above the GPS coordinates indicated at the bottom of the screen; her camera reveals no more than wilderness. She shudders as a strong gust swipes the icescape, and the screen view blurs for a moment. That high-tech de-icing system is working beautifully. I even built a defroster on her camera because I knew fogging would be a constant problem.

The group makes annoyed, angry noises.

"It's here! I swear!" I turn back to the screen. "It can't *not* be here."

"Well, you were right about the slabs, but it's not there, CJ," Ricardo says, an edge in his voice. He slumps back onto his sleeping bag, arm resting over his eyes.

Michael grimaces. "You were lied to, CJ. We were all lied to. Evil goat daddy figured we'd sail right onto the thin ice. We should've known it was a Krampus trick to lead us to our deaths."

Judy huddles on her sleeping bag, arms circling her head as she rests her forehead on her knees. Hiding. Shivering. "I'm sick of being cold," she cries. "It hurts. Everywhere!"

Ghost shudders again, snow swirling over the circle of ridges.

Failure. We came all this way, in danger of frostbite, hypothermia, homicidal blizzard creature, arrest, murder accusations, insanity...

Snow swirling.

Michael puts his arm around me. "CJ, why don't you retrieve Ghost and call it a night. We can try again in the morning. Maybe Ghost needs recalibration or something."

I start remembering that reoccurring dream. His voice fades behind the static crackling between my ears. I'm standing before the fortress, leaning on the ski poles. Enraged. Dying with desire. I'm shouting in a language I don't understand. The words baffle me.

Dream words.

Ahn-sai-ra-potem. Na-ren-hi-gatow.

I repeat them.

"CJ? CJ!" Judy's voice fades in the distance.

I repeat them. Louder. Mesmerized by the shimmering, hazy screen. Snow. *Snow.*

Louder. Movement around me. Warmth.

Ghost's camera settles, focuses. Realigns.

Reveals.

A massive curved disk of ice appears, surrounded by the slabs.

It's the fortress roof. The rest must be underground. But how? It's seawater below the ice. And...

Seamounts. Dead volcanoes.

"Whoa!" Ricardo says. "What just happened?"

"Oh, my God!" Judy gasps. "No way!"

"Holy crap," Michael says. "Where did *that* come from? And what the heck is it? A UFO or something?"

"It's the fortress." My head clears. "Remember what Aidan said about his dad being able to take any form? Think about it. He's been able to cloak everything. Aidan gave me the words in a dream to unlock the cloaking."

"Like magic words?" Judy asks.

"I wouldn't say magic," I reply. That word makes me grumpy. "Words unlock meaning in our brains. Why not visual perceptions? A picture's worth a thousand words, right? It only takes one word to unlock an image in our minds."

"Even if that hypothesis is true, your words didn't make any sense." Michael says. "How can babbling unlock anything?"

"Babbling to you. Maybe it's another language. An old language we once all knew as a species." I shrug. "I don't know. I'm talking out of my butt now. It worked, whatever it was."

I guide Ghost to the base of the fortress. Strange, angular picture-symbols like Egyptian hieroglyphs are carved into the circular fortress's ice wall. They shine with that eerie blue light that Aidan's eyes radiate.

The blue of ancient ice.

Another jolt in my body as Ghost soars past a dark opening in the ice wall.

"The hell?" Ricardo yells.

"Ghost, stop!"

She halts. I then guide her with another command to double back to the opening: an arched portal covered in more of those hieroglyphs. Everyone crowds around me, leaning toward the screen. As ghost hovers in the opening, we stare at the dark portal, breathless. Outside our tent, the ice creaks like rusty hinges on a giant dungeon door. Winds buffet the tent walls.

"Look at those symbols!" Judy says. "I don't think I've ever seen anything like that before. They're not runes or hieroglyphs. Are they pictographs, maybe?"

My mouth is dry. I take a swig of cocoa and try to steady my breathing. I'm terrified of what we're about to see.

"Ghost...night vision."

The screen floods with sickly green light to reveal a vast circular cavern swarming with those loping nightmares.

Elves.

148

Goatish and demonic looking, they drag dead seals and shiny slabs of creature meat to a far corridor, the slick floor smeared with dark fluids in their wake. Others huddle together, jabbering and weeping. Hundreds of stalactites jut from the high ceiling like the fangs.

Michael whimpers and hyperventilates. We all feel how he sounds.

"I don't hear anything. What's wrong with the sound?" Ricardo asks.

I fiddle with the microphone keys. "I don't know. Maybe something got damaged in transit after all."

Judy rests her chin on my shoulder. "That's okay. I don't want to hear anything anyway."

I remove the outer mitten of my right hand so that I can maneuver Ghost around the cavern, keeping her back high up against the wall. My fingers feel stiff and painful.

There are three entrances, roughly one each facing Europe, Greenland and the U.S.

"We're so — "

I shoot Michael a look that dares him to finish that sentence.

"I was *not* going to say doomed."

"Better not. Map?"

"On it." Judy whips out her sketchbook.

"I was going to say 'We're *so* going to need a lot of cookies and milk.'"

Toward the back of the cavern sits a monstrous chair.

It looks empty. The elves scuttle around it casually. Two corridors branch off behind the chair. Ghost moves closer.

"Ghost, zoom in."

Ominously broad, the chair's made from antlers, human skulls, and —

"Mammoth tusks!" Fear flares in Judy's eyes. "See? They arch over the back!"

"Whoa!" Michael's mouth hangs open. "That's a bad Santa throne if I've ever seen one."

"Are mammoths, like, dinosaurs?" Ricardo asks.

"No, but they're still hella old," Michael replies, dour. "CJ, there's no light in there, is there?"

"Maybe some sunlight comes from outside. We'll have the night vision, so we should be good."

The sound is still cutting in and out. Whispers. Growls. Shouts. The elves interact in no language I know. I wonder if the dream words are part of that language.

Can't believe Ghost is working so well except for the sound. It's difficult trying to focus on what's happening onscreen with this technical problem happening.

I turn Ghost toward the opening of the left corridor. The ceiling is rocky and covered with frost but no stalactites.

Suddenly, light floods the camera. Blinding. "Ghost, standard cam."

Ghost scans the corridor. Some sort of glowing symbol now hangs in the air right at the same level as Ghost. The shape reminds me of something I can't quite put my finger on, like a stretched out "M," but with more angles. I could have sworn it wasn't there a second ago. We didn't detect any light at all.

"What the heck is that?" Michael asks. "It looks like some crazy, glowing emoji thing." Michael says. "How's it hanging in the air like that? And what's it even for?"

Below the symbol, someone in animal skins and bare feet huddles against the wall. A silver bowl of water sits nearby with another silver bowl half filled with something lumpy and oily. The walls and floor are crawling with shaggy rodents. The person holds his arms against the wall, another symbol drawn into the stone above them. The creature lifts its head to see what's fluttering above it. I see its scarred, disfigured face.

It's human.

It's Charles.

Chapter 35

One of Charles' ears has been eaten away, his hair wild and bushy where it's not melted from the side of his head. Even like this, I'd know that jawline and those eyes anywhere. His brows furrow as he examines the drone. He doesn't seem to know what it is.

"No way! It can't be him!" Michael sputters.

We all stare at the screen for a moment.

"Krampus must have taken him Christmas night after the battle," I say at last. "I thought he'd let him go!"

"And look what he did to him," Ricardo says.

"Good." Judy glares at the screen. "Glad to see he's still in prison at least."

There goes the guilt again. It's not that I love my brother. I hate him almost as much as I hate Krampus, but it's not right for him to be in that state. He should be back home at the detention center where my folks can visit him. They're worried sick about the jerk, especially since an escape will lengthen his sentence. But if we can attest to his kidnapping, that would both help him and make my mom feel better. It would also go a long way towards her accepting what really happened and reuniting the whole family.

"We have to rescue him," I say.

"Why?" Michael asks. "He should be in jail. And, oh look, he's in Santa prison!"

"He's being tortured!" The tent warms with my outrage. "He's been mutilated and kept like a dog chained to a tree. It isn't humane! It goes against our entire justice system."

"CJ's right." Ricardo gulps the last of his cocoa. "At least, in theory."

"I am *not* rescuing that guy," Michael says. "Judes. Come on. Back me up!"

Silent, Judy watches the screen.

"You ever have a family member in jail, *güero?*" Ricardo says to Michael.

Michael rolls his eyes. "Oh. Here we go again. The privilege thing. This has nothing to do with — "

"This has *everything* to do with it! You don't know what it's like, in your nice white neighborhood, with your educated family and the opportunities you've had. But I do. It's bad enough when your brother is in regular prison. But this." He indicates the screen. "This is worse. Seeing this would kill his mom. She would die of heartbreak."

"He tried to get us *killed*," Michael argues back. "Sorry if the needle on my compassion tank is spankin' Empty, y'all."

Ricardo throws his cup against the tent wall. Michael makes calming noises, but Ricardo continues over them. "I love you, Miguel, but I'll be damned if I let anyone suffer like that."

"Stop!" I yell. "Look, we all hate Charles. He deserves to pay for what he did to us. But he needs to serve his sentence in the institution that convicted him. Not Krampus Court."

Judy remains unusually quiet. She closes her eyes. Since the big battle, she's been getting panic attacks. And nightmares. Post Traumatic Stress Disorder, the doctors say. She's on medication. This doesn't feel like a good quiet. More like a holding-back-Hiroshima quiet. She told me once that she blames Leo's death on Charles as much as she does on Krampus. This can't be a good discovery for her. Or is it? Maybe she thinks he's fine right where he is and doesn't want to upset me.

Michael offers a compromise. "Fine. We'll try. If we fail, Charles isn't going anywhere. Once we get Aidan out, we can come back with reinforcements to get your brother."

Ricardo puts his arm around Michael. "*Gracias, amorcito. Te amo.*" They kiss and make up. It's the first moment of affection I've seen between them since the beginning of the expedition, come to think of it.

152

"You don't think Krampus would get revenge on us through Charles after we leave?" I ask.

"Doubt it," Michael replies. "Why would he think killing Charles would hurt us? He knows we hate the guy."

"But why would he take him in the first place, then?"

"Maybe Charles asked him to in that damned letter he sent telling Bad Daddy where Aidan was," Michael suggests. "You know that as soon as Charles got here, he probably did something so stupid that Krampus decided to thrash him and stick him to the wall like a Post-It note."

Charles is yelling. Voice choppy. "...is...hey!...come...what..."

"CRAP!" I yank Ghost out of that part of the corridor and switch her night vision back on. She sails with the green light, past the throne and into the opposite corridor.

"Pull out!" Michael says. "They're gonna catch us!"

"No," I reply. "It's our only chance for reconnaissance." Over my shoulder to Judy: "Mapping?"

"Yup." Her voice is colder than the ice we're sitting on.

The gloomy corridor widens and branches into three passageways. The left seems to bend back and then burrow downward into the mountain. The middle is dark and narrow. I figure we might as well start with the right-hand passage, which is a bit wider. I have Ghost's cam split/flip to check for pursuers. No one. She follows the passage as it winds down and up again to an obsidian archway etched with more of those symbols. No door. Beyond is an open room.

"How far was that?" Judy asks.

"Under a quarter of a mile," I respond, checking the readouts at the bottom of the screen.

More of those angular symbols hang in the air beyond the archway. Instead of the cool glow of the symbol that was hanging over Charles, these symbols are on fire. Suspended in the air, they turn in space above what appears to be an enormous platform pushed against the far wall. A bed?

Ghost creeps beneath the archway and into the sparse room. Closer. Deep in shadows. Small tables beside the bed hold more

153

bowls of that lumpy substance.

Something dark and bulky lies on the bed under a massive cover. Dark fur. Giant twisted horns.

We stare, breathless.

At Krampus.

Chapter 36

Krampus lays lifeless on his side under several layers of what looks like animal skins. Eyes closed.

Vulnerable.

His snake-split tongue slips from his lips between his fangs. Pointed ears protrude like bat wings. Beneath that, he now has a beard that more resembles gnarled black tree branches than fur. His eyes are squeezed shut as if he's having a nightmare or wincing from a loud noise. The night vision's green cast makes him appear even more alien and monstrous than I remember. White wisps of smoke escape his body, unfurling into the air and flying off into the corridor.

I wish more than anything that Ghost had weaponry. That I could shoot Krampus in the head with a VA bullet. Destroy him once and for all. I'm dying inside all over again for Aidan. I would give anything to have him back.

Anything.

Michael lays a hand on my shoulder. "You okay, CJ?"

I nod, smoldering with rage. And fear. We found Charles. What happened to Aidan? What has this monster done with him? "I'm seriously upset, though, that he's not dead."

"Are you sure about that?" Judy asks.

"Yeah, I think he's dead. Things don't decompose around here."

Michael shakes his head. "Nope. He's breathing." He points at the barely perceptible rising and falling of Krampus' chest. "See?"

Ricardo frowns. "Didn't Papa K have white fur?"

"Maybe it changes depending on the season? Or maybe he made it white just for us," I offer. "We've got to find Aidan."

"I'm not liking that we haven't seen Aidan yet," Michael says. "If that's what Krampus did to Charles, I don't want to even think about what he's done to Aidan."

The ice outside groans like a wounded beast. I feel a stab of anxiety. Ricardo volunteers to check what's happening. He pulls on his full outer gear and crawls out of the tent. The Arctic Ocean is constantly moving, the terrain changing every minute. We put up our tent far from the nearest pressure ridge, but not too far as it protects us from the wind.

While Ricardo scouts, I bring Ghost out of the Krampus room and float her deeper down the passage, descending into the seamount, surrounded by glossy porous walls.

"UGH!" Judy clutches her sketchbook, grimacing at the rodent things lit up by the infrared. "No no no no no no. Seriously? I can't do rats. Those don't even look normal."

Michael also makes noises of disgust. No one can identify the species skittering and skipping along the passage surface, but they have humpbacks with bristly spines.

Ghost pulls out of the passage.

"But what if Aidan's down there?" Michael asks.

"He might be," I reply, "but I don't want to get too far down any one corridor and not be able to get out quickly before we have a better idea of the general layout."

Ghost spins around and heads the other direction, passing Krampus' room. A deep, sharp chill cuts into my lungs as the obsidian archway flashes on the screen. Maybe this is what they call blood lust. This overpowering thirst for revenge. For a moment I forget how much my fingers hurt. It's a good thing there's no Hell because I'm pretty sure that's where I'd go if there were one.

Ricardo squirms back into the tent. "I think we're okay, but I can't see a better place for us. Find anything else?"

"Just hundreds of rat things," Judy says, wrinkling her nose. "There's a reason my family has a cat, okay? And she's *not* fat from kitty treats."

Ghost re-enters the throne room, stealing around the seat, climbing up along the wall as she circles to find another passage entry. As she rises, her vision blurs. A rapid clicking sound floods the speakers. Flurries encrust her lens faster than she can dissolve the frost. Misty images flicker on the screen. Whirring and clicking. Growing louder. The blurry images shake violently.

A sharp jerk to the right.

Everything goes black.

The satellite phone beeps. Startled, we look at each other. It beeps again. Someone from base camp is calling.

Shaken, I answer. "Hello?"

"Charity!" It's Viktor's voice, crunchy with static.

Shouts. A cacophony of multilingual voices. Viktor's voice is suddenly garbled. A loud thump, as if the phone has hit the floor. Or something. And then in the background I hear:

Hrrrreeeeeeeeeaaaaaaaw!

More static. An engine sound crescendo splinters into the grinding of tearing metal. Screams.

Explosions of gunfire.

Fading voices. Crying out.

Hrrrreeeeeeeeeaaaaaaaw!

Static.

The line dies.

Everyone gathers around me. Worried looks.

"What's happened?" Michael asks.

I almost can't speak, I'm so horrified by what I heard. "Viktor's dead. Base camp is gone." I take a deep breath. "The blizzard creature killed them."

Chapter 37

I feel sick picturing what's just happened to the men and women at the base camp.

We're in bigger danger than ever.

If anyone is injured or even if we succeed in our mission, there's no one to come get us. We'll have to call the outside world. It could take *days* for help to arrive. And whom would we call? Barneo, the Russian ice base that's closer to the geographical North Pole, might be there. They usually pack up by the end of April. We could call one of the scientific drift stations, but what are the phone numbers? And do they have planes?

Probably not. Who knows?

We have three days of food. Four if we could go back and pillage Sergei and Vasily's sledges, but it's unlikely we'd ever find them again.

Not just that: Ghost is broken. I can't leave that technology sitting out in the world for someone to find.

Instead of forming a geek group hug, the team splinters in despair. The winds assault the tent, the temperature plummeting.

"What're we going do now?" Sobs choke Judy's voice.

"We have to keep going," I say.

"You're joking, right?" Michael replies angrily. "We've got to get out of here!"

"We're too vulnerable, CJ. We need to call someone outside." Judy says. "I hate to say it, but we've got to call your dad."

"NO! We can do this! Besides," I add, "I'll be in serious trouble if I try to go back to the States without Ghost and someone else finds her."

Michael flips out. "So that's why Interpol was after us? You stole CIA property? The freaking kill-first-ask-questions-later State Department? *Goddammit*, CJ!"

"I didn't steal anything! How do we know it wasn't because of you?" I counter. "You and your dark web stuff? How do we know you didn't build some kind of Amazon for kiddie porn and heroin? Haven't you thought about the implications of building evil techno crap?"

"I did it for you!" he says, eyes darkening to coals, cheeks reddening. "I did everything for you and Aidan. So that we could rescue him and you two could be together. And maybe if we're lucky we'll get revenge for Leo. Maybe you've forgotten him, but I sure as hell haven't."

"That's low," I growl. "I can't believe you would say something so mean!"

"I can," Judy cries. "Tell her the truth, you bastards, or I will!"

Michael shoots Judy a look of death. Ricardo's face drowns in sorrow, his gaze falling to the tent floor.

Judy lunges at Michael, shoving him off his knees. "You saw Aidan on Christmas! Tell her what happened!"

Shock.

Rage.

Anguish.

I throw on my outer clothing and squirm out of the tent as they argue. Stumbling onto the bright white drifts. I forgot my goggles. The sun's glare blinds me, each tiny flower of frost throwing thin shards of light at my retinas. I run some yards before I fall onto the snow. Chest heaving. Face scorched with chilled tears encrusting my cheeks. Exhaustion wringing emotions from my body. My knees ache as the cold bites into them, but my body is so hot with resentment that I ignore it.

159

Betrayed. By everyone.

A scuffle breaks out at the tent opening.

"Tell her what happened!" Judy shouts. Snow sprays across the drift. She's throwing snowballs after Michael as he heads toward me in the snow. "Asshole! Tell her!"

I don't want him here. I'm so mad at him and Ricardo that I can't speak, much less acknowledge, his presence as he shuffles through the snow to my side. My fingers hurt more. I shove my hands into my armpits. Teardrops run off my chin, freezing before they hit the ice. I pull the parka around my face, yanking up my facemask. I've got to pull myself together or I'll get frostbite.

"CJ? I'm so, so sorry. He made us promise not to tell you. And when we swore not to, it was like a magic spell or something. We couldn't! But now we can somehow. Maybe it was Judes. I don't know."

My eyes squeeze shut. More tears. "You *saw* him."

"He'd stolen the sleigh. He only came to us first because he wanted to clean up before he saw you. He was super worried you wouldn't believe us if we told you it was him. He thought you'd think it was just Krampus fooling us."

"How...do you...know...it wasn't?" I sob.

"He answered questions that Krampus couldn't have. Stuff about my dad."

Winds whip the frozen surface. Wraiths of snow rise, snaking across the bright blue horizon. Michael cries, voice cracking.

"He had this sort of Arctic Tarzan look going on and smelled like seal piss. So, we let him use the shower and gave him some clean clothes." He hesitates. "And he wanted to know if you still had feelings for him. He couldn't tell anymore. Bad Daddy had done something to his radar, and he couldn't measure you. He needed to talk to you."

Dying.

"Last night, I just blurted it out to Judes, I guess because it'd been bottled up and we didn't have any restrictions with her. We literally couldn't say anything to you. We tried! It was crazy! Any time we called you, the line died. Or the text bounced. Or the letter

160

was returned by the post office. We finally gave up. You've got to believe me, CJ. Please, *please* believe me! Do you honestly think I'd hold out on you about something as huge as this if I could help it?"

Aidan did show up.

He must have been the person who broke into Volertech. And I let him get chased away by the security personnel because I didn't know he was there.

I'm shaking hard, teeth chattering. From the freezing cold. From the anger lashing its way out like a tornado. But "Get away from me," is all I can say.

"*Get away!*"

Chapter 38

Without another word, I repack the sledges with the weapons and ammo before I get ready to sleep. Or at least try. Judy helps. I kick my way into the sleeping bag, which crunches as I try to slide inside. My torso scars flare painfully. Everyone is quiet. Michael and Ricardo go outside for a bit and whisper to one another. Judy leans over and kisses my forehead. Our eyes meet briefly; hers are brimming with sorrow.

"I'm with you to the end," she whispers.

She sniffs several times and blows hard into a handkerchief before she herself fights with the sleeping bag.

We both brought sleeping masks to create nighttime. I slide mine over my face, but I wish I'd thought to bring earplugs. Who knew ice was so noisy? The sounds of the ice creaking and moaning outside would have drowned out Leo's snoring.

I feel like I have a heavy bag of cinders in my chest. I can't think straight, I'm so angry, bitter, and disappointed.

After a short while, Ricardo and Michael return to the tent. Ricardo cleans up the cookware, starts thawing new ice, and tidies up before he and Michael both finally climb into their respective bags, moving them to the southern side near the computer. He's probably doing it to give me space, but it sucks all the same. I feel like I'm lying in a grave.

I heard Michael and Ricardo's plans. They have the satellite phone. Michael wants to call Ricardo's sensei tomorrow with our coordinates to get a rescue plane. Ricardo is reluctant.

They probably think I'm giving up. I won't go back. Not yet. I'll take the weapons and food that I can, and I'll move forward. But I don't tell them that.

It sounds like Judy will go with me. I won't be mad at her if she bails, though. She's clearly suffering from the extreme cold despite the top-shelf gear. I'll complete my plan no matter what. I'll get back Ghost and Aidan at the same time.

My weapons will work.

After a while, the Arctic booms and groans along with everyone's soft snores. I fall under the heavy footstep of exhaustion.

I dream. Aidan and I kiss in the rain. His lips crush mine, hands pulling me against him. I want him so badly. I can't take another breath without him. Someone is coming. A rustling in the blackberry bushes. I pull up his coat hood. Black curls spill over his forehead but his face is obscured in shadow. Blue eyes blazing.

A long tongue slithers out of his mouth, flickering.

A distant cry.

I'm standing on the hood of Noah's car and jump off. Floating. Snow blankets the ground beneath the tires. Landing.

Freezing. Lurching.

Screaming.

Michael. Judy.

Charity! Wake up!

BANG! BANG!

Ker-BANG!

Someone rips the mask from my face. Light blinding.

Judy. "ICE BREAKING! GET OUT!"

The ice wails as it cracks around and beneath the tent. I wrench myself from my sleeping bag, my brain foggy with dream sickness.

Chaos.

Everyone starts packing like crazy. Ricardo is outside, moving the snowmobiles and sledges, monitoring the cracks. The rest of us throw on parkas, boots and outer mittens. Judy is tossing things out of the tent to Michael. I try to stand up but the surface lurches underneath. My foot slips and I fall to my knees. The freezing cold and lack of sleep lock my brain.

"HURRY!" Ricardo cries from outside over the grinding of the

163

snowmobile engines.

The computer. KEDs. Night vision goggles. And more.

Sleeping bag in hand, I run-crawl-shuffle to the other end of the tent to snatch the laptop from its perch and shove the equipment inside the bag.

Another lurch.

Having turned off the stove, Judy shoves the cookware as she squirms out of the tent. Most things are out.

Except me.

Michael and Judy call my name. I dive toward the entrance, dragging the heavy sleeping bag. Pushing it through first. Someone grabs the bag, but hands reach inside for me. "Come on, CJ!" The two haul me out of the opening. Blinding sunlight, winds blasting our bodies. At first, I can see nothing through the glare except vague body movements. I don't know what happened to my goggles. Searching. Focusing. A massive pile of stuff lies in the snow a dozen feet away in total pandemonium.

The tent is stretching at an odd angle, buffeted by the winds. The ice is cracking right underneath, ocean water swirling in the opening.

Michael and Judy untie and yank at the anchors, loosening them before the ice can tear the tent in half. I run to the other side of the tent and try to untie the anchor in my bulky mittens. In despair, I just pull on the thing. It's stubbornly wedged in the ice, as designed.

The ice breaks open beneath me.

I plunge into the black water.

Chapter 39

The shock of immersion is so powerful, I forget to swim. I almost swallow a mouthful of dark, salty water that I've sucked in. Instead, I spit it out as I pop back up to the surface. The water is warmer than the snow, but still insanely cold. My heartbeat slows, head throbbing. As the water laps my chin, my arms and legs wake up. Flailing.

Can't breathe. Cold crushes my lungs, pinching my legs. Icy skewers drill into every scar of my torso. It's like Krampus squeezing me all over again, claws sinking into my flesh.

Judy calls my name. Again and again.

The survivalist instructor yells in my skull. *Kick, damn you! Kick!*

The frozen water's edge is floating away. Turn around. There. Another edge. Kick!

KICK!

Ricardo offers me his arm, coaxing me to the edge. "Hook in! Come on! You can do it!" Flat on his stomach. Judy and Michael hold his legs.

Exhaustion. Depression...

Survival instinct takes over. I try to surge forward. Kicking. Swimming. Panic overriding exhaustion. I hook my arm into Ricardo's arm. Everyone pulls me up and onto the ice surface. I slide right over like a fat seal.

My body shivers uncontrollably. Teeth chatter so hard I think they'll crack and fall out. A screech comes out of me I've never made in my life. Can't. Think. So. Cold.

Vision is blurry.

I feel Judy and Ricardo stripping off my clothes, hear them

rolling my parka and pants in the snow to dry them. I'm so cold, I think I'm going to die. Right here. A million needles pushing through my skin. Michael digs through the giant pile of equipment. Judy pushes me inside what's left of the sagging tent to get me out of the wind. Eyes blazing, focused, she straddles my torso, unzips her parka, pulls up her shirts and shoves my hands under her bare armpits. She yelps, panting.

"Stay with me, CJ. Don't go into hypothermia, okay?"

Two sleeping bags jettison into the floppy tent.

"I need help with her feet!" Judy calls. Then, to me. "Shivering's good. It means your body is trying to warm itself. Keep it up."

Violent tremors. Every muscle on fire. Jaw spasms. Body numb. Brain blank. Wait. Am I naked? Dooooooon't. Caaaaaaaare.

Ricardo scuttles inside, pulls the sleeping bag around me. "Michael's got the stove going." He then drops his pants and squats behind Judy. My feet slide between his hairy, muscular thighs, which he closes over them. He's trying to warm my feet to keep away frostbite. "Hiiiiyeeee! So that's what it's like to have a girl on my *cojones*," he says, rubbing my legs. I twist slightly, feet now closed flat between his legs. "We got you, CJ. Hang on."

Winds howl, the tent material weighing on our heads as it sinks on us. Drowsy...

"No sleeping!" Judy shouts and pats my cheeks. "Wakey wakey, lady! If you lose consciousness, we'll lose you for sure!" Her hands rub my face, neck, shoulders.

A backpack thrusts inside the droopy tent. "Dry clothes!" Michael announces.

Judy grabs the bag and throws it aside. She keeps rubbing my neck, shoulders. She giggles.

"What's so funny?" Ricardo asks her.

"It's just...CJ's feeling me up. And her feet are on your junk. It's like we're having a threesome."

He bursts into laughter. "Never thought it would be with two ladies, but hey!" He shouts outside of the tent. "Gotta go where the love is!"

"Oh, *fine*," Michael replies. "It's okay. I'll just play caterer to my

166

boyfriend's Arctic orgy." He sticks his head in the tent, making a mock serious face. "Rick, when did you *choose* to become straight? Hmmm?"

My whole body hiccups with giggles.

"You laughing, icicle lady? Yay!" Judy says. Everyone laughs. We're all punch drunk. I feel a tiny squiggle of warmth working its way into my body.

Michael wades in with a steaming cup of tea. "No, no! Don't remove your hands. Just...keep feeling up Judy." More laughter. "That looks kind of hot, actually. And so's this. It's tea. Sit her up a bit, please?"

Over the next hour, the team nurses me back to being only semi-frozen as opposed to half-dead. My brain is foggy. Judy helps me into what turns out to be Michael's spare clothes. Baggy but adequate. They get the tent back up on some hard-packed snow. The ice that broke is now filmed over with tissue-thin new ice growth.

I'm just slipping back into my less-crunchy sleeping bag to settle down for more sleep when Michael enters the tent, clutching the satellite phone in his mitt. He kneels beside me and sweeps back his fur-lined parka hood, his face and eyes red, puffy.

"I know you want to go home," I say. "Go ahead and call Ricardo's sensei or whoever he wants to fly in. I'm not going with you. I'm going to finish this."

He looks surprised and then hands me the phone. "You're the team leader. You decide what happens next. And if you'll still have me as part of your team, if you can forgive me for what happened, I'm with you to the bitter end. Although I hope it's sweet."

"You still want to be part of Expedition Eldorado?"

He nods, sniffling. His eyes are tearing up.

I hug him. He hugs me back so hard it feels like he's going to snap me in two.

It's horrible hating Michael. It's almost as bad as breaking up with Aidan. Although I don't hate him anymore, I still don't know if I can trust him. Who knows what other secrets Aidan's making him hide? Or maybe Michael's been keeping secrets for so long that he doesn't know when to let go of them.

Groggy, body burning with grief, I fall back to a fitful sleep. Krampus nightmares poison what little REM sleep I get. His horrible, slimy tongue slithers over me as I shiver in disgust. Chest tightening.

Shadows in the shape of elves loom outside the tent. My eyes wrench open.

Nothing's there.

Chapter 40

Michael's watch alarm awakens us. My head throbs like sharp rocks have been banging around inside. Everyone takes turns going to the bathroom, using the little fur-lined potty seat outside. I will myself to pee as fast as possible into the little toilet. The best feeling in the world is to pull up my pants.

Ricardo goes outside and cuts some ice to melt for cocoa. Judy and Michael make breakfast. I dry swallow some ibuprofen from the first aid kit. Wrapped in our sleeping bags, we settle near the stove to talk. Everyone is strangely calm, which I guess is better than crazy agro like last night. It's surreal to be actually sitting here in the wilderness ten miles from Aidan talking about killing his dad.

Time to plan the death of Krampus.

"Did we lose anything last night?" I ask. "Anything, that is, other than my dignity?"

Judy looks sympathetic, pats my knee. "I respect you this morning."

"Good to know," I say.

"Judy's snowmobile sank partway into the water," Ricardo says. "I got it out, and it seems to run okay, but it probably froze overnight. It might be hard to start. Let's see...two of the sledges fell in the water, but thank goodness they just float. So, they were okay. I kind of suspected they would be."

"I can't find several of the petroleum bottles," Michael says. "We're screwed if we're stuck here more than a couple of days. I mean, we still have the snack food, but we won't be able to cook, melt snow for water, or make hot drinks."

The bad news settles on us in silence as the cups of hot cocoa warm our hands and insides.

"How many days can we last?" I ask.

He shrugs. "No idea. Maybe three if we're really careful. To be fair, we only had extra petroleum because I took a few from the dead dudes. I'm feeling less like a creep for that."

"Feeling creepy was a luxury before the blizzard creature destroyed base camp," I say. "Now it's life or death, especially if someone else falls into the water."

He nods, grim.

"Don't forget Charles," Ricardo says. "He's going to need food, too."

Michael groans. "Can't we just tie him to the back of the sledge like a horse thief and drag him across the ice?"

"And then there's Michael's clothes," Judy says.

Both guys look confused.

"You can't get wet until we're rescued," Judy reminds him. "Charity's wearing your spare clothes and you won't fit in anyone else's."

"Did *my* extra clothes survive?" Ricardo asks.

"Probably," Michael says. "We're not sure."

I look to Ricardo. "What about the guns, the ammo, helmets..."

"We're mostly good, as far as I can tell," he says. "But I'm really more worried about those ice slabs. They looked huge and unnatural."

I start up the laptop and we review the footage that Ghost sent us last night.

Ricardo is right. Unlike a normal pressure ridge — or at least the ones we've seen so far — the ice slabs ring the fortress. That didn't register last night, probably because I was so fixated on the empty space where the fortress should be.

"What are we going to do?" I ask him.

He shrugs. "I don't know how we can possibly cut through ice that thick," he says, staring at the paused screen. He rubs his nose idly. "Unless you know more magic words."

I shift in place to relieve the shooting pains in my legs. I'm worried about my left foot. My toes don't feel right. In fact, I can't feel them. My heart flutters. Frostbite? Oh, no. No, no, no, no...

"We'll cut our way through the wall from the back. We should come around, two on each side, and then rush the entrance," Ricardo says. "Go in shooting."

"Or," I counter. "We slip into the Alaskan entrance and make for the tunnel where we saw Charles. He's going to have way more information than we can get on our own. He might even know where Aidan is. If we time it right, it'll be a major surprise when we emerge. They won't see us coming." I rethink that last statement. "Well, the elves won't see us, anyway."

"You mean Krampus will?" Judy asks.

"The List will tell him we're there."

"But he looked really sick or like he's passed out," Judy says. "I don't think Krampus is going to be as big of a problem as the elves. At least not at the beginning."

"What if he puts up one of those barriers over the doorway?" Michael asks.

"We disrupt it with the KED," I reply. "It's going to work. Trust me."

Everyone exchanges doubtful looks. I start to lose confidence, too, but it suddenly feels suicidal to give in. And I'm *not* suicidal.

"Listen! Do you guys even realize what an incredible thing it is we're doing? We might very well be at this moment four of the bravest, most badass people on the planet. Four teenagers from California shouldn't be freezing their booties off in a tent in the Arctic. If I believed in miracles, I'd say just being here is a miracle in and of itself. But it's not. The planning, the sacrifices, the hustling we had to do to get here was un-freaking-believable. And you know what's awesome? We're about to right a whole lot of wrongs. Remember how you felt Christmas Day. The terror and grief and outrage. And now think about how you'll feel when the monster is the one who's dead, the world is safe, and we have Aidan back."

I almost lose it when I say his name. Yes, I want to avenge Leo, but Aidan is everything.

Judy rises on her knees. "For Leo and Aidan!" she yells. Michael

171

and Ricardo follow suit, wiping tears from their eyes.

We then start packing. Michael's the first one to go outside with his gear. I pick up the GPS and check where we are, as we undoubtedly moved in the night...

I'm just comprehending what I see when Michael shouts, "No effing way!"

We're used to Michael overreacting. So, everyone just glances up at the tent wall.

"How is this possible?" he yells. "What were you just saying about miracles?!?"

We scramble out of the tent. I'm not sure why we didn't notice it earlier when we were using the potty or getting snow to melt. Maybe because the horizon was misty, the sun hidden behind the blur. Maybe because we were too damned cold to care. Or maybe because we weren't expecting it. We certainly weren't looking for it.

Not yet.

The ice wall. We can see it half a mile away.

Chapter 41

Judy stands next to me, jaw slack in her parka hood. "Is it because of Aidan? Or Krampus?"

"Probably neither. This is the Arctic."

"You mean it's a thermal inversion?"

"A thermal what?" Ricardo asks.

"Inversion," I explain. "It's a kind of mirage, but this isn't a mirage. Remember how the ice kept moving us off course as we were riding? Today, it moved in the opposite direction and brought us closer to the fortress. I don't think it was anything magical. That's just how the Arctic Ocean works. It keeps moving, even while we're sleeping. It could have easily taken us past without us knowing until we used the GPS."

Even though the phenomenon is perfectly natural, my body and face warm with overwhelming awe. The sun crouches on the horizon, brilliant golden light reflected by the walls and the fortress dome that peeks over the top dappled with shades of rose. The ground between us is covered with gray ice chunks where the pressure ridges have been grinding together for the last few days. Tiny crystal "flowers" blossom from the snow around us.

Judy documents everything with her camera. "The slabs remind me of gorilla teeth," she says, and then falters. "Elf teeth, actually. Like a giant jaw opening up and biting up through the ice." I can almost see the images behind her eyes. Sketching. Creating.

Ricardo and Judy volunteer to circle the wall on snowmobile to search for openings. It's not even a mile around; the fortress circumference is at most half that, probably smaller. Should be a short trip. Michael and I help them unhitch their sledges and then wait in the tent, drinking more cocoa as we strategize from our sleeping bags. We review Ghost's footage once more. Eventually our talk turns to yesterday's atrocities.

"I don't think Interpol is after us because of Ghost," I say. "If Volertech was after stolen goods, they would have confiscated our stuff and put us in custody. Full stop."

"But what if they thought we were selling it to someone," Michael offers. "Wouldn't they want to follow us out there to see who our buyers were? Assuming that they weren't able to figure out who they were from tapping our communications."

I shake my head. "No way. They wouldn't risk anything falling into the wrong hands, and they certainly wouldn't leave it up to a lone cop." I swirl the cocoa in my plastic cup and chug it before it cools. "Something feels off about this. The same way the blizzard creature looked past us. It's like there's something bigger happening just out of the corner of our eye."

"Then why did they want to follow us?"

"I think they wanted to know where we're going."

"But why?" Michael stands and paces in the tight space, thinking. "Are they after Aidan? Or Daddy Satan Santa? Or both? Or just the fortress? It's probably not the cops because all they knew was that he was a runaway."

"No, remember? I told you I saw Detective Bristow when I was in the hospital."

Michael pauses. "That rings a bell..."

"He wanted to know why we didn't trust him. And I told him it was because he and his friend laughed at me when I told them the truth about the elf. So, he was told Aidan was more than a runaway. Whether or not he believes it is another story. But let's say Bristow suddenly believes us. Why wouldn't he just ask us where Aidan was after I'd been so honest with him? I think whoever sent Vasily and Sergei doesn't trust us. They want to trick us into revealing where Aidan and his dad are."

Michael's voice becomes brittle with emotion. "Aren't you scared? I don't know what that was about, but it's bad news, either way."

My mouth goes dry. "Yeah. I'm more afraid of what's behind us than what's in front of us." I gesture to the ice wall. "Krampus is terrifying but he's just one dude. And we know how to handle the elves. But those bodies back there? What happened to Sergei?"

"No, see, this is going to sound totally cray-cray, but I don't think the Abominable Snow Dude is a threat. Hear me out: He's had two chances to rip us to shreds and instead he just struts by like it ain't no thang."

"That could be luck."

Michael rubs his knee. "Maybe. But I also think there's more in that fortress than we can possibly know. More nightmares than just Krampus and elves. I just can't escape the feeling that Aidan — well, it's not that he lied, or even lied by omission. He just didn't tell us everything because he didn't have time or reason to give us the full low down. For all we know, time and space and everything else works differently there. I don't want to find out exactly how differently. I want to get in and out. That's it."

He's right. I've been so focused on the two known enemies that I figured we could handle everything else with bullets. How bad is that? Really bad. "We've got to crush this," I tell him. "Aidan is our only hope. At least short-term. We can still call a plane but it could take days to get here."

"Days we don't have," he says glumly, staring at the cook stove.

Neither of us says anything for a moment before I inquire about Ricardo. "I'm afraid to ask this but...what is up with Ricardo?"

He shakes his head. "I wish I knew. He went to some martial arts seminar in Virginia for a weekend. And when he came back, it was like he was a different person. I mean, still Ricardo, all badass and sweet and everything. But he'd run hot and cold with me. At first, I thought maybe he'd met someone because he'd get these texts that would throw him into these unbelievably bad moods. And it only got worse after we met with you to talk about the expedition. He's been hitting the gym and running like crazy."

"You've talked to him, right? What does he say?"

"Just that he's got tons of family stuff going on. He thinks I don't know about his sister, Ariana, but I do. His mom told me Ariana's dying from Stage 3 brain cancer. I'm sure that's a big part of it, but..."

"But?"

Michael pauses, emotional. His bottom lip trembles. "I dunno, CJ. It's sucked these last few months, but I love him and I'm not ready to break up."

We hug.

An hour after they left, Ricardo and Judy's snowmobiles sail up to the tent. Judy makes a sad face as she enters. "It's solid."

"No holes. No nothing," Ricardo says. "How did Aidan ever get over that wall the first time without the sleigh?"

"Maybe he's a really good jumper," Judy offers.

"Maybe. But how tall are they on average?" I ask. "How thick? They're sitting at angles, sort of like teeth, right?"

"Sort of," Judy looks to Ricardo. "What do you think? Maybe twenty, twenty-five feet tall? No idea how thick, but I wouldn't be surprised if they were at least three to five."

Ricardo nods. "I'd say that's about right."

"So, no hacking it down with axes," Michael says.

An idea sparks in my freezing head but I don't want to spook anybody with it yet. "Let's pack up everything and go take a look. I might have an idea."

After eating a few peanut-filled candy bars, we load up the sledges and take off for the ice wall. I shiver at the sight of it. It's like we uncovered an ancient civilization in the Arctic, its terrible secrets sealed up behind an impenetrable fortification. And should the wall come down, the world would be exposed to the evil within.

Kinda already true, actually.

The winds pick up, snow stinging our faces. Checking the GPS, keeping my head low, I lead the group around to where the opposite side of the fortress entrance should be. The ice slabs tower over us. No leads, no cracks in the ice. Just piles of icy rubble that crunch under my boots as I approach one of the giant slabs. Judy was right. It's at least twenty feet. Maybe twenty-five. It leans inward slightly and is fairly flat on top. The bluish white ice gleams in the dimming sunlight. Oppressive dark clouds roll over us. They glide in like the Imperial Star Destroyer, trapping the warmth from the sun's ray. Everything will soon heat up, weakening the ice beneath us. We don't have much time.

"Why don't we just pile a bunch more snow against the wall and climb over?"

"How? We don't have any shovels. And even if we did, we don't want to exhaust ourselves. We've got business on the other side and we've got to be ready when we hit the ground."

"How are we getting over, then, Ms. Smarty Pants?" Judy asks, waving at the wall top. "Without breaking our backs, anyway."

"We have to take apart one of the snowmobiles."

"Whoa! Hold on," Michael asks. "How in the world is *that* going to get us over?"

There isn't time to explain. "Ricardo, you get the kit and I'll take apart the machine. Judy, please find the nylon rope, the axes, and one of the metal tent spikes that has a loop. Michael, we've got a pair of crampons, right?"

"Just one pair," he says. "Not four."

"We only need one to get over," I explain. "Get it."

"What about getting back?" he asks.

"We won't be able to without Aidan." The sky is darkening, the winds whipping the loose flaps of our sledges. "We've got to hurry."

Chapter 42

The team scrambles to pack and organize their gear, loading the rifles, strapping on the KEDs and night-vision goggles. As they prepare, I take apart Judy's Viper to remove the drive train and set it about fifteen feet from one of the leaning "teeth." The rope weaves through the drive train.

I give Ricardo the crampons and the axes. "Once you reach the top, drive that stake into the ice block, putting the loop facing me. Then, pull the nylon rope through the loop and toss it down to me. Michael will bring up both of your packs."

Ricardo nods, hefting an axe in each hand. I tie the one hundred-foot nylon rope to his waist. The other end dangles. I then make sure his parka hood is secure around his face. Ricardo won't be able to put it back on right away if it slides off. He turns to the base of the wall. I imagine his powerful muscles flexing and rippling under his parka. His face is stony with concentration, the axes turning in his hands. One, two, three...

HUCK!

He plants one axe in the ice high above his head. Assured that it's anchored, he leaps up and plants his feet against the block, the crampons clawing at the ice until they find purchase. Simultaneously leveraging the planted axe, he reaches up and sinks the other axe in the block.

HUCK!

It's like watching a superhero or one of those ninja athletes on TV as he creeps up the sheer surface. The Arctic winds tear at his body, pulling this way and that. If his arm was sore earlier, it's not a problem now.

He slows as he nears the top, breathing heavily, winds pummeling him. The sweat is freezing inside his parka, lowering his body temperature now just when he needs it most. His feet scramble against the slippery ice. I am woozy watching him. If he falls, he could be seriously injured.

"You can do it, Ric!" Michael says. "You got this, honey."

He's dangling too long. He's strong but he can't hang there forever. If we lose him to the ice, to a nasty fall, it's over.

And I'll never forgive myself.

With an explosive kick, Ricardo digs his foot into the ice and then wrenches the axe out of the ice wall before slamming it into the top ledge. He wobbles as he swings his leg over the edge, finding his balance. We all breathe a sigh of relief as Ricardo rests a moment, scanning the fortress and all else on the other side of the wall.

"YESSSSS!" Judy and I hug, but Michael reminds us with fingers pressed to his lips to hold onto the victory or further risk revealing our presence.

I'm just super relieved that Ricardo made it. "The view must be amazing," I say.

His gaze is indeed riveted to the incredible sights around him. He reaches into his parka for a snack to refuel quickly, as the other hand motions for us to hurry.

I thread the rope through the drive train and a makeshift trolley with handles that I've put together using snowmobile engine parts sticky with oil. I'm shivering, dropping things, covered in oil streaks as I put the finishing touches on the reverse zip line. It's the first time I've felt like myself since we left the U.S. Designing. Building.

Monster hunting.

Watching Ricardo as he prepares to drive in the spike, Judy looks unbelievably badass with those NV goggles sitting on top of her head and a rifle hanging over her shoulder with her pack. Shanks of blue hair escape the edges of her hood, mingling with the gray fur lining. The whole team *looks* about ten years older. I'm sure we all *feel* ten years older. Maybe twenty.

Using the back end of one axe, Ricardo drives the spike into the ice with a resounding *crack* that he times with the booming of the ice, startling us all. He hits it twice more before it lodges deeply enough and then gives me the thumbs up. Once he threads the rope through the loop, he gives me the other end, which I use to complete the circuit on the zip line.

"Ready?" I say to Michael.

He nods, shouldering both backpacks, and grabs onto the trolley as I instruct.

"This is true tech genius, CJ. I should have never doubted you."

"Just wait until you get to the top before you thank me." I start the engine. The drive train groans as it churns the rope. Michael hitches off the frozen ocean surface and rises to the wall into Ricardo's waiting hands, which heft him up and onto the Sentinel. Michael then scoots over gingerly, trying to make room for the next team member as the trolley retreats.

When Judy grips the trolley, I say, "Hey, Judy!"

"Oh, no. Am I doing it wrong?"

"No, you're cool," I laugh. "I just wanted to say thanks for joining my dopey club."

"Safety in numbers," she says. A glimmer of her old self in her eyes.

"Safety in numbers," I reply, and the zip line carries her up to the Sentinel. Not smoothly. It hitches a few times, three brief hesitations before continuing to her destination. My heart's in my mouth until Michael and Ricardo heft her up onto the ice slab.

I check the zip line. The machine looks great but the rope is already badly frayed. I should have realized everything is more brittle in subzero temperatures. After I get over the wall, that's it. I was hoping we could use the rope for something after the battle. Unfortunately, it looks like it's barely going to survive getting us over once.

We definitely have no way to get back over.

Not without Aidan.

Chapter 43

On the inside of the wall, each ice slab is carved with those massive hieroglyphs. I run my hand over the surface of one of them. The edges are perfectly smooth, as if cut by lasers. It shimmers like a mirage, giving off a peculiar vibration.

Chest tight. Breath ragged. Head light. Seeing this aberration, I feel the way I did that night as Krampus crushed me in his claws. Like I'm going to start screaming and never stop...

"CJ!" Judy turns her back to me. She wants me to adjust her pack. I shake off the distress drumming in my head and help her. I hear the goat-things bleating in the distance. More of them must have just returned from having baby goat-things.

I'm startled by a cry from Ricardo. He was just rappelling down, but I look in time to see him plummeting to the ground. The frayed rope must have broke. Michael dives to break his fall. They both tumble onto the ice.

Judy and I rush to them. Ricardo winces. Michael and I help him up. It's slippery but we get him standing.

"I'm good. Don't worry." He stands, but he doesn't *look* good. He favors his right leg as he moves away from the wall. We're still at least a quarter mile from the fortress.

Time to move.

We quickly recheck our gear, retesting the walkie-talkie microphones in the NV goggle headsets. Hyper alert. Electricity washing over my skin under the parka. I grip the rifle. White puffs of breath, body heavy with thick clothing. A slow run, *one-two-one-two*, ears twitching at every noise. The hieroglyphs etched into the fortress wall come into focus. They're like the symbol thing that hung over Charles' head. Angular drawings with nodules. Like electronic schematics. Can't shake the feeling that the hieroglyphs are cranking out some kind of energy field. A vibration that slices right under my skin and makes my innards shudder.

We make it to the Alaskan entrance. Guarding Ricardo's back. He tries to hide his limp but I notice. We whisper to one another via walkie-talkie. I take deep breaths to calm my nerves. "Remember," I whisper, "keep to the wall. Quiet. Fast. Shoot only if attacked. Save what you can for Papa. And stay close. Don't separate or we'll be more vulnerable to friendly fire. Got it?"

Everyone nods.

I give the signal.

We dive inside the fortress. My feet scramble until I regain balance as my snow boots lose purchase on the slippery floor. Thankfully no one falls. Night vision washes the hellish scene of the throne room in ghastly green light. The detail is breathtaking as the vast belly of the fortress opens before us. A thousand green stalactites threaten from above. The ground is uneven, like polished glass pockmarked by falling rocks. No sign of the seamount yet. It must sit beneath this supernatural formation.

The nauseating stench punches me in the nose. The team audibly gasps at the smell. It occurs to me that nothing in the rest of the Arctic has much of a smell. It's like sticking your head in the freezer at home. And since we've not smelled anything except some cooking since yesterday, the odor is especially overwhelming.

The guttural chatter of the elves freezes my blood with terror. Those round eyes are reflective like a cat's with a black slit for a pupil. Goatish snouts and ears. Filthy jagged teeth jutting from the gums. Some of them have horns. They're just as I remember. They gather near the passage that opens next to that creepy bone throne. Memories from that night threaten to lock up my arms and legs. Seeing Leo's body fly through the glass sliding doors, shattering, bleeding, dying. Krampus clutching me, ribs cracking. Claws sinking into my body. Pain flooding my insides. My breath shortens. Michael presses against me as we move against the wall. Urgently. And then the sweetest memory flutters like a butterfly through my thoughts.

Kissing Aidan outside the gym that night.

Snow.

Aidan is here.

Aidan, if you can feel me, please help us. Please tell us where you are!

We move toward the tunnel as quietly as we can. Although cold enough for stalactites, the cavernous throne room is surprisingly warm. Sweat trickles down the back of my neck. I fight the urge to tear off my parka and mitts. I'm suffocating with heat.

Suddenly, a wraith with antlers reminiscent of the blizzard creature escapes the biggest tunnel opening. The wraith flies around the stalactites before it soars out the nearest fortress opening. The elves wail in its wake. They emerge chattering grimly.

I spot Ghost lying on the ground near the throne. The urge to run and pick her up is almost too much.

Stay cool, CJ. She'll be okay for a while.

Our hearing is distorted because of the echoing in the chamber, but the noise masks our movements as we slip into the mouth of hell itself. The tunnel immediately doubles back and splits in two, offering a second passage we didn't notice before. Charles slumps against the wall in squalor. He smells worse than any homeless person I've ever met. At first, he just blinks at us like a rabbit, but his eyes widen when he sees us. He sits up on his knees, checking the corridor behind him.

"Cherry! What're you doing here?" he says.

I shush him, gagging on his stench. "We're going to save you," I whisper. "But you have to tell us first where Aidan and Krampus are."

His reddened eyes well up and he starts sobbing, tears spilling over his ruined, acne-cratered face. I've never once seen him in tears except that one time when Mr. Spotty hit him with that rock. I flip up the goggles to get a better look, since there's normal light here thanks to a symbol slowly spinning above him. His face looks far worse than it did on Ghost's scan. Something like acid has eaten away part of his face, as well as the skin on his free arm and hand.

One of his hands presses to the wall beside another glowing symbol. How is he restrained? His wrist has no sores or other signs of

183

bondage.

As horrible as he looks, I still have this urge to kick him. For what he did. For what happened. For being the biggest jerkface on the planet. But I hold off because I want him to think we're on his side.

"He fucked me up, Cherry. He did this. Horrible. Shit. To my face. Out of spite. He fucking tortures me night and day. He captures kids and does this to them. You've got to kill him!"

"Where's Aidan?" I ask.

"You've got. To kill. Santa!" He sobs harder, snot running over his mouth. It's so alien seeing Charles like this. So broken and hideous. A scared, scarred little boy rather than the confident thug I last saw in the detention center. He's grown in the last year or so, too, but he's skinnier than ever.

"Okay, then where's Santa?" I ask, exasperated. Ricardo stands guard at the tunnel entrance. Michael guards on the other side. "We're not getting you out of here unless we find him."

Soul-sickening moans swell from the corridor beyond Michael. Ancient, evil. Either dying in the darkness or giving birth to something worse. My knees wobble at the noise. The gloom in that corridor is strangely impenetrable. Even the goggles only carve out a few yards of visibility.

Michael is clearly shaken. "The *hell* made that noise?"

"The elves say he's sleeping." Charles' affect is weirdly flat, his filthy finger pointing to the throne room. "Down the far passage past the throne. Keep going to the end. And then kill him, okay?"

Chapter 44

I back away from Charles and hopefully out of earshot. The team follows, gathering close. It's not like we can hide from the elves if they see us, but at least we don't have a spotlight on us.

"What if he's lying?" Judy asks. "I don't trust him!"

I glance back at Charles, huddled against the porous wall. He just stares down at the ground before him in despair. My feelings crisscross, compassion and rage. He now looks as damaged outside as he is inside. Or could he have reformed? "Why do you think he's lying? We just saw Krampus in that room not twenty-four hours ago."

"For one," Michael replies, "Aidan doesn't sleep, which means his dad doesn't sleep. You and I both know this. The very fact that he'd use that word is suspicious. Plus — listen! — it's Charles! He wants us to die. He wants everyone to die. At least he did last time you talked to him."

"He's sick," I say.

"Having one or more personality disorders isn't an illness, CJ. Maybe he does better on meds for his anger, but his other issues aren't illnesses. They just make him even less reliable."

Why am I defending Charles? Maybe I just want answers.

"I'm sorry," Michael says. "I don't mean to be a jerk about this, but you heard that horrible noise. Remember what we talked about? The nightmares we can't even conceive of? Charles knows what's here. We don't."

"None of that changes the fact that he just verified what we saw through Ghost last night. If he weren't in the equation, we'd still be heading down that tunnel because it sure looks like Krampus was

185

laying down with his eyes closed."

Ricardo cautiously peeks around the tunnel wall to the throne room. "Something's happening at the bone throne. This might be our chance."

Another sickening, grotesque moan rises from the corridor beyond Charles. He seems immune to the sound.

"You're right," Michael says to me. "As far as we know, that's the last known location for Krampus."

"Let's do this!" I check my KED. We have a shooting pattern that we've practiced to distract Krampus. Combined with the KED attack, the blast pattern will throw Krampus off guard and keep him from deflecting our bullets. We hope.

Leveling their rifles at whatever may come, the team follows my lead, rushing to the mouth of the passage that empties into the throne room. We pause as the spectacle unfolds just a few feet away.

White wisps spin like cotton candy in a wild spiral, the elves crying out to them in that alien tongue. Leaping. Bowing. Begging? It reminds me of the savagery that the elf showed that night in the shed. But it's like these guys are *praying* to the wisps. One of the wisps elongates, reaches out to a prostrate elf and grabs it in a clawed, spectral fist. The elf shrieks, kicking and clawing. The disembodied fist then throws the hysterical elf against the ceiling, skewering it on a stalactite. Its body fluids rain on its howling siblings.

"GO!"

I rush behind the throne and run full speed to the other tunnel, halting as the passage branches three ways. The others stop behind me. Just as it did during reconnaissance, the left passage abruptly doubles back toward the direction of the throne room but dips down into the mountain. Just as I step into the right-hand passage, where Ghost found Krampus, I smell something like a cross between a dead possum and ammonia.

Breathing through my mouth, I charge into the tunnel.

Judy charges forward with me, dodging rats that run out in front of us. The guys follow.

A dozen or more elves emerge from the shadows of the tunnel, blocking us. Some seem startled, looking at us with curiosity. Others bare their teeth, snarling.

"How dare you defile the Home of the Klaas!" one screeches. Its siblings curse, edging closer as if they'll rush us. Those eyes emit a hellish purple light in the green night vision. "You deserve death!"

"Or a lump of coal," Michael quips under his breath. "I'll take coal, please."

"Charity..." Judy says, voice shaking. I glance behind and see her rifle is leveled at several elves filling up the passage from behind. Michael takes up beside her.

I raise the rifle. It helps me feel stronger.

The biggest elf lopes toward me, a crowd of siblings pressing from behind. It's as tall as I am. With horns. Must be male. I aim the rifle right at his sternum. "Where's Krampus?"

"Who dares desecrate this place?"

"Charity Jones. The Klaas is expecting us."

"Leave now," he hisses, "or we'll rip you to shreds!"

"No! Take us to him now, or we'll destroy you the way we killed your other siblings."

The creature lunges at me. I pull the trigger.

His floppy goat ears fly back, terror and agony rippling across his features. Thanks to the inky smoke that camouflaged their attack on my house, I never had the satisfaction of seeing an elf die. And now it's not satisfying at all, just horrifying.

As the other elves rush towards us, a higher elf voice says, "Stop! Please!"

The elves halt as she approaches us, paw outstretched, a signal to stop or a plea for peace. Eyes wide. "You are Charity Jones?"

My name sounds haunting in the mouth of this evil goat thing. I lower the gun and nod.

"We will take you to the Father of Sin."

"Traitor!" A larger elf leads a chorus of the word that echoes through the tunnel. "We are dying and you give us to intruders!"

"The Father wants to see this human," she hisses. "We will take her if the other humans do not hurt us."

"You give orders because you have a name?" The larger elf comes forward and the two engage in some kind of stare down, hissing and baring their teeth. After a moment of posturing, the larger one backs down. "Fine. Take the dark female. We keep the others."

"Oh, yaaaay," Michael says sarcastically under his breath into the helmet mic.

I'm shaking, sweating, trying not to lose my resolve. A black shadow passes over my eyes briefly at the thought of facing Krampus again. I've always said, though, that I love Aidan more than my life.

Now's the time to prove it.

"Let's go," I say to the elf.

Judy grabs my arm. "CJ! You can't go alone!"

"I'm not alone, not as long as you guys are here. Keep your ears open, okay?" I tap the mic. Hopefully the elves don't realize we're connected by audio.

"Okay," she squeaks. We do our fist bump but end it with hands grasped.

Ricardo and Michael pat me on the back and with heavy sighs wish me luck. Hugging would require relinquishing our rifles, which ain't gonna happen.

I take a deep breath, readying the rifle. "Lay on, MacDuff." A flash of memory in AP English, when Mrs. Hohlwein corrected a student for saying, "Lead on."

Dorky high school memory? Now? Ugh.

Standing backs to one another, the team's now surrounded by snarling elves.

Judy yells, "Back off! You heard the deal!" They reluctantly move away, but only by a few feet.

The elf skitters down the sloping tunnel, not even checking to make sure I'm with her. Not even speaking. We clear a long bend before it steepens. I recognize the passage from Ghost's reconnaissance. We're almost to the Abandon All Hope room. "MacDuff is not our name," the elf says at last.

"It's just a quote from Shakespeare," I reply. Wait. They have names? "What *is* your name?"

"It is Reilly." She slows at the entrance, symbols etched into the arch over the room opening. "The Klaas is inside."

Reilly?

"He hibernates. We grieve because a part of him escapes unchecked and does evil."

The white wisps. The blizzard creature?

Stunned, I stand at the entrance for a moment, trying to process what the elf just said. Reilly. I haven't heard that name since I was at Oak. That was Aidan's favorite teacher, the one who threw us into the classroom together for lockdown. Where Aidan first told me I was pretty. A tsunami of emotions hits me as I step inside the room.

The first thing I notice that we didn't see through Ghost is a mosaic embedded in the far wall that forms an open eye. It startles me at first with its realism, like some dark Pixar animation. The vaulted ceiling is covered in ice that's been carved with stunning patterns imitating a snowflake. A faint odor of musk comes from the skins and furs covering the bed with its whalebone frame, glowing red symbols hanging in the air at each corner.

Krampus lies motionless on the bed set beneath the ice carvings, just like in Ghost's camera. He seems a bit smaller than I remember — then again, he was trying to kill us, and everybody looks less scary when they're in bed, hunched over like they have the flu. He breathes with a steady rumble.

As much as I want to, I can't shoot someone in bed. It's not right. So, I call out.

"Get up, Krampus! It's me, Charity Jones."

The rumbling sound stops abruptly. A thousand years seem to pass before the furs rustle. Sweat pours from my scalp as those twisted horns emerge from under the heavy covers. He rises to his knees, his massive head hanging with fatigue as if his body is awakening before his brain.

He then turns that hideous face to me. Tongue snaking from his mouth, matted fur covering his gorilla-like body, open eyes brilliant beams of blue light. Blinding me.

I pull the trigger.

Chapter 45

Features melt from beast to... *Aidan?*

His name echoes in this cavern. Reilly's voice. Screaming. His name.

Aidan.

"AIDAN!"

He wobbles, the ragged wound from the rifle blast smoldering with the corrosive mistletoe mixture. Blood runs from torn flesh. Eyes wide. Lips trembling.

"Charity Jones. Of course you thought I was...him."

And then he collapses face first onto the bed. Convulsing.

Devastation. Disbelief. Grief. I've destroyed everything. His life. My life. He's the most precious thing in my entire universe. My Aidan.

Aidan the Klaas.

Judy, Michael, and Ricardo yell in my ear on the helmet comlink. "We'll save you! Don't worry! We're there! Hang on!"

A volley of rifle blasts, shrieks, and snarls over the comlink.

I break down, sobbing uncontrollably. I throw aside the rifle and climb on the bed. Pressing my face to his, blind with tears. "No. No. No." Stroking the mass of tangled black hair. "I love you, Aidan. I came for you. I came to kill your dad, the Krampus, and save you. I didn't know you're now the Klaas."

It all made the worst possible sense. Aidan's Christmas escape on the sled. He could only escape because he was the Klaas now. He was afraid because he didn't think I'd accept who he was now.

Something snarls behind me.

Aidan lifts his weakened hand. And everything stops.

Reilly hangs in the air, mid attack. She was going to kill me for what I did. The voices and gunshots are silenced on the comlink. I wonder why he didn't do this at Volertech, but then his powers are probably amplified here.

A deep shudder works through Aidan. He squeezes his eyes shut for a moment. Every bit of monster is gone. A crackling noise: long streaks of ice break across the walls, ceiling, floor, running over the eye. The symbols turn from red to blue.

His eyes dim.

"NO NO NO NO!" I kiss him. Those lips so incredibly soft. Butterflies and scorpions. Roses and snowflakes.

His hand wraps around me. I pull closer. Chest heaving with sobs.

"Shhhhhh," he whispers. "Listen, my dearest love. I should have never doubted you. I thought you no longer loved me. Because of Sergei."

The boys talking that night. Sergei. He must have heard that banter and believed it. He probably picked up on the kiss, too. I want to die.

"I'm so sorry, Aidan! I had to lead him on to get contacts for our trip up here. I thought you'd know my true feelings. But how did you not know we were here? Michael told me that your dad had taken me off The List, but what about everyone else?"

"I couldn't bear to be tempted to check on everyone. So, I took everyone off The List. Listen, please," he says, swallowing hard. Milky blue eyes watery. "We have little time. If I die, the world will end."

"I know!" I cry.

"No, it's much bigger than that. If there's no Klaas... *everything*...dies."

I don't believe it. It's not possible. Then again, I didn't think someone like Aidan could possibly exist. So, I do believe him when he says something bad will happen. I just don't understand how.

He must see the fear on my face because he kisses me again, this time more tenderly, feverish. "Find the ash and take its bark. Make.

A poultice. And add three drops." Aidan's voice fades as his body shudders. "Take Reilly." Aidan's pupils elongate to cat slits. *Hurry!"*

The team stares at me in disbelief as I explain that I shot Aidan and that we have to get ash bark to heal him. The elves are crowded in the room with Aidan, lamenting his injuries while we hastily figure out what we have to do.

Ricardo slams his fist against the tunnel wall, crying out in anguish. You'd think he was the one who'd shot his boyfriend.

Reilly wanders anxiously back and forth around us, shaking her head. "Must hurry! The Klaas dies! We all die!"

Another massive ice streak runs along the tunnel wall with a resounding *crack*, startling everyone.

"What the hell does that even mean? Ash bark?" Michael waves his hands, pacing. "Ash? As in tree? There aren't any trees in the Arctic! What the hell is he talking about?"

Ricardo barks at Michael. "Stop freaking out, goddammit! We won't figure it out if we're amped up."

"*You're* amped up!" Michael yells.

"Shut up! Both of you!" I tell them. "Reilly, do you know what Aidan needs us to get?" I ask.

She shakes her head, brow furrowed.

A voice echoes in the tunnel. One I know too well.

"I know what he wants. I was with him when he got it for Daddy Krampus, but I don't know why he thinks it's going to work. It didn't work on Daddy."

Whatever kept Charles "chained" to the wall has apparently stopped working, and he now stands unfettered in the passage behind us. Arms crossed. Mocking expression on his face. The symbol lights up his scarred head from behind like an obscene halo.

Reilly hides behind me. "The Cruel One is loose!"

"The Cruel One, huh? Don't worry," I assure her. "He can't hurt you now."

She takes off down the passage at a gallop. "Reilly!" I call after her, but she's gone. Despite Aidan's orders, she probably doubts that anyone but Aidan can control Charles. She might be right.

192

Judy explodes. "No way. He can't come!"

"He has to," I say. "Do *you* know what the heck Aidan needs? Because I sure don't."

Michael sides with Judy. "Great. So you want to let a psychopath lead us into god knows where? I think we're better off on our own, thanks."

I approach Charles. His scars are terrifying to behold, making him look infinitely more sinister than when he was at the detention center. He's the very last person on this earth I can trust, and it takes everything in me not to kill him for what he just did, but I have to trust his will to live. "What does he need, then? Tell me or I'll just shoot you now."

"What, no love for your brother, even though the fate of the world is in my hands?" he says. "If you want to save your boyfriend and everyone else, you better listen to me. Maybe in fact you should bow to me."

I shove the muzzle in his face. He went from wounded to smirking so quickly I want to kill him just on principle. "Can you at least pretend you don't want to die?"

Another vein of ice creeps and crackles across the ceiling, causing us both to glance upward. If everything is going to die, it makes sense that the fortress will be the first thing to be destroyed.

"Sure," he says. "But I have conditions."

"We don't have time for conditions!" Ricardo yells. Now he's the one totally losing it. "Spill, you lying bastard!"

"First," Charles says calmly, "when we get out, you will release me in Alaska without turning me over to the authorities. And second, you must let me go with whatever I can carry from the vault."

"What vault?"

"YES OR NO?"

"Whatever!" I reply, knowing I'll regret it. This isn't what I wanted at all. Then again, maybe Mom will be happy just knowing he's alive. "What do we need to do?"

Chapter 46

Charles leads us down the left-hand corridor to two colossal wooden doors. "We'll hit the vault first because you'll need a tin or something to carry the ash."

Michael and Ricardo lean with all their might against the doors and, with a deep groan, they part to reveal the most spectacular sight I've seen since we first laid eyes on the Arctic.

Scenes from the movie, *The Monuments Men*, run through my head as we enter a massive room filled with gold bars, jewelry, artwork, and other stuff that must be incredibly valuable. The Vault. A reverence overtakes me as I register how ancient some of these treasures are. This room has preserved them beautifully. But not all of it has market value. Many things are just lockets with photographs, combs, baby booties and other precious mementos. I even notice a stack of laptops and other electronic devices against one wall, useless without electricity and probably outdated mere months after they were stolen.

Standing at the vault opening with a smirk riding his lips, Charles won't lift a finger to help.

Judy approaches one of the marble sculptures of a young Pan and mimics his impish pose. "Oh, look. Krampus found a statue of himself. Bastard probably stole all this stuff!"

Ricardo and Michael seem just as absorbed by the sight of so much wealth and beauty as I am. They keep getting distracted as they search the room. "I thought Santa was supposed to bring gifts, not steal them!" Michael says, training a gun on Charles.

A dirty feeling settles like coal dust on my heart. "Maybe when he's Santa, he gives. But when he's Krampus, he takes..." I bury the rifle muzzle in a mess of lace scarves, brushing them away to reveal a basketful of cigar boxes and snuff tins. "YES!" I seize three of the latter and dump out the contents on the floor, wiping out any tobacco remains. I really don't know how much of this ash bark we're supposed to bring back. Three should do it, right? "Let's go!"

We file out with Ricardo lagging behind. He hangs in the doorway, an intense sadness marking his features as he lingers. He realizes I'm waiting for him and rushes to catch up to everyone.

Charles next leads us back up to the three branches and then down the middle corridor to a room with wide, half-moon doors that stand partially open. No locks. No doorknobs. Michael and Ricardo push the doors inward with a heavy *creak* to reveal a room with dull stone walls. The open ceiling that wasn't visible to Ghost yawns above us, drinking in the hazy Arctic light. Snowflakes dust the floor where a flat stone circle about fifteen feet in diameter surrounds a polished obsidian circle. The circle radiates with more of those symbols carved into the stone. The obsidian reflects the sunlight to create an inky brilliance. I stand at the edge and peer at my reflection. I look like the Arctic *Mad Max* with my crazy hair and Sub2000 in the reddish black radiance. A murmuring percolates behind us: the elves have gathered at the doorway, nervous and weepy.

Charles paces around the circle, eyes furious and flashing.

"What's wrong?" I ask.

"Nothing," he says, halting on the opposite side of the circle from us. He raises his hands and speaks with a booming, authoritative voice. "*Machet daz Tatzlewurmstor uf!*"

If something is supposed to open, I can't see it. The goggles are pushed up from my eyes because the glowing symbol following Charles is so bright. It reminds me of something, but I can't put my finger on it.

Charles huffs and kicks the obsidian circle. "We need one of these little shits to say it. It has to be a Krampus."

The elves cower behind the doorway. I swing around to face them, which sets them quivering. "Don't just stand there! Help us!"

The elves retreat further behind the doorway.

195

"What was it you said, anyway?" I ask Charles.

He repeats the phrase.

"What does that even mean?" I ask. "Machet...daz...Tatzle? Wurmsstor...uf..."

Freezing winds funnel down from the open ceiling, whipping around us. Everyone's eyes snap to the surface of the obsidian glass as it ripples like a pond of crude oil before it spills inward and melts away completely, revealing an enormous opening that plunges down into the mountain. A foul smell wafts up from deep inside. Sulfur. Stone steps with a shaky railing wind downward into a gigantic cavern.

The volcano. That's what a seamount is.

"So you're a Krampus now?" Charles says. "Figures."

A wave of annoyance washes over me that I haven't felt since we were home with Mom and Dad. "Don't be an idiot. It has something to do with us not being on The List."

"What do you mean, we're not on The List?" Ricardo asks, confusion and concern in his voice.

"Aidan removed us." As soon as I say that, I regret it because a sly smile creeps over Charles' face. Now he knows that Aidan is disconnected from us. We're truly alone.

The obsidian glass reforms over the hole. The opening must only last for a few moments.

Judy commands, "*Machet daz Tatzlewurmstor uf!*" with a sharp German accent, and the portal instantly reopens. "Let's go!" She points her gun at Charles. "You first, beyotch."

Chapter 47

My life no longer feels like *One Hundred Years of Solitude*. More like John Carpenter's *The Thing*. And I'm not a fan of horror movies.

The stairwell clings to the wall as it winds down into the seamount. The cavern dims. I glance back up to find the portal has closed over us. It's now pitch black except for Charles' symbol, which lights up only a few feet in front of us. I debate whether this is a curse or blessing. The lumpy, rough wall to our right is striated with gold, crimson, aquamarine and muddy brown that reflects the light like wet stone. The stone steps are awkwardly steep, carved for a stride much wider yet feet smaller than a typical human.

Krampus hooves.

Charles halts before he reaches a gaping hole in the wall.

"What's wrong?" A demand more than a question.

He shrugs, eyeing the hole with obvious trepidation. "Nothing. Just checking it out."

"Liar," I say. "What's in there?"

Silence. He keeps walking. Slowly. I'm next up to the gap. I flip on the night goggles and peer inside.

The narrow hole drives far back into the mountain. Holes like this one repeat throughout the walls at intervals. Anything could emerge and attack us as we make our way down. I shudder as I imagine what could possibly be in there, but the real shock hits when I turn away from the gap and glance over the stair railing into the seamount. The dizzying drop from the staircase winding down into the darkness makes my throat tighten, breath shallow.

"Oh, crap. CJ, do we have to look inside?" Michael asks.

Ricardo flips on his goggles. "I'll look for you, baby," he replies. Leaning bravely over the rickety handrail, he whistles like a bomb dropping.

Charles spins back to look at Ricardo. "Shut up!"

I lift the rifle barrel to his stupid, panic-stricken face. "*You* shut up and move!"

"I hear something," Judy says. She flips on her goggles. "There!"

Thousands of rustling, flapping, slithering nightmares emerging from the myriad openings.

Scrrrraaaaaay!

"Get ready!" I yell, aiming the rifle at the cavern below.

The rising swarm of thick albino pythons soars upward toward us on batwings, mouths open wide as they make that horrible noise, rows of fangs bared in each jaw, talons extended. Their faces are vaguely feline...

Judy lets loose the first volley of rifle fire. *Crack! Crack! CRACK!*

She kills two creatures that drop into the abyss of the hollow seamount. My ears ring from the ensuing storm of rifle blasts and the ear-piercing cries of the snake things. A shot ricochets off the far wall with a spark. "Drive them down!" I yell. "Down, down!" I don't think anyone can hear me. I can't even hear myself.

Charles scampers further down the massive steps, the "halo" bouncing behind him.

Judy curses. She motions to me that she needs a new cartridge. "*Cover me!*"

Scrrrraaaaaaaaaaaaaaaay!

The swarm closes in. I "blade" off, placing the butt of the rifle against my shoulder, but the kickback smacks me against the lava wall. Aim shaky. Heart racing. My stomach lurches as the creatures slither through the air towards us. The smell of blood and ripped reptile flesh mingles with sulfur and gunpowder.

There are too many of them. The rifle blasts recede...

"BOOYAH!"

The cavern lights up with crackling electricity as reptiles convulse mid-flight. Reptiles plummet into the void below, wings and heads snagged by the barbs of Michael's KED. Ricardo lets out a whoop.

198

The remaining creatures retreat to the cavern holes, screeching pitifully. I'm not sure why the gunfire didn't scare them. Maybe they're deaf and smell draws them.

"Good thing that worked. I'm out, too," Michael says, attending to his rifle.

Judy slumps against the wall, trembling. She reloads her rifle as she takes deep breaths to steady her hands.

"Where's Charles?" Ricardo asks.

"Down here, fools," Charles says, voice echoing. Arms crossed, he stands further down the winding staircase in his angelic haze. I bet the light scared the beasts, which is probably why he's still alive.

My toes burn from the frostbite, and now my thighs ache from going down so many of those monstrous stairs. There's least another hundred to reach Charles. Maybe more. The cavern rustles with faint sounds of the snake creatures. Gurgling and hissing. We halt at an outcropping that leads to another passage. The outcropping is just far away enough from the stairway that we can't easily reach it. It's going to be a terrifying leap. Down. Over a dizzying breach.

Crouching, Charles seems lost in thought as he rubs his chin and stares at the ledge. It's still a mystery what actually happened since he got here, and I get the feeling he's not spilling that story — at least, not the truth. The urge I have to push him off the ledge is only held at bay by the fact that now, ironically, only he can save Aidan. And he has to in order to save his own life.

"This is it," he announces, gesturing to the outcropping. "I got a ride last time. So, looks like we get to jump."

"A ride?" I ask.

"I rode one of those snakes and it dropped me off on the ledge."

Liar. Charles could barely ride a bike, much less a flying snake. "Right. Why didn't you do that *this* time?"

"How could I?" he huffs. "You were massacring them! They wouldn't let me on them like before. They probably won't at all now because they're scared."

"Oh, yeah. They looked totes scared, Mr. Psycho," Michael mocks.

Ricardo breaks in. "Fine, but how do we get back?"

"We worry about that when we come to it." I shrug off my backpack. "Let's jump."

Chapter 48

As I assess the dimensions of the jump, my head is woozy, tortured leg muscles tense.

"Me first," Ricardo says, pulling me back.

"No way!"

"I have a better chance of making it," he says.

"You're hurt!"

"So are you." He points at my foot. "You think I haven't noticed you're injured?"

I should have known he'd see it if no one else did. "But if I can make it, then that means everyone else can, too," I argue. "And we need the whole team to get through this, not just one gun."

Ricardo's nostrils flare as he looks away, thinking. "Everyone get out of the way," he orders, taking my pack and rifle. "She needs as much of a running start as she can get."

The sharp edges of the volcanic rock wall cut through my parka and gouge my back. Three feet. That's all I get before I cross a gap of twice that length to land on a shelf maybe three times as large as the step I'm standing on. I try to ignore the possibility of another creature shooting out of the nearby passages.

Calculations fly through my head. Trajectory. Horizontal velocity. Body part masses. Arms. Head. Torso. Every bit of mass that can move forward must. Plotting the trajectory of the center of mass. Calculating the pushing force and the work. The timing of the jump determines the power needed...

And I go.

Tilting like a knight on horseback. Running.

201

A spasm tearing through my legs, hips, foot...

...falling...

...ledge closing in...

...foot slips...cliff edge scraping open my shin...

...sliding...

...off. Into dead space.

Screams. Mine. Theirs.

Reflective eyes with cat slits flash before me, claws cuffing my wrists.

A female elf holds me tight as my feet dangle over the ledge. Fear and elation. Who knew such contradictory emotions could surge through me as I look in the eyes of my enemy? *Please don't hurt me. Please don't let me go...*

"Charity Jones," Reilly says, "we have you."

I'm too surprised to cry as she hauls me onto the ledge. Sprawling on my back, staring upward, I can't even see the obsidian door anymore. It has disappeared in the darkness above us beyond the reach of the night vision goggles. The relieved cheers of my friends echo around me. But my pant leg is ripped, skin stinging and damp beneath.

"Thank you," I mumble.

"You are hurt," she says. "There is another way. Safer for your friends. We must go, then show the others."

A brief rumble beneath us. Earthquake. That would explain why I missed. I was trying to hit a moving target. My gimpy foot didn't help. "No!" I say, sitting up. "I can't leave them!"

"CJ, are you okay? What's going on?" Michael yells.

"Reilly says there's a safer way!"

"Yay, Reilly!" Judy says. "Thank you! Now please get us out of here!"

202

"She's lying!" Charles says. "*This* is the only way! Besides, are you seriously going to believe that thing? She just tried to kill you earlier!"

"Seriously?! I almost died just now, thanks to you! And Aidan said to take Reilly. Clearly he didn't think you could be trusted, either."

Those cat eyes widen suddenly. "We must leave, Mistress Klaas," Reilly says.

The snake things are emerging from their holes again. I can hear the rustling. My pant leg is damp with blood. The smell of blood must be a powerful lure.

Ricardo steps forward, gripping my gear as if holding it hostage. "Where are you going?"

Standing hurts. I'll be able to get around but not very quickly. I look to Reilly. "They're going to jump if you don't explain," I tell her. "Tell them where to go."

A volley of screeches pings the cavern. Reilly looks nervously to the group. "Go many steps. Another opening lies below."

"Hey! How many steps is 'many'?" Michael asks. "We didn't learn that integer in calculus."

"I don't know. It's...*many*!" I shout back. "Just give me my gear and go, okay? We'll pop out somewhere down there."

Ricardo still hesitates.

"What's the matter?" Judy asks him. "Give her her stuff!"

He reluctantly tosses the bag and gun to me. I feel a queasy distrust.

"Be careful," he says at last.

Reilly nods and whimpers. She's already disappearing into the passage, tugging me along.

I grab my gear and follow. After a few moments, I realize what she said.

"Did you just call me Mrs. Claus?"

I hate these murky, winding tunnels. They're stinky with sulfur and other gases. I thought seamounts were extinct volcanoes. Maybe I'm wrong. Plus, anything can be lurking ahead as we plunge into unchartered territory. Fortunately, I can still breathe. The narrow passage closes in. Small rubbery blobs wiggle and hop along the ground. Frogs! That must mean there are insects and other life forms inside the seamount.

Normally seamounts have crazy huge ecosystems teeming with life because of something about the way the water swells attract plankton at the base of the mount. But that's outside the seamount, not inside. These seamounts are extra-mysterious because they've not been studied very well. Especially not the Arctic ones. This thing must be millions of years old. And technically these passages were created by magma rising up from the magma chamber. I feel even queasier as I realize that the darkness below those winding steps must conceal the drop into an extraordinarily large cavern.

My lower right leg feels weak, like it's on fire as I stumble after Reilly. We stop at a junction where the passage breaks off into three totally inscrutable directions that all at least seem to veer.

"Which way do we go?" I whisper.

She shakes her head, sniffing at each entrance. "We have only been here once long ago. We are the first to explore these tunnels. It has been forbidden for centuries."

A groan rises in my throat. "Reilly, I thought you knew where we were going!"

"We are sorry, Mistress Klaas. We try to remember." Reilly's nose wrinkles, sniffing before she heads into the far left passage. A chill brushes my ankles and nape of my neck. There is something very wrong about this corridor.

Sniffing?

I know how to find the ash! Maybe she's already doing it.

"Reilly, listen! Are you...?"

The world goes black.

Chapter 49

My. Head. Hurts.

I wince and gag from the foul smells. My body feels like it's been dragged over every rock and tree twig of every path in Oak County. I didn't hurt this much in the hospital recovering from Krampus' injuries.

Something skitters over my hand. GAH! Bugs! I yank my hand up from the ground, frantically brushing off whatever. My brushing turns into a frenzy of shaking, sloughing, and freaking out as I try to make sure nothing is on me.

Am I blind? Or is it just incredibly dark? It's crazy intense, like coal dipped in black ink rolled in midnight with a side of uncomfortable East Coast heat. I feel for my goggles and they're gone. I don't know where my pack, gun or anything else is. Bone-chilling moans ripple around me. I cough, rolling over onto...feels like...dirt. Dirt would require rock decaying. Tree leaves, bugs, organic matter... Okay, maybe it's sand. I'm afraid to reach out and explore my surroundings. But if I don't, I'll never know what's here. Or not here, for that matter. My parka feels loose. I wrap my hands around myself and find big tears in the outer shell.

Aidan...I've failed you. I've failed everyone. We're all going to die because I'm *so* stupid. Mom was right. I'm totally self-absorbed or whatever it is that would let me walk into a trap. I should have been watching more closely. I could have at least looked behind me, but no.

Did Reilly betray me? If so, why would she save me and then betray me? That doesn't make sense. It's more likely we were ambushed by the elves that were opposed to Reilly helping us. If so, then she might be even more badly injured than I am.

But it's worse than that. I let revenge take over my brain and my life. This is the price.

Almost imperceptible gusts of wind disturb the air. Movement.

A pair of blue eyes suddenly appear about a dozen feet from me. They don't illuminate much beyond those cat slits, which by their shape tells me their owner is hella mad.

"Reilly!" I whisper. My throat is sticky-dry. I hope my backpack is nearby because a couple bottles of melted snow water are inside. I suspect it's nowhere to be found. "Are you okay?"

"SILENCE!" It's definitely not Reilly's voice. The elf charges toward me.

I scramble out of the way and crash into a coarse mass of rumpled, rubbery flesh. Shivers run through me. I can't move because the elf is threatening me, eyes boring into me as they gleam with hatred.

"Humans defile the House of Klaas," the elf continues. Its hideous breath hits me in the face as it closes in, fangs bared. "Humans try to kill the Klaas! We will destroy the humans."

"Why haven't you killed me, then?" My voice is shaky and weak. The thing behind me shifts and groans like the damned. A stronger quake hits the chamber.

The elf scowls, grinding its hideous teeth. A confused expression tightens its face. "We not kill Mistress Klaas. We would upset her sibling."

"Her sibling? You mean...The Cruel One?"

"He was not cruel to all of us. He was a friend. And now he's angry. We will destroy the humans that make him angry."

Wow. Even here, Charles' friends aren't very bright. How could Papa Krampus have ever hoped to get Aidan back by sending these creatures into the world? They're not just feral. They're dangerously dumb.

And yet Aidan loves them.

"I get it. Charles is your friend and he's mad, or whatever. But you have to let me go or we — WE — are all going to die if I don't find the ash to heal Aidan."

His ears flop as he vigorously shakes his head. "No! Humans die! We kill all!"

I wish I had my goggles, even one of those glowing symbol things. What powers them? Are there packets of energy just floating around, waiting to be tapped? If so, where does it come from? How is it generated? How is it stored? If I had one, I might be scared by what I see, but at least I could get my bearings. Or find out whether or not I'm two inches away from a ledge.

"We're trying to help you!" I explain. "Aidan is good. Elves are good." I try not to gag on that. "We want to save you. Save the fortress. If you don't let me go, you're going to kill everyone, including Aidan!"

"You lie!" the elf growls. His paw strikes me on the shoulder, knocking me to the ground. "Kill her!"

Chapter 50

The thing behind me bellows. A leathery tentacle whips around me, squeezing as it lifts me off the ground. At first I struggle against its grasp but then I sag into the crush, too weak with thirst, hunger, and pain to fight. My one free hand lamely smacks against the creature's hide as I protest.

I realize what that glowing symbol behind Charles' head reminds me of:

A circuit.

Picturing the circuit pattern that appeared behind Charles' head, I reach out into the air, and with my index finger I draw with the vague intent of harnessing the fortress energy to power it...

Light explodes from my fingertip. Crackling. Shining.

Searing.

The tentacle slackens. The creature wails pitifully. I'm blinded for a moment but my eyes quickly adjust in time to see the ground just before I hit it. My injured leg buckles, throbbing. My foot feels like it's on fire. It's not a hard fall but I'm winded.

I then brave a glance up at the creature that held me and immediately wish that I hadn't.

An amorphous nightmare towers over me as its mammoth body lurches away from the light. Tentacles attached to its mouth flail in the air like tree branches in a wild Oak County storm. The rest of its body is elephantine, legs so swollen they can barely bend. Its eyes are pinched shut. It rests on its front arms, with hands that bare a remarkable likeness to those of the elves.

These are the things Aidan told me about that Krampus mated

with. The Mothers.

Fighting the urge to heave what little is left in me, I scramble away from the monster. The circuit remains in the air, moving with me. I scan the space. It's a filthy underground den swarming with creepy-crawlies, flittering flutteries, and more of these lumpy squid monsters. But everything is fleeing the light. Even the lumpy monsters are trying to escape, but they're trapped by their bulk. The elf that held me captive cowers from the circuit trailing me.

"Where's Reilly?" I demand, wondering if I'm even still in Tatzlewurmstor or whatever. "Tell me where she is or I'll summon something worse!" I have no idea what the heck I'm saying or how I'd do it, but it's worth a shot, right?

The elf drools as he covers his head with his long furry arms. "We are cursed for helping humans," he sputters. "We are sealed in the tunnels and left to die."

"*Which* tunnels?" The words are more of a rasp through my parched throat.

"Secret tunnels we know. We follow Reilly to them to stop the humans."

This "we" business is making me crazy. What the heck is he saying? Maybe they're like The Borg — all elves are one elf. I just have to find Reilly. She's the only hope we have of finding the ash and saving Aidan.

Saving the world.

Another earthquake hits the cavern.

"Get me my backpack and to Reilly. NOW!"

The backpack is a hot mess when the elves return it to me. It smells funny and they've eaten all the peanut M&Ms. When I confront them about it, they look at me sheepishly.

Cookies and milk on Christmas night? Yeah, they'd *love* that.

One of the elves runs off and returns with an icky bag that he explains is made of...bladder? Intestines? I'm too grossed out to inquire. Inside, he says, is chopped whale blubber.

"Oh, you mean *muktuk*!" That's the Inuit word. I open the bag. It smells like dead whale all right. The fortress must allow them to come and go, at least to where they can get seals and whales.

"Is very good for elves," one elf explains.

"And for humans!" corrects the one who gave it to me. "Replaces delicious things in Mistress Klaas' sack."

I drain one of the water bottles and gulp down a couple of handfuls of high-calorie trail mix, wishing I knew where my goggles and headset are. At least if I had the headset I could communicate with the team, who are at the mercy of Charles. Sort of. I don't think Ricardo, for one, would listen to him if he thought for a second Charles was leading them somewhere dangerous. Ditto for Michael and Judy, although their instincts aren't as honed as Ricardo's.

Most of all, I wish I still had my gun. The elves claim it's still in "Tatzlewurm." They probably ditched it there on purpose.

Muttering at the sight of my newly acquired light source, the elves lead me so far down a narrow tunnel that I worry they're just taking me somewhere else to kill me, but they seem too frightened for that. Thin lines of ice streak the walls.

When we reach a dead end, they stop and point to where the tunnel puckers, creating an ovoid shape in the wall. Like the other gate, this one is covered in obsidian. I know nothing about geology, but that hole doesn't look natural. More like something incredibly strong tried to break through from the other side and someone tried to cover it with black rock. More crimson symbols are drawn around the opening like the ones around the obsidian gate.

"I have to go in there?"

The nasty elf nods. "We dare not return to sacred Tatzlewurm," he whimpers. "We are afraid. Please do not make us, Mistress Klaas."

The ground trembles. A single ice vein runs under my boots to the lip of the gate, crackling. "And Reilly is still in there, right?"

They huddle together, blinking at me with their big blues. I have to risk it and go inside. It's not as intimidating as the obsidian gate that liquefied before our eyes, but there's something about diving head first into a dark hole that just makes me go *nope*.

Except that my sweet Aidan — and maybe everyone else — is dying.

"Machet daz Tatzlewurmstor uf!"

210

Chapter 51

The obsidian melts away. The circuit slides forward as I tilt my head, shining light into the crevasse. Once I'm inside, every step deeper into the passage feels like I'm wading into nothingness. I look back and find the passage is closed, the opening covered by one big, blazing, crimson hieroglyph.

This one is a symbol diagram of a closed circuit. It's possibly the weirdest thing I've ever seen here so far. And I've seen a lot of weird stuff.

I stagger forward, foot burning with pain, legs wobbly from exertion and injury. Ricardo's behavior still bothers me. The way he freaked out even more than I did about Aidan. He couldn't have known about the consequences already, could he? He was even more emotional than Michael, and that's saying a lot.

A rumbling. I jog, watching for uneven surfaces. When I come to branches, I choose whichever takes me down at a steeper angle.

"Reilly! Judy! Michael! Ricardo!"

Unintelligible whispers rush at me from the shadows. Sometimes it looks like things are moving just out of the light's reach. My breath hitches, lungs squeezed by anxiety. A whiff of a bitter gas smell makes me feel slightly light-headed. I bet that's what they used to knock me out. A gas. Or maybe they just got lucky and came across me after I'd already passed out.

Keep calm, Charity.

I pull my shirt up out of my parka and over my nose, doubling back and pressing on until I find a series of branching passages. Once the gas smell is gone, I pull off the shirt and tear it up, marking each branch choice with a shred of cloth, calling out everyone's names.

My GPS! I pull it out. It doesn't track altitude, but at least I'll know if I'm going in a big circle.

After about twenty minutes of this, I hear a weak voice. "Mistress Klaas?"

Hope soars. "Reilly! Where are you? I can hear you but I can't see you."

"We are here, Mistress Klaas," she says. "Here! But we cannot reach you."

I double back and turn down a passage I passed on because it was too narrow. Sure enough, the walls close to a thin gap. But Reilly is on the other side of that gap, her eyes lighting up the corridor. Well, one eye, anyway. The other seems swollen halfway shut. I wish more than ever I had some mint. The small first aid kit in my backpack is only for humans. She got mugged by her own siblings for being smart. I can totally sympathize.

"Mistress Klaas, you have a sigil!" she says, eyes widening.

A sigil, huh? Okay. "I guess I do," I say. "Are you okay?"

She nods, her lids heavy. As I get closer, I can make out a head wound with blood clotting over her swollen eye.

"Reilly, can you pick up Aidan's scent down here? Basically anywhere he's been? I know it's an old trail, but I bet if you can follow the scent, it'll take us to the ash."

"We can follow the Klaas," she says, nodding. Her nose twitches. She turns back, peering down her passage. "This way!"

"Great!" I say. "But how can I get to you?"

Reilly looks frightened. "I do not know. There are many tunnels."

"We don't have time." I study the gap. Reilly could probably fit through if she tried, but it would be much faster if I were on her side of the gap. I test the surfaces to make sure. The walls are sturdy. There's no crumbling or rubble to push out of the way. And the magma is smooth with lots of bubbles.

"I'm coming to you, Reilly. Stay there."

I drop the backpack and dig out the bag of muktuk. The oily pieces glisten in my hand. I might starve, but we'll definitely die if I

212

don't get that ash. Taking handfuls of muktuk, I slip off my parka and smear the oil over my body. It's the grossest thing I've ever felt, but I keep going until I'm greased up. Arms. Feet. Torso. Even my head.

Reilly watches with a concerned look but says nothing.

I take off my clothes except for my pants and flatten the backpack as much as possible, sticking them all through the gap. Reilly moves everything aside and steps back. Turning sideways, I then take the ultimate, getting-into-my-tightest-jeans tummy suck-in, raise my arms over my head, and work myself into the space. Every inch of my body that's ever been injured is in agony as the rock digs into my flesh, front and back. Despite my best effort, my leg drags. I have to stop mid-squeeze to keep from hurting my leg anymore. But creepy bugs are drawn to the muktuk and they pour out of the wall holes, swarming my bare arms. I start moving again, wiggling and maneuvering, shaking off the diners, until my body is through. Exhausted and feeling like I need a thousand-million showers, I throw on my clothes and reset the backpack on my shoulders.

Reilly runs off ahead of me. "I smell him!"

I wish with all my heart that I could, too, as I follow her.

Chapter 52

Reilly is better than a bloodhound. I follow, GPS in hand, sick with the smell (and gross feeling) of muktuk. We're moving in a tight space, so the GPS barely registers our movement. As for elevation, that's dicey, too. Depending on the position of the satellites, the measurement I'm getting could be as much as four hundred feet off, up or down. But if I take the GPS readings at face value, we should be nearing half a mile under sea level. I shudder because the average Arctic depth is around thirty-four hundred feet. That means we're surrounded by crushing ocean waters, protected only by the walls of this seamount. It's held this long. But can it withstand the tremors that rock the mount every fifteen or so minutes?

Strike that. Ten minutes.

"Reilly, do you still smell his trail?"

"Yes, Mistress Klaas. Faintly."

"Have you heard of this place?"

"We do not know the name. We heard the Klaas once say Hel is somewhere in here."

"Wait. We're going to Hell?" Well, the so-called Christian bullies at school said I was going there. Maybe they were right after all. "This is a real place?"

"It is not a place but a person." I then hear only the rasp of her breath as she hastens down the tunnel.

We only seem to follow tunnels inhabited by the yellow frogs. My foot feels like it's on fire, my leg throbbing, throat raw. I don't care if I wake the dead. I've got to find them. I call out to the team.

No answer. My heart sinks.

Just as I feel like dropping to the ground, we stagger into a massive cavern about two hundred feet square, floor wavy with obsidian rock. A heavy mist clings to the cavern walls, which means it could be larger than it appears. The ceiling must be at least forty or fifty feet high. I see what might be other passage openings to the left and ahead. Just patches of midnight behind the mists. One of them must have been the passage that Aidan took. Deep red rock drips from the ceiling like the stalactites, a dark mirror image of the throne room above. This place must have the same mojo as its twin upstairs. There's no throne, but an even scarier sight stands against a far wall.

A circle of trees grows up out of the black rock, the branches piercing the wings and body of a grotesque creature. It's like the grownup version of the snakes, a stone dragon with a woman's face twisted in agony. A tree branch drives right through her throat. Everywhere she's been pierced she seems to bleed this red substance that sparkles in the light. Maybe this is a sculpture made in honor of some demon. Hey, Christianity is just as dark with its gory crucifixes.

Reilly's face is horror-stricken as she examines something around the base of the tree. "Mistress Klaas, come quickly!"

I take a closer look, carefully stepping over the roots. If I rush, I could easily twist an ankle. That's the last thing I need. The backpack is lighter without the muktuk but it still weighs on me. As I consider setting it down somewhere or handing it to Reilly, I notice something blood chilling.

What I thought were lumps of rock or even tree roots around the base of the dragon-thing are actually bodies. As I get closer, I'm stunned to see who it is.

It's the team.

"The Klaas, too, was here long ago," Reilly says, her voice cracking.

Ricardo, Michael, and Judy are lying motionless at the base of the tree trunks that seem to have broken upwards through the rocky floor, leaving jagged heaps of rock in their wake. I sob as I think the worst. Saying their names over and over, trying to coax them to wakefulness, I first check Judy's pulse. It's low. So low, I'm not sure I feel it at all. Same for the guys. They have no obvious wounds. It's like they're in a deep sleep. They still wear their gear. I check their guns. Spent shells are scattered around them. Magazines are empty.

"It looks like they were shooting at something, Reilly. What could they have possibly been fighting?"

Charles. Where is he?

Reilly turns in place, swatting and blinking at the shadows around us. "Mistress Klaas, we must go. Take the ash and return. Only evil is here. We are very afraid. Please," she begs. "Please let us leave. Now!"

She's right. I have to move, even though it's killing me to see them like this.

The ash tree! Aidan said to get the bark, and this looks like the only tree for hundreds of miles. It must be the right one. I retrieve my Swiss Army knife from the backpack and scrape off the bark into two of the tins. I keep fumbling with the knife and I almost cut my hand. That shiny red stuff is intriguing. It seems to have dripped from the creature's body in thumbnail-sized droplets that prove easily crushable with my knife. I open the last tin and put in some of the shiny red droplets. I then zip the little knife into one of the zillions of pack pockets and give an ash tin to Reilly, just in case we get separated.

A weak voice calls to me from an adjoining passage. "Charity?"

Charles?

"They hurt me. Real bad." He moans, his voice more a hoarse whisper rippling through the mists. "You've got to help me."

Reilly looks frantic, hopping this way and that, edging toward the opposite passage. "No! Mistress Klaas, do not listen!"

"Charles? Is that you, bro?" I quietly reload Judy's rifle with a spare magazine in her backpack. I then step gingerly toward his voice. "Where are you? Come on. Let's take that thing and get going."

"The actual tree is in this cave," he says. "Aidan got the wrong tree."

Reilly whimpers.

It's possible. Exhaustion and pain are making it hard to think. "Where are you?" I ask, knowing full well he's in that other passage. It's hardly big enough to walk inside, and there is no way I'm doing

216

that. I don't trust him, but I also know there's something else here that Reilly is afraid of. "What hurt you?"

"*The ghosts.*"

I roll my eyes. Seriously? The circuit eats through the mists clinging to the passageway opening, which is even smaller and darker than the opening we entered through.

"Please, Cherry. You've got to help me," Charles says again. His sobs ratchet up. "You've got to get the right tree or we'll all die."

Reilly is beyond inconsolable. She mewls and weeps, covering her head with her paws. Seeing her so upset makes me crazy, but we have to be practical.

"You've got to come out. I'm not going in there after you," I say. "Get the bark if you can. I've got a tin for it."

"Okay," he says. "I'll try."

After several breathless moments, Charles' grisly visage emerges from the small passage as he crawls out. Wobbly. Snot running from his face. He then collapses halfway out of the opening, hand extended before him, patting the ground. Grasping. Twitching. He then lies still. His hand is clenched closed over something. Probably the bark.

Crap. He really is hurt.

I move toward the entrance as fast as I can. I kneel beside him, reach for his shoulder.

Then Charles looks up at me, cool and emotionless. His other hand comes up and he throws something at my face.

A handful of that shiny red dust.

Chapter 53

Sunlight sears my vision. Gasping from the sudden brightness, I cover my face and turn away. The light feels like it's stabbing straight to the back of my skull. I haven't seen sunlight for at least several hours. Maybe that's why it seems abnormally bright? Before I open my eyes, I shield them with my hand like a visor, scanning my surroundings.

It's the campus of Oakmont High School.

I stand in front of the library, heavy backpack slung over my shoulder. In the distance, I hear the bus engines rumble down the street as they leave the school, faint traces of exhaust in the air. It must be just before first period. I drop the bag and tear open the zipper. It's my school backpack, not my supply pack.

Mr. Vittorio, our *mafioso* librarian, hustles inside the library. He's dressed in a black suit, not carrying anything. "Get to class, kid," he says before the door closes.

What class? I've already forgotten where I'm supposed to be. Need to check the schedule I printed out. I look in my bag. It's not there.

It's like one of those "first day of the school year" anxiety dreams. I've been having them since third grade. Could this be a dream? It feels incredibly real.

The bell rings as I scan the grounds. No other kids are around. An eerie stillness settles on the campus like one of those apocalyptic movies where the town is deserted because everyone's been killed by a virus.

Unfortunately, it's more likely everyone is in class rather than dead from the plague.

A cool breeze rushes over me. The air smell changes from exhaust to freshly cut grass and faint remnants of perfume lingering in the hallway. The cloudless blue sky stretches above me. Pristine. Sunny. My eyes no longer hurt.

Second bell. I'm late again.

I can figure this out. Block days are Wednesday and Thursday. I *think* today's Monday? It would explain why I feel so much dread. Let me check my phone. I'm sure they emailed me my schedule.

I search my bag, coat, purse — can't find my phone anywhere. Great. If it's lost, I'm going to be busted. Big time.

The anxiety about my missing phone gives way to more confusion. Why am I here at all?

Aidan. That name bleeds through the static in my head.

My heartbeat quickens. A sense of urgency surges forward.

Aidan. He was kidnapped by his father on Christmas.

But how could someone like that even exist? I must have dreamed him. A fantasy to fill the loneliness. Maybe I should spend less time making trouble and more time doing girly things so that I can have a boyfriend.

But I don't want a boyfriend. I want...Aidan.

I feel empty and cheated. I've got to make my life better. I want to go to Carnegie Mellon. They have the best robotics program in the country. Maybe I'll put up a new video on YouTube of my latest bot, Ghost. Like my other videos, no one will believe I made that, either.

Ghost is better than Les Femmes Nikitas. She can fly in sub-zero temperatures to spy on Russian military operations in the Arctic...

Me, building spy tech? No way. First, I don't do war. That's my dad's territory and I hate it. Second, I'd never have the courage to go somewhere like the Arctic. That's not me. I like my bed, bots, and Mom's lasagna.

Leo rounds the side of the music building. He must have just dropped off his trumpet in the band room, which is what he usually does first thing in the morning before heading to his locker. I wave to him. He's walking funny. More like shuffling. Head down, staring at the ground.

"Hey, Leo!" I call out.

No response. Instead, he changes course, heading towards me. He isn't wearing a backpack, but he does wear his thick wool scarf. His hands burrow into the pockets of his long grey winter coat. It's much too warm for that coat and scarf. Is he sick? His shuffling speeds up. Too fast.

Abnormally fast.

He lifts his gaze from the ground to my eyes. Dark, angry circles smudge the skin under his bloodshot eyes. He's talking either to himself or to me, I can't tell. I can't hear what he's saying. It's like he's talking in fast forward, his lips a blur.

Blood drips from his nose, running over his lips, down his chin.

"Leo, you're bleeding!"

His feet now blur as he speeds up. Tearing off his scarf...

A long gash on his neck gushes blood. Soaking the scarf, his collar, shirt and coat. Skin pale as white candle wax shot through with bluish veins. Tongue black.

I run.

The nearest door is the library. It's locked. I bang on the door. "Mr. Vittorio! Let me in! Please!"

"I told you to get to class, kid!" he yells from somewhere inside.

Leo is suddenly behind me. He grabs me, nails blackened, eyes as bloodthirsty as they are bloodshot. The stench of rot and dirt overtakes me. The backpack slides off my shoulder and I slug him with it. He staggers backward, howling like a wolf. His head now sits at a strange angle on his neck. I drop the pack, terror flushing into every synapse as I run to the next building.

The science rooms. Doors locked. No one in sight.

Leo isn't far behind. Screeches pop from his mouth, punctuating his senseless gibbering, his torn throat oozing blood. His mouth opens wider, revealing broken teeth. I don't understand why this is happening, but one thing is certain.

He wants to kill me.

Storm clouds blow across the sky, throwing shadows over the campus as I race to the football field. I need space around me so that I can see Leo coming. He isn't running but somehow he's never far behind. I'm winded, a stitch biting my waist. I can't keep this up. He's going to wear me down. Soon.

The bleachers loom before me. The clouds blot out the sun, casting twilight on the sprawl of mud and grass. The cool breeze is freezing. Arctic. Ice crystals spread over the grass and mud, crackling as they carpet the ground. I slip and fall, hands splayed out before me. Pain sears my left leg and foot. I scramble to my feet. Fall. Try again. Keep moving. Or die.

A figure stands in the middle of the football field. His back to me, arms folded. Shoulders like a gorilla. Blue and white football uniform and helmet. A football player?

"Help me!" I cry. "Please!"

His head tilts as if he hears something from far away. When he turns toward me, he pulls off his helmet.

Darren.

His intestines spill from huge, grisly rips in his flesh and uniform. Like Leo, his face is webbed with bluish veins, tongue black, eyes hellish. Unlike Leo, he darts at me with the frightening speed of a professional athlete.

I can't move. He's too big. Too fast. At the last possible second, I will my feet to start running. I run no more than ten yards before I slip again. His hideous form closes in on me, feet thundering on the ground.

And then I hear nothing. The ground is still.

I dare to look up.

Chapter 54

Aidan.

The winds bluster around him as he raises his arm, undead Darren defying gravity at Aidan's command. Long scraggly black hair, a haze of facial hair dusting his jaw, rough with acne. He wears a sleeveless sealskin tunic that reveals sculpted arms. Sealskin boots and pants. His bright blue eyes bathe the field in a soft, unnatural light.

"I can't hold him for long," he says. "You *must* break out of this."

"Out of what?" I ask.

"This nightmare that Hel's blood has induced," he says. "Charles did this to you."

I sit up, puzzled. Shivering. My brother the psychopath trying to kill me? Sounds about right. "So, this is a dream?"

Darren thrashes in the air, growling and hissing at Aidan. Leo is heading toward us on the horizon, head now knocked off kilter from when I slugged him with my backpack. He's gibbering and yelping.

"A very powerful nightmare from which you're not meant to wake up," Aidan says. "Michael and the others can't. But you can."

Everything feels so real. Not like a dream. But my memory is returning. An awareness. It happens at times when I'm dreaming, when I realize I'm doing something I'd never do when I'm awake. Remembering. Aidan. Dying. Because of me. Judy. Michael. And Ricardo. Half dead by the ash tree in Hell. Because of me. I did this to them.

Guilt. Self-hatred. I have to make things right.

"How?"

"Question what you see. You have a stronger grasp of reality than they do. Do it! If you die here, I can't help you. The entire world will die. You know this. I told you. Please, Charity. It's up to you and your amazing mind."

As he talks, I remember the glittering red dust flying into my face. The bodies of the team lying at the foot of the great ash tree. Aidan dying...

"But how can you be here?" I ask.

"I'm in a coma," he replies, "traveling in my dreams."

Whether or not he's real, my feelings for him definitely *are*. I struggle to stand, my foot and leg aching. The memory of Reilly catching me after I slipped flashes before me. A smart, kind elf that helped us. So smart that Aidan gave her a name.

Forget the facial hair and acne. I kiss Aidan fully on those lips. His beard scrapes my chin and his breath is acrid, but I don't care. His mouth is the sweetest thing in the world. His eyes resume their normal hue, and his smile is breathtaking, like sunlight breaking across earth as seen from the space shuttle.

"Let's do this," I say. Turning to Darren, I shout, "I graduated from this school. I'm a Freshman at Carnegie Mellon and an intern at Volertech. This isn't my school and you're dead. You, Darren, can no longer bully me. Not in dreams, and certainly not in life. You're not just dead to me, you're fiction courtesy of Charles and the red dust."

Darren suddenly appears on the ground, motionless. He lies as I last remember seeing him when I snapped those photos — his corpse mangled, a bloody mess under the bleachers. And for the first time ever, I feel sorry for him, his life over before it had even begun. Sure, I hated him, but his death was a tragedy. Maybe he would have grown up to be a good person. He might have gone on to do better, have a loving family of his own. Now he'll never get that chance.

Leo, too, has fallen just a few feet away, lying in the position he was in as he died on my parent's deck, a glass shard embedded in his neck. Grief chokes me. I don't want to believe sweet Leo is dead, but I have to accept that reality in this moment. He was an adorable guy who loved his friends, not this undead phantom trying to kill me. He was a true friend who died trying to save Aidan. To save us all.

The world fades. The football field ripples with ink that solidifies. Aidan's body fades and pixelates like a character in a corrupted video game.

And then I remember. "Aidan! How do we open the gate back?"
He opens his mouth to answer but then vanishes.
"*Aidan!*"
Leaden clouds billow over the sky. A brilliant flash of lightning briefly reveals the chamber of Hel behind the façade of Oakmont High School.
"*Help us!*"
A second flash of lightning tears across the sky, this time hitting the basalt. Rocks explode nearby, the ground rolling under my feet. Terrifying. Ducking, running, mumbling to myself. This isn't real. This is a dream.
It's. Not. Real.
I wake up. I lie on the hard floor, my shoulder aching from the way I hit it when I passed out. The circuit must still be working because I'm surrounded by feeble light. Charles tried to drag me through the crawl space into that other room, but he must have given up halfway. I wish people would stop moving me when I'm unconscious. It hurts and it's really making me mad!

As I stagger to my feet, shivering, I notice that the heavy mist has been burned away from the walls now streaked with those terrible icicles. Strange, incandescent words are carved into the now bare wall.
Machet daz Niklaustor uf

Chapter 55

Niklaustor? Is that like Tatzlewurmtor? More importantly, *where* is it? Or is it a person?

Michael, Judy, and Ricardo remain in that death sleep, bodies unmoved. Charles and Reilly are both gone, as are both tins and my rifle.

Pressing my hands against my cheeks, I close my eyes, willing myself to calm down. Leaving the team is the last thing I want to do, but I have to. I have to chase down my terrible brother.

Alone.

At least he left my backpack. I dig in the pack until I find a plastic baggie. Digging out the small Swiss Army knife, I extract more ash and tie the bag closed. I hope it's enough. The big question is: how do I get back? I might be able to retrace my path back through that far passage thanks to those shirt pieces I left as breadcrumbs, but I don't know if I can get through that gap again.

It's my only hope.

Before I leave, as I take another rifle and reload it with trembling hands, I kneel down beside my friends, fighting tears, shaking them, shouting in their ears. "Guys! *Wake. UP.* It's not real." And then, "The world depends on you."

The ground rumbles almost constantly as I shuffle through the tunnels like a zombie. The GPS helps me keep oriented. When I reach the gap, I place my hands on the stones and despair. I'll never get through again. I'm out of muktuk and the oils have dried on my skin enough that they won't help. In fact, they'll just gum up my passage.

I try anyway and almost get stuck.

I dislodge my foot from the gap and slide down onto the ground. The deep ache of failure and despair racks my entire body. I don't know where or what "Niklaustor" is. I don't know anything. We're all going to die.

I try to make peace with it. At least I'm dying doing what I thought was right. Then again, everyone is dying because of me. My selfish, horrible insistence on being right, as Keiko once said. Not just being right, but getting revenge.

"Sorry, everybody, like, in the world," I mumble through the sobs.

And then I hear her voice.

"Mistress Klaas?" Reilly peers through the gap from the other side. She looks unhappier than I am. "Please forgive us. The Cruel One made us open the gate for him. He mocks the Klaas who is close to death."

"Reilly!" I pop up off the ground. "Thank goodness you're okay! Do you know what the heck Niklaustor is?"

Reilly tilts her head, looking puzzled. "We can go the gate. But first." She slides a book through the gap. "Please."

"I don't have time to read. We've got to get going!"

"Please!" she says, more frantic.

Inked on the rough leather cover is one of the symbols, although it looks less like a circuit and more like the graphic depiction of a molecule. The first few pages are covered in an unknown language. I turn more of the brittle, ancient pages. I can't believe what I'm seeing. "What is this?" I ask.

She nods vigorously. "It helps, yes?"

"I don't know. I can't make it out!"

She points at the pages with her sloth claws. "Turn." She holds up three claws.

I turn three more pages. My chemistry isn't the best, but if I didn't know better, I'd say the symbol looks like an acid molecule.

"Melt," Reilly says, stroking the rock. "Like snow."

Like snow, all right. This book and the light thing on my head goes against everything I've ever believed or thought. It's one thing if someone else appears to manipulate energy out of the air. But it's quite another when you're looking at a cookbook to whip up a recipe for magic acid to save your life.

The problem is, even if this works, how do I control it? Sometimes when acids hit certain rocks the chemical result can be a deadly gas. If inhaled, the gas could combine with the calcium in my body and cause cardiac arrest. I'd be dead in seconds. Or blinded if it got in my eyes. Also? I have no idea what's even in these rocks. If drawing this symbol actually produces this acid, it could combine with any other metal or substance in these rocks to produce yet another deadly poison, gas or otherwise.

And that's assuming it is what I think it is.

"You've seen this work?" I ask Reilly.

She nods. "Oh, yes. The Father used it many times."

"Did it make a gas?"

Reilly looks confused.

"A cloud?"

She shakes her head. "No clouds. Like water."

A thick ice rivulet drives under my feet, pushing me off balance. I grab the gap rock to stabilize. I then give the book back to Reilly. "Back way up!" I say, shooing her until she is no longer visible in the passage.

Hefting my backpack, I then take a deep breath – it might be my last — before I think about the energy storage in the fortress. Those freestanding energy reserves that I drew on once before, half-crazed and desperate. With my finger I then quickly draw the figure I from the book onto one side of the rocks.

The lines of the molecule sizzle. The rock quickly dissolves under the symbol, turning to molten slush that runs off into the passage before me, a puddle on the other side of the gap. It looks dangerously hot, and I can't jump. I'm in too much pain.

I slouch by the gap. My leg throbs but my foot feels like it's being eaten alive by piranha. I don't want to give up, but I just can't go any further.

And that's when I hear it.

Chapter 56

CJ!

I *think* I hear someone calling my name. It's probably just the pain messing with my head. I focus on the molten puddle blocking my passage. The steam cools, settling. Hardening? Maybe. I rummage in my backpack for something to throw to test the puddle and see if that's the case. Or if it's still hot.

"Reilly! Give me the book!"

She shakes her head, hugging the book. "Must keep book safe."

"I have to know if it's safe to walk through there! We're going to die!"

Reilly freezes as she stares past me into the tunnel we came through.

"CJ!"

It wasn't my imagination. It's Michael!

A clatter of footfalls fills the passage behind us. Michael leads the charge with Ricardo and Judy on his heels. Ricardo is no longer limping. Judy's got her "Uncle Anyu" ready for action.

"Are you okay? And what's up with the light thing?" Michael asks. He slides off his goggles as he slings his rifle. I hold out my hand and he pulls me to my feet. Or, rather, foot. Everyone hugs me.

"It's a long story." I point at the puddle. "We need to test that to see if it's safe. Could be acidic."

Judy digs a peanut M&M out of her pocket and tosses it at the formation. The candy bounces off the hard surface. Reilly dives after it and stuffs it in her mouth.

"We're good! Let's go!" I shout.

"You okay? We thought the mountain ate you!"

"It kinda did, but I'm okay." It's a lie. I hurt like hell. I realize as Michael grips my hand how much I need them all. I couldn't have gone another step without them.

"How'd you guys wake up?"

"*You* woke us up!" Judy says, sliding off her goggles. "I was terrified and shooting zombies like it was *Call of Duty: The Reality Show* when you stepped in front of me and waved your hands, saying, 'Hey, Judes! Wake up!' I shot right through you without hurting you and you gave me stink eye. Like you do." She laughs, nudging me on the back.

"Awesome!" I say, triumphant. "I didn't think you could hear me. Aidan didn't think you would wake up at all."

"Really? When did you talk to Aidan?" Ricardo asks. He sounds very anxious.

"He's in a coma, but he was somehow able to reach mentally into my dream." To be honest, I'm still not totally convinced it was really him in my dream. Maybe my subconscious raised him to give me incentive to break out of the power of the red dust. But I keep my doubts to myself.

We're moving, Michael helping me walk. I tell them about escaping the dark cave filled with hideous creatures. My encounter with Charles. Fighting undead Leo and Darren in my dream until Aidan appeared. Everyone falls quiet for a moment at the mention of Leo. I probably shouldn't have said it, but exhaustion has disabled my brain. I want more than anything to hug Judy, but she pushes forward, her face somber.

Reilly moves ahead of us, book under her arm. It's amazing how fast she can move when she needs to. She periodically glances back to make sure we're following her.

As we close in on the gate, the team recounts how Charles led them to the tree and threw the red dust in their eyes. How the dust disoriented them and eventually knocked them unconscious. They were already shooting at imaginary enemies before they hit the ground. Zombies, dinosaurs, rabid elves, whatever. At least not each other. They say Charles must have then hid in that crawl space, waiting for me to come so that he could hijack Reilly and use her to get out.

"Why did he need you?" I ask Reilly. "He knows how to get out."

"The Cruel One...can speak the words...but gate does not open," she says, breathless.

I've been trying not to think about what he's doing to Aidan while vulnerable and dying. Maybe nothing. He certainly doesn't *need* to do anything if he wants him dead.

"But he seemed like he was really helping us for a while," I say. "Why would he go to the trouble of taking you all the way to the ash tree if he didn't want what he originally asked for?"

"Dunno," Michael says. "But dude definitely changed channels at some point as we were taking that alternate route. Towards the end, I think. Like, just before we got to the tree? He kept looking at us, especially at Rick, as if he wanted to say something, but then he just shut down and wouldn't look at us at all." He asks Ricardo, "You saw that, right?"

"Yeah. Just before the tree room he sort of slowed down and started acting weird," Ricardo replies. "Well, weirder, anyway."

This is bad. If I know Charles, a new plan hatched in his brain and he ran with it. But what made him decide to ditch any chance of escaping to Alaska? Was it something about Ricardo?

I've always trusted Ricardo. Not only has he been in a relationship with Michael for a couple of years now, he was with us at that final battle against Krampus on Christmas. But now that I think about it, he doesn't talk much about himself. I should never have accepted his help without question. I should have considered there might be strings attached. Then again, if I could go back, I'd probably still trust him all over again to get the gear for the expedition because I couldn't have gotten here at all otherwise.

Of course, if we never came, the world wouldn't be in danger.

I lose it when we reach the small obsidian gate, its opening surrounded with angular crimson symbols. "Reilly, this is the Tatzlewurmstor gate! We need the *Niklaustor* gate!"

"Forgive us, Mistress Klaas, but here is the Niklaustor. *There*," she indicates the other side, "is the Tatzlewurmstor."

Of course! The gate is on the border between the land of Tatzelwurm and the land of Nicholas. So, the other side, it's the gate that *goes to* Tatzlewurm. On this side, it's the gate that *goes to* Nicholas (or at least where he normally lives). As insane as this place is, it does have an internal logic.

"Sorry for yelling at you, Reilly," I say, scratching her ears. I shouldn't. She's a sentient being, not a pet. Still, she blisses out when I do that, which makes me happy. Her fur is rough but not totally unlike a dog. "Machet daz Niklaustor uf!" I shout.

The obsidian ripples and runs off into nowhere, revealing the hole I originally entered to find Reilly. I step through first.

And the tunnel begins to shake violently.

Chapter 57

We run as fast as we can. Reilly leads us, book spine clamped in her jaw. The walls are covered with those ice rivulets. The entire fortress is collapsing, as Aidan lies dying. Ceiling debris works loose and rains down on us, the dust making it hard to breathe.

When we emerge in the throne room, it's nothing but blood and chaos. Stalactites have fallen from above and are now either shattered or embedded in the floor, impaling elves that still writhe and twitch. Hapless elves pour from the opposite tunnel behind the throne, racing for the outside. But the blizzard creature grabs them as they pass, flings them up at the ceiling, and impales them on the stalactites. Their dripping blood forms dark puddles on the icy floor.

Reilly brings us around the back of the throne. We slink by, trying not to draw attention to ourselves. Even if the blizzard creature can't see us, the elves can as they flee the fortress *en masse*.

Not that it will do them any good if Aidan dies.

"Get out of here!" I say to the team. "Go outside!"

"No way!" Michael shouts. "We're looking out for you!"

"Then find Charles."

"Roger that!" Ricardo shouts, readying his rifle muzzle to seek and destroy. Judy falls in step with him as they leave, gun ready.

I stagger painfully to Aidan's room, where massive rivulets of ice are puckering the walls. Aidan sleeps on his back now. He's paler than I have ever seen him. I shiver as I remove the backpack. Reilly whimpers as a terrible clattering-clomping noise rushes towards us from the passage.

"Careful, Mistress Klaas! He's coming!"

Charles.

Bound in skins and furs, he rides past us on one of the goat things, rifle and reins gripped in one hand. With the other he snatches my backpack, tearing it out of my grasp as he thunders out into the chaos of the throne room.

I follow him. "Coward! Why don't you just shoot me?"

At the throne room, I keep to the wall as I edge around the insanity toward the opening I just saw Charles use. Freezing winds blast my body once I'm outside, tugging on the gloves clipped inside my parka. Damn, it's cold! My jaw chatters uncontrollably. The worst sight I can imagine rises above me: Charles flying into the sky on the back of the goat creature.

"YOU! ASSHOLE!"

This is it. We're done.

The fortress is about to be destroyed. And so will the world with it. The ground shakes beneath me. I can barely stand as it is from my injuries.

Just as I crumple to the ice, the team races to my side from around the fortress bend.

More clattering behind me. Reilly and the others lead one of the flying goats. It's one of the big daddy goats with thick, twisted horns. It mews at me, catching a falling snowflake on its tongue. I've never seen one up close like this. The look in his eyes is almost sentient. Maybe it is.

One of the bigger elves lifts me up onto the creature's saddle. My brain howls into a bullhorn, *Don't Do This! Heights Scary! Die Die Die...!*

With a leap, we rise into the air. I've only once ever ridden a horse. It was at Griffith Park on one of those trails that leads to a Mexican restaurant for dinner. It was a slow, gentle ride on solid ground.

This is nothing like that. More like hugging the back of a rocket as it soars into the sky. I cling to the creature's neck, figuring the lower I am against its body, the less chance I have of falling off.

Oh, God. I'm flying.

Flying!

Don't look down. For the love of not-God.

(Seriously. Don't.)

Charles goads his mount to greater heights, clearly an experienced rider.

"Catch up to him!" I tell Daddy Goat. He bleats as he rises. Cheers of encouragement from the team float up from the ground. The Arctic winds whistle in my ears and blast through the tears in my coat. Like in my Leo and Darren red-dust nightmare, the sky roils with massive thunderclouds that crackle and rumble overhead. A thick mist is forming over the horizon, blotting out the Arctic Ocean for miles. The slabs crumble and fall, one by one.

Apocalypse.

I don't know exactly what I'll do when I catch Charles, but I am *so* done with this guy. I am *so not* going to die because of him.

The goat flies far more gently than I expected. It moves with the winds. Dances. Like a kite but more controlled. Honestly? I'm way too mad to notice more as I focus on Charles. His goat rises into the air, its legs churning like the limbs of an Olympic swimmer in the currents. Wearing my backpack, Charles looks startled as my goat catches up to his.

I had no plan when I jumped onto this thing. My thigh muscles quiver. My foot burns. My arms are fatigued. I don't know how much longer I can hold on.

"Hey!" I yell. "Give me my backpack and I won't kill you!"

Charles stares at me a moment, jaw dropped, but he jerks away as I draw closer. "You aren't going to hold up your end of the deal," he says. "I know it. You're taking me back. And I'd rather die than go back."

"What are you talking about? Of course we'll take you to Alaska! Whatever! Just give me my damned backpack!"

"Liar! You brought a fucking bounty hunter!"

Stunned. "What are you talking about? We're not bounty

hunters. We're here to save Aidan!"

"That's Emilio Zepeda's little brother. The biggest bounty hunter on the West Coast. Everybody's scared of him. Took me awhile to recognize him, but that's definitely him."

And then it's like the sky crashing down on me. Everything I thought I knew about friendship. Trust. Love.

"Look at me, Cherry! I can't go back! Not like this!" His ruined face cracks, revealing his torment. "That's why I threw the Hel dust in everybody's eyes. I read about it in the library months ago. If I can't go, nobody goes."

As I stare at Charles with a mix of hatred and pity, the real hunter bobs up behind him on the winds.

Chapter 58

Ricardo rides the creature into the sky above the fortress like he was born to it. And maybe he was. Someone trained to chase people with his strength, cunning, and deadly skills. To bring them to the police. Or worse.

But is he chasing Charles?

Or Aidan?

I'm an idiot. He not only brought us guns, but I gave him the KED and the AV bullets. It's everything Ricardo would have needed to take out Aidan — at least before he became The Klaas.

Charles doesn't see Ricardo. I can't conceal my surprise. Just as Charles turns his head to look at whatever is behind him, Ricardo throws an arm around his neck and puts him in a headlock.

"Lower!" he orders his steed. Both goats obey.

Charles passes out, hanging like a rag doll in Ricardo's arms. Ricardo drags him off the goat and drapes him over his own as we move closer to the ground. He then wrenches off the backpack and tosses it to me when we land. And, boy, am I relieved to be back on the ground...

"Go, go, go!" he shouts.

I ride straight to Aidan.

My head buzzes with adrenaline. We plunge into the fortress at top speed, me clinging tightly but slipping from side to side. Reins cutting into my hands. Holding on for my life and everyone else's. The blizzard creature has disappeared.

We reach the bed where Aidan lies still as death. The symbols that once hung in the air are gone. The Daddy Goat brings me to the bed's edge. I tumble onto the surface and fumble with the backpack. Here's the baggie full of tree scrapings. *A poultice.* I pour in what little water I have left in my bottle into the baggie — three dashes? Drops? I don't know how to measure the water as I mush up the shavings into a pulp.

The ceiling cracks and buckles above me.

I crawl across the bed to Aidan's side. Locate the terrible, gaping, sucking, blackened wound from the mistletoe bullet. He's not breathing. Cold. Got to try. I plaster the wound with the ash.

"I love you. I love you. I love you, Aidan the Klaas..."

Nothing. More dust rains down on me as I sob. Giant cracks scrawl across the walls, ceiling. A guttural howl of self-hate flies from my throat. An animalistic wail. I've killed the one person I love more than anything. I fold over Aidan's body, resting my head on his chest. My tears soaking his wound. The world is passing. The molten core breaking through the plates. The fortress ceiling breaking above us, ice rivulets melting. The great Arctic Ocean dissolving in a tsunami that will crush the surrounding continents for hundreds of miles inland. My selfish jihad destroying billions of lives.

Eyes closed. Ceiling raining rocky debris. Pelting my head. Shoulders. Back. Legs. Tears pool under my cheek. Wet and sticky. Warm...

Movement under me.

The shower of debris halts.

Stillness.

A soothing sensation heats my cheek, floods my face, body. Every tortured muscle, wound and frostbitten part of my body relaxes, feeling warm and feel whole.

Healed.

A hand brushes my hair. Plays with the strands. Caresses the back of my neck.

"Three drops," Aidan says.

Aidan. I open my eyes. There he is, awake. Smiling.

"Three *tear* drops," he continues. "I should have known that's what he meant. My father died because I didn't cry for him when I applied the ash tree bark. But how could I? He was a monster. A

237

Krampus."

My thoughts scramble with incomprehension. I raise my head. Covered in granite dust like a gargoyle coming to life. Heart bursting with gratitude.

Aidan smiles even wider. Healthy. Whole. He lies beneath me, his delicious mouth inches from mine. Eyes incandescent. The scent of nutmeg, cinnamon and pine faint on his skin. His hair is shaggy, unruly, a riot of black curls. His cheeks are still Arctic Tarzan rough. But you know what? Don't care. Not even a tiny little bit. He could be Zit Boy from Planet Acne and I would take him.

"Kiss me, Charity Jones?" he asks. "And don't ever stop. Please."

"Oh, HELL yeah," I say before devouring that mouth. Forgetting everything else. Brushing my hands over the new landscape of his upper body. Even the muscles in his neck are thicker. Ropey. He responds to my touch everywhere. And I to his. That crazy chemistry. Yet he's no longer the boy with the chartreuse skin. He's transformed to meet his destiny.

He's changed so much. But so have I.

I tear off my parka and snuggle into him. He feels more amazing than ever. My tears of joy and relief soak his shoulder as we cling to each other. I wipe them off self-consciously.

"Um, Charity, I don't mean to spoil the moment." He sniffs. "But are you covered in muktuk?" I notice he's crying, too. "Not that I care," he adds quickly. He sits up, wrapping his arms around me as we kiss. His mouth on mine. Heaven.

When the kiss ends, he says, "I'm sorry I doubted you. But I couldn't read you. I read Sergei and found you'd kissed him. I...I wanted to die."

Oh, boy. Here it is.

"Aidan, I was just leading him on so he'd give me the contacts I needed for some of our equipment. I thought you'd know what I wanted for Christmas. Heck, I even sent you a letter! Well, it was for your dad, but..."

Aidan smiles. "It was the best thing I'd ever read. But I can't read *you* anymore. And now that I've taken you off The List, if you're away from me, I don't even know if you're alive."

"I'm alive. And so are you." In more ways than one. I feel him against me in ways I never could before.

Oh. Wow...

"Can you forgive me?" I ask.

"Totally." Kiss. "Unconditionally." Kiss. "Forever."

Whispers outside the doorway. The elves crowd the opening, eyes wide, chattering. Gamboling in the passage. A song breaks out in a language I've never heard before. Jubilant. Festive.

Not a Christmas song. But it could be one.

The chorus swells. Such glee! And another set of voices joins the song, infinitely lower, in that same strange language, bass notes vibrating from deep in the earth. Soothing. Spirited.

"The Mothers," Aidan whispers. His face beams with awe. "I've never heard them sing before."

I shudder as I realize he means the tentacle monsters in the pit. But you know what? Like me, my bae is mixed, except he's half human, half Other. He sees the world in ways I never will. And it's all good. We cling to one another in the warmth of the bed, breaking only to look into each other's eyes in absolute wonder.

"How did you know where to find me?" Aidan asks at last.

"The map coordinates came to me in dreams. They pointed to a location in the Arctic Ocean. I figured that must be where the fortress is and that you were putting out some kind of homing beacon for me to find you."

"I wasn't aware of it, if I was," he says.

"I never told you, but after our first kiss, my dreams went totally crazy. I had these intense dreams about you that felt random sometimes, but they always had some kind of meaning. I even dreamed of the ice wall the morning before we came here." I kiss him. "Leo said that swapping spit with you was changing my brain and more. I think he might've been right."

"Leo," he says sadly.

"He didn't make it."

"I know," he replies quietly.

My heart sinks thinking of that stupid "hell dust" dream.

He squints at my head. "And how'd you get that sigil?"

"You mean the circuit?" I tell him. He doesn't speak at first. When he eventually does, his words are slow and deliberate.

"I had no idea what taking you off The List would do to you. I hope it's entirely good, like this. For all of you."

"You mean, if I'm not on The List, I can do things like you?"

He shrugs. "Or maybe it's just the spit-swapping. Either way, Charity Jones, you're very special indeed. And always have been."

No talking after that. We just bask in being together. I won't lie, though. Part of me wants to run out and try to throw people around by waving my hands in the air. My brother would be a good start.

As it occurs to me to ask Aidan if he can add people back to The List, another voice cuts through the doorway.

"I'd say, 'Get a room, you two,' but you kinda got one." Michael hangs in the doorway, grinning. Seeing him brings everything rushing back. "We figured you'd succeeded in saving the world and stuff, what with all the singing and bouncing elf action." His expression falls. "But you might want to come outside. Something's up."

I wonder what effects being taken off The List have had on the team?

"Michael, can you leave us alone for another moment?"

"Nooooo problem." He winks as he ducks back into the corridor.

I look at Aidan, sobering. "I've made a lot of mistakes getting here. This one's kind of huge. Can you forgive me for this, too?"

"You've done the impossible just coming here, not to mention everything else," he says. "I refuse to entertain the idea that anything you've done needs forgiveness."

"Well, okay, but just so you know, I'm not sure Ricardo is who he says he is. Charles seems to think he's a bounty hunter. If he is, he could be hunting more than just my brother, especially since he has weapons that could kill you."

Aidan frowns. "I wish I could tell you. I took him off The List, too."

It's time to find out the truth, however hurtful.

Chapter 59

My parka goes back on much less easily than it came off. I especially hate having to put the bulky gloves back on, but I need to be ready for the worst. I wiggle my toes in my boots. Everything feels good again.

"I'll come with you," Aidan says.

"No!"

"Charity Jones, I can take care of myself." As he slides out of bed and stands, it's like I see him for the first time. Holy crap. He looks like a Greek god. Or maybe a Norse one. His body is absurdly ripped. He even seems taller than I remember. And with his full Krampus-Sinterklaas powers, whatever those might be, he's obviously a force to be reckoned with. Or should I say, a much greater force.

"I get that," I say. "But let me lead. I need to talk to them first so that we can get as much information as possible before they see you. They don't realize how you've changed."

"Fine, but first..." He draws an invisible symbol over me. Nothing appears but the parka feels warmer. "Now you will be as warm or cool as you wish," he says. "Anywhere."

I pull him close to me so I can get another mouthful of crazy-amazing kisses before I face the team and Charles.

Wow.

Rifle in hand, I step out into the hallway where the elves continue to dance and sing in the midst of carnage. Aidan stares at the bodies, clearly upset.

"Dear Gods! How did this happen?"

"I'll tell you later," I whisper. "But you probably never want to

241

hibernate again."

The blizzard creature is gone. It was probably as Reilly said, a part of Aidan that broke away while he was in hibernation and went off unchecked. A sort of unbridled id. Who knows how far it would have gone if Aidan had remained in hibernation? I'm not looking forward to telling Aidan about what it did to people on the ice and at camp.

Elves are already cleaning the throne room, dragging the bodies of their siblings outside. Mists rise from the battered, elf-stalactite-horn-littered ground. Ghost still sits battered near the throne under a blanket of ice crystals. The fortress creaks and groans as it repairs itself. The effect is deeply eerie.

Aidan follows at a pace, hanging back. The elves throng him, bubbling with happiness. I envy them. They've been with him this whole time, enjoying his company. When he isn't hibernating, he must be such a welcome change from his horrible dad. Their joy is so pure, untainted by whatever human drama is unfolding just outside. The Klaas lives and that's all that matters to them.

Not just the Klaas. A Nicholas instead of a Krampus.

Outside, the sky is a brilliant blue I've never seen before, golden sunlight washing over the wall wreckage, ice shimmering a shade of mystical azure created over thousands of years as it formed. The glorious wilderness surrounds us as far as the eye can see. But in the midst of the breathtaking Arctic beauty sits Charles, hands tied behind his back as he's propped against a crumbled slab. Ricardo stands guard over him with his rifle as Judy paces, her face red with fury. She kicks snow at Charles, cursing at him. Michael gives me a hug that would break a bear.

"Well done, CJ," he says. "And thanks."

Ricardo steps away from his ward. "Aidan is okay?"

"He's recovering." I can't take my eyes off of him or even answer. It's like I'm seeing him for the first time. "Why did you lie to us?"

"What?!" Michael says.

Ricardo breaks eye contact, his face pale.

"What's the real reason you came, Rick?"

Michael looks stunned.

"I think I know why he's been such a jerk to you these last few months," I tell Michael. "He's been keeping a much bigger secret than anyone else on the team. And he kept it from you, too."

Ricardo breaks down, tears pouring down his cheeks. "I couldn't tell you. They'd kill me!" He sobs. "They're going to kill me, you guys."

Judy watches, mouth open. But she doesn't leave Charles' side.

"No, I *don't* get it, Rick," I say. "Who's 'they'? Tell me before we get it out of you."

"You don't understand!" His voice booms through the air. "How could you possibly?"

I feel that familiar stab of fear in my stomach. I fight it and stand my ground. Aidan's watching. He won't let anything happen to me. "You're a bounty hunter, aren't you?"

"What?" He looks genuinely surprised. "No. No, that's not it at all. My brother's a bounty hunter. But I'm..."

He falls silent. Although I might be protected from the cold, a chill worms inside me, spreading goosebumps over my arms and legs. *To accomplish a mission, you might have to hurt things besides Krampus. A lot of things.* That's what he said. I guess he was talking to himself more than me.

"You're what?" I ask.

He casts his gaze at the ground before looking at me again. His eyes flit like he's in REM sleep as he reveals his waking nightmare. "I'm sorry. They have my sister's life in their hands."

"Who's 'they,' Rick?" I ask. "What are you talking about?"

A sad, serious look. "I wanted to tell you everything. I really did. But they promised to take care of my sister if I did this one thing for them. And of course they paid for everything. They had to."

"Do WHAT one thing?" Michael rages.

Ricardo rubs his arm the same way he did earlier on the expedition. "They kidnapped me and implanted a tracking device inside of me."

"Who did this to you?" I ask.

"The Perchten," he says. "That's what they call themselves. They approached me about finding Aidan shortly after Christmas. After the

243

Volertech break-in. Volertech tried to hush everything up but word got out about what really happened. The Perchten knew that Aidan was not only alive but that something big had happened back at the fortress. They just didn't know exactly what. I think they sent Sergei to keep an eye on us."

"Are they human?" I ask.

"Half human," Ricardo says. "Like Aidan, but they've never been to the fortress, so their powers have never been activated. That's what they think happens when Krampus brings the mother and baby here. And they think by coming here, they'll get that power, too."

Tears flood Michael's face. As he melts down, Ricardo casts his gaze down at the frozen surface, withering.

The Perchten, whatever that means, probably feel cheated because they never got to have the power that Aidan has. And now they're coming to take what they were denied.

As Aidan approaches us, face somber, everyone looks startled to see him, including Charles. Michael walks up to him. The two throw their arms around one another, Aidan nearly lifting Michael off the ice.

Ricardo trembles.

At last Aidan speaks.

"They're not true perchten, of course, but I see why they took that name," he says. "They're offspring like me, but they're on The List. I just didn't know how to measure them until now."

True "perchten"? I wish I knew what that even meant. "I thought you could see everybody on The List."

Aidan shakes his head. "I can see far more than ever before now that I'm the Klaas, but it takes practice and concentration to separate out the billions of names. Up until now, I've only guessed that these half-siblings must exist, given my father's appetites." He closes his eyes, pauses. "Even then, I can only barely read them. They're not fully human, which makes it harder." He steps close to Ricardo. "You don't realize the trouble you've brought on the world by leading them here. Depending on how many there are, they could become an army with all the power but none of the restrictions and certainly none the responsibilities I bear. Or maybe nothing will happen." He sighs. "But it's too late. They've tracked you here already."

"So they're coming here?" I ask.

"Yes," Aidan replies. "And they've brought reinforcements."

Michael explodes. "WHAT THE HELL, RICK?"

"I didn't have a choice!" Ricardo says. "What was I going to do? Let Ariana die? They knew I'd do anything for my family."

"But what else have you lied about? What about us? Have you been lying about your feelings for me so that you can stay in the group and keep your word to these Perchten assholes?"

Ricardo looks absolutely stricken by this question. "No, *mi cielo*. I love you so much. You have to believe it. But my family needs the money to cover my sister's medical bills. I didn't want to burden you about her condition, especially after you lost your father. So when the Perchten approached me."

"Screw those guys!" Michael punches the air, spittle flying. Face and neck flushed with rage. "Do you even know how badly you've been treating me these last few months? And how much it hurt? I felt like garbage. And the whole time you were going to screw over everybody, including me! How could you do that?"

Now Ricardo's crying. "I'm sorry," he sobs.

"It sounds like these people are dangerous," I say. "We've got to have a plan before they get here. We've all got to work together."

A bloodcurdling scream. And then a single gunshot explodes nearby, the sound shredding the crisp air. Echoing. Fading. Ears ringing.

Nobody moves. Not even the elves make a sound.

Judy stands between us and Charles, her Uncle Anyu smoking as she raises it.

"What have you done, Judy?" My voice cracks. Hysterical. "*Judes! What have you done to him?*"

She steps aside to reveal my brother slumped over, his skull weeping blood where the bullet blasted through his temple. Eyes glassy.

The girl I met outside the library that day is dead, too. The new girl blooms before us like belladonna, reborn wild and dangerous. A murderer. Defiant, she holsters the gun. "He needed to die."

My brother has been killed in cold blood. Bound and delivered. Butchered on the ice.

Dead.

My vision swims with shadows. I stagger over to his body and kneel beside him. Of course Aidan didn't know what Judy was about to do. She's no longer on The List. And, like Michael and I, he was probably too absorbed with Ricardo's drama to notice.

"Human beings are too cruel to be trusted." His eyes throw spears at Judy. "I had every reason and opportunity to kill Charles, far more reason than you because he killed me in cold blood. Unlike you, I showed him mercy."

"You call leaving him chained to a wall like an animal mercy? You're no better than your dad," she says. Aidan looks stung by her words, but he says nothing as she continues. "He got my first love killed and just tried to destroy the entire planet because he didn't want to go to jail. Well boo fucking hoo!" Her fury builds. "I literally did the entire world a favor, Aidan. He didn't deserve to live! He would have only made things worse!"

I break down. I'm grieving for more than Charles' death. Now I'll never be able to heal my family. We'll never be together again.

"Mistress Klaas."

The elves watch me, wide-eyed and morose. Reilly pushes to the fore, the book under her arm. The sight of her and the elves warms me, oddly enough. I see them with new eyes. I love my family, but maybe this is my family now. I'm far too young to marry Aidan, even if I can't imagine loving anyone else. Not after this. Nothing can replace my parents, but maybe now this is my extended family.

Stroking Charles' lifeless hand, I look to Aidan. "Can you?"

He shakes his head, stricken, and wipes away a tear. "I wish I could, my love. You know I'd do anything for you."

Judy falls to her knees, keening. She flings the gun away from her. Maybe she's not as hardened as I thought. Or maybe she's just realizing that Charles' death isn't bringing back Leo or her old life.

Still, I don't know if I'll ever be able to forgive her.

I stand. Aidan curls one arm around me and the other around Michael, whose face is bruised with heartache. The three of us hug.

Aidan looks up at the sky, questioning. "Do you hear that?"

I listen. A faint rumble.

Michael nods. "Is it the Arctic maybe? It could be recovering from the apocalypse."

"No, Miguel," Ricardo says, face upturned. "Those are helicopters."

"And a plane," Aidan says. "Quickly, before they see us!" He ushers us inside. As Ricardo enters the fortress, Aidan says to him gruffly, "If you'd told me, I would have healed your sister that night."

"We didn't know how bad it was on Christmas," he replies. "Honest."

I think everyone detected something was off about Ricardo, but no one, not even Michael, guessed what his true purpose was. He effectively infiltrated the group the way I thought someone should.

I'd make a great bad guy.

Once we're inside, I say to Aidan, "I thought this place was invisible without the words. How can they see us?"

"The Sentinels have fallen. They were marked with invisibility glyphs that cloaked the fortress." Aidan then motions to the elves and says something in that other language. They bring inside Charles' body, laying it by the wall with more reverence than I would have thought they'd have for The Cruel One.

Through the fortress entrance, we see on the horizon a swarm of black and grey helicopters heading straight towards us.

"Maybe it's a rescue looking for us," I say, trying to comfort everyone. "The science base was destroyed and we'd be considered missing." This looks far scarier than a rescue, though. More like the U.S. Special Ops coming to wipe out a global villain.

"They probably found the bodies of Sergei and the Interpol agent," Michael replies, wiping his nose on his parka sleeve. "That is, after they found all the dead people at base camp. I knew we should have called for help."

Aidan shakes his head. "It's not help." He throws a poisonous look at Ricardo. "In fact, it's quite the opposite. It's *them*."

The helicopters hover over the fortress, the churning blades thundering. Terrifying. They then spread out to land on the ice.

A lone figure emerges from one of the helicopters and approaches the fortress. The winds buffet the thick mane of his hood opening. Someone staggers behind him, hands behind back.

Aidan raises his arms. The fortress shudders. The "sentinels" rise like beasts shaking off sleep, groaning and snapping as they stand from the ruins. The hieroglyphs are faded. The wall eclipses the figure just beyond, cutting off his approach.

And then the figure speaks on a megaphone. A woman. "Aidan MacNichol, we're here to claim what is rightfully ours. Let us in or we'll kill this man."

A familiar voice calls out faintly: "Charity? Baby, are you there? Stay safe! You hear me?"

It's my dad.

The real war on Christmas is about to begin.

Acknowledgements

This book would not have been possible without the generosity of many people, but primarily that of the ever-astonishing Ann Daniels. A famous polar explorer who's led numerous exploratory and scientific expeditions to the poles, Ann loaned me her expedition journals for both her Arctic and Antarctic polar expeditions. These beautiful journals allowed me to experience the Arctic wilderness through the eyes and skin of a brave woman facing unbelievable adversity with her sister explorers. I'll always be grateful for her incredible generosity, and not just for her journals. She reviewed the book for errors in terminology and other issues regarding the Arctic. Any remaining issues are my fault, not hers. I never dreamed of making such an awe-inspiring friend. She's forever my hero.

One other expert helped bring this book to life in an entirely different way. Many thanks to Dr. Glenn Ehrstine, Professor of German at the University of Iowa, who translated various phrases into medieval German, most notably the commands to open the various gates in the book. Again, any errors are mine, not his.

Many thanks also to Jonathan Reilly for his engineering expertise, as well as Marc Cameron, who taught me about gunfire in the Arctic.

But I'm lucky to have a great many golden folk in my life, like my teen beta readers: Jonathan, Olivia, Miri, and Hannah. You guys rock! Unfortunately, one of my other teen beta readers couldn't join us for this book because her father had just been killed in the San Bernardino shootings. Her mother and I agreed maybe it wasn't a good idea for her to read *Snowbound* — at least, for the time being. I hope someday she can and that she can find some healing and kinship with Aidan. But moms like Betina Shaltout and Judy Stewart Wingerden-Jones were also a great help as beta readers. Their excitement went a long way towards encouraging me, as did my beloved agent, Alex Slater, whose advice is always sound. I can't wait to see what the future brings us in my next book!

And then there's my dear husband who read at least two drafts. I'm eternally grateful for his notes, which were absolutely invaluable because, being the incredible partner he is, he shined light on my blind spots, helping me see the things I didn't want to see that were holding back the story, and ultimately me as a writer. Thank you, honey. I'm the luckiest gal in the galaxy.

Most of all, I want to thank the many fans of *Snowed*, with special shout outs to Kristopher Zgorski of Bolo Books; the attendees of both BoucherCon and StokerCon; Sunday Assembly of Los Angeles; Noir at the Bar Los Angeles; the Writer Types Podcast; and the Horror Writers Association. Your esteem of and enthusiasm for the story were what made Book 2 of the trilogy happen. Thanks from the bottom of my grinchy heart for your support. You guys are everything to me. I promise that the final book in the trilogy will absolutely blow you away.

Also, super sorry for the cliffhanger. Again. But it'll be worth it. Klaas promise.

About the Author

Maria Alexander is a multiple award-winning author of both YA and adult fiction. Her short stories have appeared since 1999 in publications such as *Chiaroscuro Magazine* and *Gothic.net,* as well as numerous acclaimed anthologies.

Her debut novel, *Mr. Wicker,* won the 2014 Bram Stoker Award for Superior Achievement in a First Novel. *Publisher's Weekly* called it, "(a) splendid, bittersweet ode to the ghosts of childhood," while *Library Journal* hailed it in a Starred Review as "a horror novel to anticipate." Her breakout YA novel, *Snowed,* was first unleashed on November 2, 2016, by Raw Dog Screaming Press. It won the 2016 Bram Stoker Award for Superior Achievement in a Young Adult Novel and was nominated for the 2017 Anthony Award for Best Children's/YA Novel in mystery writing.

When she's not stabbing people with a foil or cutting targets with a katana, she's being outrageously spooky or writing Doctor Who filk. She lives in Los Angeles with two ungrateful cats, a Jewish Christmas caroler, and a purse called Trog. Want more? Visit her website at www.mariaalexander.net.

Lightning Source UK Ltd.
Milton Keynes UK
UKHW011843041020
371004UK00001B/131